"I didn't come back to stir up old wounds."

Riley kept her eyes on Jackson. "As long as you understand things have changed."

"So you want me to step back and let you go on as if nothing's changed?"

"Well, you always were better at stepping back than stepping up."

Jackson moved his hands down her arms and took her fingers in his. "Riley, listen. It's just me and you here, honey. Nobody to impress or mislead. Just us. We had so much when we were together, but we lost a lot when...our little baby died."

"Don't speak about him."

And that was part of the problem.

"Don't you want to remember him, to talk about him?"

She seemed to shrink as she fell against him. Jackson didn't stop to think. He lifted her up into his arms and carried her through the house and straight up the stairs to her room.

Their room.

Dear Reader,

This was both a fun story and a heartbreaking story. I laughed at times and I cried at times, writing about Riley and Jackson and their pursuit of love and being parents. The subject matter of losing a baby is serious. We all know someone who's been through this. It's not an easy subject to tackle, but I tried to respect that kind of pain while depicting the reality of life.

Riley and Jackson both suffered through a traumatic crisis that changed them, but in different ways. They both learned to compromise and let go of their past hurts and pain in order to start over with a new life and new hope. This is reality for any couple, but it's especially hard when dealing with the loss of a newborn.

I hope this story will bring laughter and comfort to anyone who has experienced similar circumstances. I enjoyed writing this challenging story so I hope you will enjoy reading it. You can let me know what you think at my website, www.lenoraworth.com.

I enjoy hearing from my readers!

Lenora Worth

The Life of Riley

LENORA WORTH

HARLEQUIN®
entertain, enrich, inspire™

Recycling programs
for this product may
not exist in your area.

ISBN-13: 978-0-373-60739-6

THE LIFE OF RILEY

Copyright © 2012 by Lenora H. Nazworth

ABOUT THE AUTHOR

Lenora Worth has written over forty books for three different publishers. Her career with Love Inspired Books spans close to fourteen years. In February 2011 her Love Inspired Suspense novel *Body of Evidence* made the *New York Times* bestseller list. Her very first Love Inspired, *The Wedding Quilt,* won Affaire de Coeur's Best Inspirational for 1997, and *Logan's Child* won *RT Book Reviews'* Best Love Inspired for 1998. With millions of books in print, Lenora continues to write for Love Inspired and Love Inspired Suspense. Lenora also wrote a weekly opinion column for the local paper and worked freelance for years with a local magazine. She has now turned to full-time fiction writing and enjoying adventures with her retired husband, Don. Married for thirty-six years, they have two grown children. Lenora enjoys writing, reading and shopping...especially shoe shopping. This is her third Harlequin Superromance book.

Books by Lenora Worth

To Barbara Robinson, mother of my crazy twin friend Tina/Gina and avid reader in charge of my Oklahoma connection.

Thanks, Miss Barbara!

CHAPTER ONE

"It's official, Riley. You're pregnant."

Pregnant.

Riley Sinclair touched a hand to her stomach, her manicured fingernails scraping across her red linen sheath. "Thank you, Dr. Reynolds. Thank you so much for letting me know."

The good doctor laughed. "Congratulations. You look to be about six weeks along. I'll see you next week for your first checkup."

Pregnant.

Riley now stood in her office, remembering her earlier conversations with her doctor. After all this time, after all these years, she was finally going to get another chance to be a mother. Her stomach fluttered, nerves hitting against nerves. She touched a hand to her womb. She felt faint. She should have eaten breakfast. She'd have to take better care of herself now.

Sitting down in the white leather chair behind her ornate Louis XIV–style desk, Riley tossed back her shoulder-length blond hair and stared out the window. It was a lovely spring day in the tiny town of Sinclair, Georgia. She thought about the playground in the town square. Imagined taking a tiny tot there to swing and climb on the slide.

"A baby," she said out loud, just to test the words. Her little Yorkie barked his glee. Riley picked up the little dog and held him close. "Don't worry, Killer. Mama still loves you, too."

But it was official.

She was about to become a single mother.

JACKSON SINCLAIR DROVE the slick roadster up the main street of the quaint Georgia town his great-grandfather had founded. He shifted gears at the First Bank of Sinclair, drove past First Sinclair Church and kept right on going past the creamy yellow art-deco-designed The Life of Riley Gift Shop.

He'd deal with his ex-wife later.

Right now, he wanted a juicy hamburger from the Hamhock Café. And he wanted to see the expressions on the faces of all the people he'd left behind five years ago. They'd all given him up for dead, or worse, given him up as washed-up and put out to dry. But, he thought with a sense of revenge mixed with regret, he was alive and breathing and in better shape than he'd been in a long, long time. He'd had a revelation.

And he'd come home to shout the news to the rooftops.

And to his darling ex-wife.

He parked the red '57 Corvette convertible and ran a hand through his shaggy dark brown hair. His brown cowboy boots clicking on the hot sidewalk, Jackson opened the screen door of the popular eatery and stood there, his aviator sunshades blocking out all the unpleasant memories of his hometown.

When everyone looked up, he grinned and said in a voice loud enough for all to hear, "That's right! The prodigal son has returned." Walking straight to the long Formica counter, Jackson hit his hand on the aged patina. "Dorothy Lyn, before you call Riley to let her know I'm home, would you serve me up one of your best Hamhock-burgers? With seasoned fries on the side and the biggest Coca-Cola you can find, suga'. Oh, and peach pie, too. I'm starving."

"WHY, YES, I'D be delighted." Riley sat grinning from ear to ear while her sister-in-law and assistant Margie Sue danced around the room, Killer racing to stay with her. "Y'all just come on down tomorrow morning, then. We'll be here. We can talk about the shoot and the magazine article then."

She hung up and came around the desk to dance right along with Margie Sue and the little dog. "Can you believe? *Magnolia Magazine*—as in Sharon Butler herself—wants to do a blurb on our shop?" Hopping on bare feet since she'd long ago kicked off her red high-heeled sandals, she held Margie Sue's hands in hers then grabbed her excited little dog. "Could this day get any better?"

"I don't see how," Margie Sue replied, her salt-and-pepper bob not moving an inch. Drenched in beige linen and wearing her favorite Birkenstock sandals, she looked as relaxed here in the busy retail shop as she did at home cooking for the entire family. "A baby and a spread in *Magnolia Magazine*. Can't get any sweeter than that, honey."

"No, I can't think of another thing that would make this day more exciting." Riley touched her tummy again. "I still can't believe it, Margie Sue. After all this time."

Margie Sue hugged her close. Twenty years older than Riley's thirty-five, and with four grown children of her own, Riley's sister-in-law had been a rock through everything. She was one of Riley's best friends. "Honey, I'm so happy for you. I can't wait to tell Delton. Your big brother is gonna just burst a gut with pride."

Tears welled in Riley's eyes. "I hope so. I hope Delton and Curtis and even Bobby will be happy. I know my methods were...different, but it brought about the same result."

"Those boys don't care about all that. They know how much you've struggled with this," Margie Sue replied with a wave of her hand. "Those Atlanta doctors are the best at what they do. I'm sure they'll take real good care of you."

"Let's hope so," Riley replied. "Dr. Reynolds plans to consult with my local ob-gyn doctor, too, just in case. Now I need to finish this paperwork that's piled up all week." She stopped, memories flooding her mind. "I want to redo the nursery. Oh, I'll have to take a look at furniture and baby accessories when I go up to Atlanta next week for my checkup."

"Good idea," Margie Sue replied. "I'll get back out on the floor and tell the girls we need to spruce this place up for the possibility of a shoot in *Magnolia Magazine*. I mean, *Southern Living* last year and now one of the most popular women's magazines in the country. They'll just be over the moon about that." She whirled at the double doors. "Our traffic will pick up through the holidays for sure."

Riley rubbed her hands together. "Good. I'll need extra income to put away for a college fund." She gave Margie Sue a solemn stare. "And nothing about the baby yet. You can tell Delton after the fall barbecue next week, okay? I'll tell Mama and Daddy then, too. I'd like to wait a while longer. Just in case."

Margie Sue gave her a sympathetic look. "Okay, suga'." She did a zip across her lip. "Our secret for now."

After Margie Sue closed the door to her office, Riley settled Killer into his little four-poster bed and sat back in her chair, her heart caught between glee and agony. Holding her hand over her stomach again, she looked down at her womb. "I sure hope you take to me, little one. I love you already. So don't go away. Please don't go away. I can't take that again. Ever."

She thought of Jackson and accepted that this baby might never have a father. The pain of that situation made her want to protect her child even more. "It's just you and me, kid. I need to get used to that."

Riley straightened her spine. She'd been on her own for so long now, having a baby by herself should be a piece of cake. She'd make it that way by taking care of herself and this baby.

Ten minutes later, Margie Sue came back into the office, her brown eyes wide-open in that way she got whenever she had something either good or bad to tell Riley.

"What's up?" Riley asked, turning from her computer to stare up at Margie Sue.

Margie Sue shifted from foot to foot. "Honey, remember earlier when you said this day just couldn't get any better?"

"Yes," Riley said on a questioning note.

"How about if it went from good to worse?"

"What are you talking about?"

The door burst open and Uncle Floyd, all six feet of him in his standard overalls and John Deere cap, came strolling in, a massive frown on his furrowed brow. "Girl, you got trouble."

"What is going on?" Riley asked, standing up to hold on to the desk. "What kind of trouble? The livestock, the crops? Are our pecans bringing a fair price?"

"Ain't none of that," her uncle said, his eyes wide.

"He's back," Margie Sue said, a grimace on her face.

"Who's back?"

Riley's phone rang. She automatically put it to her ear. "Hello?"

"Riley, are you sitting down?"

"Dorothy Lyn, what's wrong?"

"He's back," Dorothy Lyn said.

A charge hissed through her system. "I'll call you back in a minute. Uncle Floyd is here."

She laid her cell phone down, her nerves jingling like Killer's rhinestone-studded collar. "Go on. Who's back?"

Uncle Floyd leaned across the desk, nose to nose with Riley. "Jackson Sinclair the Third," he replied. "Your ex-husband just rolled into town. And from the talk over at the Hamhock, he's here to stay."

AN HOUR LATER, Riley pulled her car up the driveway of the home she'd won in her divorce five years ago. Southern Hill was the ancestral home of the Sinclair family. Or had been. Since Jackson was the last remaining male after his father's death, he had inherited the vast farm. But Riley had wrestled it out from under him during the divorce proceedings. Or rather, he'd practically given it to her before he walked away.

"Wasn't that hard," she said on a huff of breath after parking in the three-car garage behind the main house. Jackson had just about let the whole place go to ruin. Somebody had to be the adult. Somebody had to save Southern Hill for future generations. *For her baby,* she thought now.

She'd tried to convince herself she'd done the right thing when her marriage had dissolved like a swamp mist. But now she had to wonder. Why was he back? What did he want?

And how in the world was she going to hide this pregnancy from him?

Her hands shook as she went through the mail that Aunt Verde always left for her on the back hall table near the sunporch, but Riley refused to let Jackson Sinclair scare her. The man had been gone for five long years, gone and out of her hair. Why was she so worried now that he was back?

Because he had that kind of power over her. Still.

Putting Jackson out of her mind, Riley headed up the back hallway to the kitchen, Killer trotting behind her like a little shadow. "Aunt Verde, I'm home."

"In here, sweetie."

Glad that she had her aunt and uncle here with her, Riley often wondered why she'd stayed in the huge Victorian mansion after Jackson had left. She couldn't explain it. Most people around here thought she'd stayed because she'd won the keys to the kingdom. She'd won two thousand acres of Sinclair land, and in Georgia, that was worth more than gold.

They'd never understand that she'd mainly stayed because it kept her closer to the man she'd once loved and to the room down the hall from her bedroom that she'd planned to use as a nursery. She's stayed because of the power and history of the Sinclair family and all that meant to this town. She wouldn't let this place go, and she certainly wouldn't let it be sold off to some stranger. Let the townspeople think what they wanted.

She was saving her ex-husband's legacy. Whether he wanted it or not. Maybe she'd subconsciously done this so she could wait for the day he decided to man up and come home.

"Well, darlin', today's that day," she said to herself as she rounded the corner to the big, sunny country kitchen.

"Talking to yourself?" Aunt Verde asked with a knowing grin. Killer ran to her aunt, ready for his after-work treat.

"Always," Riley replied. "What's for supper? Smells divine."

"Baked snapper with rice and turnips fresh from the garden. Corn bread. Sweet potato pie for dessert."

"I'm starving. I think I can handle that kind of meal."

Verde came around the big planked table where they usually had their more casual meals. "I heard your news."

Riley's heart did a little sprint. Did someone already know about the baby? No, of course not. Her aunt must be talking about that other news.

"You mean, that Jackson's back in town?"

"Yes." Verde held her hands together. "He'll kick us all out of here, I reckon."

"He can't kick us out," Riley replied with a sigh. "I won the entire estate in the divorce, remember?"

"Yes, but…he's a Sinclair."

"And what am I?"

"His ex-wife."

"I got this place in the settlement," Riley said again, trying to be patient.

"So, we're safe."

"You're safe," she said, giving Verde a smile. "Do

you think I'd let anyone put you out on the street again?"

"No, honey, I believe you'd fight to the finish. And I thank God every day that you're my niece."

Riley opened her arms and hugged her aunt close. "You're safe here, Aunt Verde. As mean as Jackson can be, he wouldn't dare put my kinfolk out on the road."

She prayed.

He might put her out on the road, but she'd deal with that day when it came.

JACKSON PARKED HIS car at the end of the long drive near the curve. From here, he could see the house still glowing bright in the gloaming of the day. Two-storied and Victorian in a stark white, rambling and creaky, old but sturdy, with good bones and a pretty lady facade. Old moss-covered live oaks stood along the drive and around the big front lawn. Azaleas and crape myrtles thrived here. Roses bloomed here. Love grew here. Or rather, love had been a part of this house until he and Riley had changed things up. This was Southern Hill. This was his home. Or it had been.

Until vindictive Riley—debutante and society girl Riley Priscilla Buckingham Sinclair—had decided to take him to the cleaners in a nasty, splashed-across-the-headlines divorce. Left with nothing much but the clothes on his back, a small yacht and his convertible, Jackson had taken off to parts unknown. And he'd tried to stay there but…a lot had happened since the

night five years ago when he'd left Southern Hill and
Riley behind.

A lot.

He wanted to see her tonight, here in his home.
Wanted to touch her and kiss her and smell that sweet
perfume that only Riley could bring to life like a garden of blooming flowers.

He wanted to hate her and make her suffer, too.

He thought he could pretty much do both by teasing
her and taunting her and working her up into a tizzy.
That might bring him some satisfaction. Or it might
make him even more miserable.

If only they'd had a child together, things might
have been so different.

Jackson didn't drive on up to the house on the hill.
Instead he hopped back into his car and headed to the
town cemetery behind the church. Dusk was falling in
shimmering waves of yellow-gold across the church-
yard. The old pines swayed in the wind, hissing and
singing. The crush of brown pine straw mixed with
yellow sycamore leaves made a pretty carpet over the
grass. Jackson moved through the rows and rows of
some of his more recent ancestors, stopping briefly
in front of his parents' side-by-side headstones, until
he came to a small grave with a tiny cherub sitting
with its head in its hands, looking down on the stone.

"Hi there, little fellow," Jackson said on a long sigh.
"I know it's been a while since Daddy's been by, but
I haven't forgotten you. I think about you every day."

Every day. "And mostly, every night."

Every night when he was alone in his bed, wherever he'd been in the world or on the sea, he'd thought about the baby he and Riley had lost. And he always thought about the "what-ifs" and the "what-might-have-beens" in those long, dark hours. There, alone in the darkness, it was easy to dream about happy things, about the good life he'd had at his feet.

But the nightmares always came later when he'd dream dark, terrible dreams and wake up in a cold sweat, the light of a too-bright day daring him to live again.

No more, that. No more.

"I'm back now, son. And this time, I'm not running away. Just wanted you to know that."

He touched a hand to the name on the tiny grave. *Jackson Thomas Sinclair the Fourth*. "Daddy's here. And somehow, I'm going to make it all up to you, I promise."

FROM HER VANTAGE point in the turret room that now served as her bedroom at the top of the house, Riley had seen the red convertible parked on the curve in front of the sloping yard. She'd watched through the cover of mossy live oaks and towering pecan trees, her eyes burning from staring too long into the setting sun. Watched and held her breath, in anticipation and dread, while her ex-husband stood there looking up at the house.

Would he come up that drive and confront her?

Or would he get in his car and leave again without a fight?

So many memories, so many emotions. From grammar school to high school, during cotillion and college, they'd been together in one way or another. Sunday school, Vacation Bible School, summer camp, pool parties and hayrides, football games and cheerleading practice. Always, always, Jackson had been there by her side. They were the golden couple, the couple whose names were said together. Jackson-and-Riley. Always Jackson and Riley. As one.

Their wedding had been the social event of the season, the ceremony held at the church, the reception held right here at Southern Hill. The honeymoon had started right here, too, in this very room when they'd sneaked away from the crowd and found each other and held each other…and started that night to try and make the family they'd wanted.

Or rather, the family she'd wanted.

"Where did we go wrong, Jackson?" she wondered out loud as she stared down at him.

Before she could even form her own thoughts on that loaded question, he'd gotten back into his car and sped away.

Where was he going?

Where did he intend to sleep tonight?

She turned to stare at the big tester bed they'd once shared.

Even though she'd redone the whole room after his parents had died and again after he'd left her, Riley could still remember the many nights she'd lain here safe and secure in Jackson's arms.

Safe, secure, loved.

But, honestly, never completely sure of that love. Never really secure in her trust of him or her hope for their future.

Why is he back? she wondered as she lay down and tried to go to sleep, Killer snuggled at the foot of the bed. Why today of all days?

Riley held a hand to her stomach, still in awe that she was pregnant again after all these years. She closed her eyes and sent up a plea. "Please let this one be healthy and whole."

But she found sleep hard in coming because for the first time in five years, she wasn't so sure about tomorrow.

Jackson was back in town. And that could mean so many different things for her.

And for this little baby.

How would she ever be able to explain this to her ex-husband?

CHAPTER TWO

"SALTINE CRACKERS," MARGIE Sue said, shoving a whole sleeve of crackers into Riley's hand the next morning. "Good for morning sickness."

Riley wondered if she looked as green as she felt. "Why today? I haven't had one iota of this until now." She grabbed a cracker and stuffed the whole thing in her mouth. "I can't even drink my latte."

"You're nervous about the magazine people coming."

"Yes, I am." She patted her upswept hair and checked her smart black-and-white zebra-print sheath in the standing mirror out on the boutique floor. "Should I change?"

"You look great," Margie Sue said, comfortable as always in her rumpled linen big shirt and smooth ankle pants. "We all look great. They said to look and act normal."

"Easy for you to say," Riley said on a low whisper. "You're not pregnant and trying to avoid your ex-husband."

Margie Sue pursed her lips. "Well, no, I'm not either of those things. But…I am concerned about you. We could reschedule."

"No. I can't reschedule something this big, this important." She ate another cracker and sipped from an ecofriendly bottle of water. "I'll be fine. Just the jitters. A lot has happened in twenty-four hours."

"A whole lot," Margie Sue replied. "I heard he's staying at the express hotel out on I-75."

Jackson. He certainly had caused part of Riley's nervousness. A large part.

"Hmm. Not quite his usual style, but beggars can't be choosers."

"I also heard he's not exactly a beggar. Apparently, he's done quite well for himself."

Riley slanted her sister-in-law a look. "Doing what? Working at a bar? He only had his share of the hunting lodge profits to live on all this time."

"No, honey, no bars involved from what I've heard. He's worked as a hunting guide for some big plantation down in Florida and from there, he got a job doing pretty much the same thing on a private millionaire island somewhere off the coast of Mexico, near Cozumel I hear."

Wondering how Margie Sue had so much information so fast, Riley shrugged. "Well, I'm so very happy for him, bless his heart."

"And I know you meant that in the nicest way, right?"

Riley frowned and ate two more crackers. "I just want to get through this. I have to get through this." She whirled to scan the shop. Focusing on work got her through most days since she really loved her job. And she loved to stay busy.

The boutique side held an array of designer clothes and accessories. The summer collection was so fashion-forward, she wanted to buy every piece for herself. But she'd have to watch that with her growing tummy. Maybe she should start a maternity section, too. She'd put it right next to the Vera Bradley collection.

The Life of Riley Boutique carried cosmetics in one corner, shoes in another. Knickknacks, some cute and kitschy, some artsy and expensive, sat on display cases and shelves in every available spot. Anything from fancy dishes and exquisite vases to plush towels, sheets and bath products filled the other half of the big two-story boutique. This was an all-purpose girlie-girl shop. A destination store for people traveling out from Atlanta and heading on South to the beaches of Alabama, Mississippi and Florida. Women from all over the South flocked to her shop. *Southern Living* said she'd put Sinclair back on the map. She wondered what would happen if the *Magnolia Magazine* people did give her a blurb.

Riley did one more scan of the whole floor and decided the place looked as inviting and adorable as she could possibly make it. But she still felt a little green in the face.

"It looks good," she said to Margie Sue. "Tell the girls they did a great job straightening up for the magazine people."

"Fresh flowers and a pot of our own special coffee,"

Margie Sue replied. "And I made brownies. With good ole Georgia pecans on top."

"Brownies?" Suddenly Riley could think of nothing else in the world but one of Margie Sue's cream cheese and chocolate brownies. "Oh, I need one of those."

Margie Sue made a face and shook her head. "Not on that early-morning stomach, no, ma'am."

Frowning again, she decided Margie Sue was probably right. "Well, save me one for later."

She had a bad feeling that she'd probably gain sixty pounds with this pregnancy. But she hadn't gained that much before—

Riley stopped that thought when she heard the front door jingling open. Running a hand over her hair, she checked herself in the mirror one more time and prepared herself to talk to a group of producers and magazine people from Nashville.

Coming around the corner so she could see, she put on her best smile and said, "Good morning. I'm Riley Sinclair."

"I know who you are, darlin'," a masculine voice said over the sounds of chattering women and cash register drawers being unlocked for the day. "And let me just say, you sure are a sight for sore eyes."

"Jackson." It came out on an inhaled breath, which caused the last crumbs of her cracker to get caught in her throat. Riley went into a spasm of coughing. Killer came running, his little manicured paw-nails tapping on the wood floor, his feisty bark in defensive mode.

Jackson stared down the little dog then frowned,

smirked and finally, grew concerned. He found the bottle of water she kept pointing at on a nearby table and shoved it into her shaking hands. "My goodness, you must have a frog in that pretty throat."

He stared at her as if he wanted to put his hands around that same throat.

"I'm okay," she said after gulping too much water. Great. Now she really needed to go to the bathroom. Her eye makeup would be ruined.

"You sure?"

Hating the triumphant color of his greenish-blue eyes, she nodded and tried to ignore his white button-up shirt, sleeves rolled up to show off some muscle, and his tight-fitting jeans over what had to be an eight-hundred-dollar pair of custom-made cowboy boots. But she couldn't ignore the way he looked.

Good. Better than good. His longer-than-usual brown hair was sun-shot with a few dark blond streaks. His vivid blue-green eyes held suntanned crow's-feet. He looked healthy and in shape, rested and relaxed. Riley did one more scan, her heart thumping right along with Killer's little snub tail.

"Riley?"

Her eyes slid back to Jackson's face and she realized she hadn't answered his question yet. "Never better. What do you want?"

He grinned and put a hand on his hip and then scooped up her yapping dog. Killer immediately turned into a wimp and licked Jackson's face. "Just came by to let you know I'm home, sweetheart. Although I'm pretty sure you already knew that."

She swallowed, regained control even with the mascara running down her face. "And I should be concerned about this because?"

He moved closer and she heard the collective sigh of Margie Sue and the three extra clerks they'd brought in to help with the tour. Jackson had always had a mesmerizing effect on women.

And apparently, little dogs, too. Killer nuzzled against Jackson's chest and stared into his eyes with a wide-eyed hopefulness.

"Nothing to be concerned about, Riley. Just letting you know how things stand. I'm home. For good."

"Nothing you do could be for good," she blurted, hoping to regain her footing. She grabbed her dog back for support. But when she saw the shard of pain cutting through Jackson's eyes and the pulse pumping against his still-strong jawline, she almost regretted speaking her mind. And yanking her dog from his arms.

"We'll see about that, darlin'." He started to say something else, but a group of expensive-looking people convoyed straight through the front door. "Friends of yours?" he asked, turning back to Riley.

The *Magnolia Magazine* people!

Riley went into panic mode. "Yes, I mean no. Business associates. And now is not a good time, Jackson. Maybe we can talk later."

"No, we'll talk now," he said, his voice echoing

throughout the whole building. "I told you, I'm home for good and I—"

"I have to meet with these people," she said, wiping at her eyes. "I'll be glad to meet you for lunch—later."

"I've come halfway around the world, Riley. I'm not leaving."

He stood with his expensive boots dug into her plush white throw rug. And he was blocking the way for the magazine executives.

"Jackson, don't start with me. Not today."

Margie Sue came between them. "Uh, Riley, they're here. The magazine people."

Jackson's face split with a wide grin. "Magazine? What kind of magazine?"

Riley wanted to smack him. *"Magnolia Magazine."* She sent him a pleading look. "Don't mess with this, Jackson. Just leave, please?"

Margie Sue grinned at the man still standing there. "Hey there, Jackson. Isn't it excitin'? They might want to do a spread on us for Sharon Butler's favorite things. She just loves our fuzzy slippers and bubble bath products. She sent some people down from Nashville for a look-see."

"Is that a fact?" Jackson grabbed Margie Sue in a bear hug. "Good to see you. I can see our girl's as ornery as ever. Did she have her coffee today?"

"No, she—"

"Needs both of you to move out of the way and let me do my job," Riley said, pushing past them to shake hands and introduce herself to the fascinated group staring at them with open wonder.

Maybe if she just ignored Jackson, he'd quietly disappear.

But he didn't leave. He stayed the whole time she chatted with the magazine group. Even posed for some preliminary pictures. Whistled to Killer to come, then found a seat over in the snack shop and moaned out loud when he bit into one of Margie Sue's famous brownies.

And, darn his handsome hide, he'd charmed those sophisticated Nashville women right into grins and giggles by the time their tour was over.

"Now, how are you related to Mrs. Sinclair?" one of the dressed-in-all-black producers asked Jackson, tossing her ebony hair while she did so.

"Me?" He smiled that lethal smile and shrugged, then stood up with a grand flair and put an arm on Riley's shoulder. "Oh, I'm just the ex-husband. My first day back in town. Could I buy you ladies a lunch at the Hamhock Café down the street?"

The camera clicked, capturing Riley and Jackson together.

Riley wanted to kill him.

But she didn't get the chance.

Instead, she turned without a word and ran to the bathroom and lost her saltine crackers.

SOMETHING JUST WASN'T right.

Jackson had never seen Riley so all-fired nervous.

He'd seen her have hissy fits lots of times. He'd kind of loved those 'cause the making up afterward had always been so sweet. He'd seen her upset or mad or fretting, but never so nervous she had to go throw up her breakfast. Did that fancy magazine spread mean that much to her?

Maybe she had a bug or something. Or maybe she really was that nervous around national-magazine-type people. Or maybe she was plain freaked out over seeing him. Or it could be all three together.

Who knew with Riley?

So why was he right now on his way out to the house to check on her?

He'd left her with those skinny producer people and gone on with his day. But he'd called the shop later to see if they could talk and Margie Sue had told him Riley had left early, with it being a Friday and all.

He still needed to talk to her so he might as well get it over with now since he was on his way to the Southern Hill Hunting Lodge out on the lake at the far side of the property.

She had to know that he planned on living and working in the lodge. Or at least that was his excuse for stopping by to check on her.

Jackson parked his car around back by habit, but he wasn't sure if he could just walk in the back door and go through the breezeway to the sunporch and on to the kitchen, or if he should knock on the side door to the kitchen.

This used to be his house, his home. Now he felt

like a stranger in a strange land. His land, no matter what the legal papers said.

He finally opted for the side door to the kitchen.

Riley's aunt Verde greeted him with a tight smile. "Jackson, how good to see you."

He doubted that, but he had always liked Aunt Verde and Uncle Floyd. "Hey, how ya doing?"

She hugged him and stepped back. "We're real good now that Riley moved us in here with her."

"She what?" That didn't sound like Riley. She loved her privacy.

Verde looked down at the floor. "We lost our farm. Didn't have a place to live. Riley sent a rental truck to pack up what stuff we wanted to bring and gave us the downstairs bedroom and den. We live here now and take care of things for her."

"Well, ain't that nice," Jackson said, thinking Miss High-and-Mighty now had a built-in maid and handyman.

Verde touched a gnarled hand to his arm. "It is nice. Nicer than living in a homeless shelter. We don't have to work too hard. She hires people to do most everything but she's got a bead on the whole operation. Truth be told, I think she likes the company we offer and she likes being in charge, too. This is a big old house."

"Yep, it is," he said. "I didn't mean any disrespect. I just never knew Riley to be so charitable."

"She's changed some," Verde said. "Now what can I do for you?"

End of that discussion, he reckoned. "Actually, I need to talk to Riley. Is she around?"

Verde nodded toward the pasture out beyond the pool and gardens. "She's out there talking to that horse of hers."

"Coco?"

"She doesn't have any other horse that I know of."

"Thanks, Aunt Verde." He started back out.

"Hey, you're welcome to stay for supper."

"We'll see," he said, waving as he strolled around the breezeway and cut through the covered patio between the main house and the big white garage. Jackson was pretty sure he wasn't welcome anytime, including supper.

He decided to focus on the many changes around his former home instead of worrying about his next meal. But it still seemed odd not to see his parents sitting out by the pool or piddling in the garden. Losing them eight years ago to a car wreck out on U.S. 19 had been one of the worst events of his life.

That and losing his baby boy a couple of years later, of course.

Closing his eyes to the painful memories, Jackson stared out over the familiar landscape, his heart settling back inside his chest.

The place looked tidy and well kept, he'd give her that. But then Riley was the queen of her domain and she prided herself on keeping up appearances.

Huge clay pots full of overflowing fall flowers sat around the newly resurfaced pool. A heavy wooden rectangular table complete with a shining canvas umbrella sat on the patio by the sunporch. The azaleas, even though they weren't blooming, were thick in the garden and underneath the tall pine trees, their bushes were bright green. His mother's prized fall camellia bushes were just beginning to bud in rich dark pinks. The whole backyard had been cleared and landscaped to an immaculate perfection.

A pretty facade, meant to hide the wild natural beauty. Just like his Riley.

He stopped at the old oak tree midway to the pasture and searched until he saw her. Jackson had to catch his breath at the sight of Riley. She'd changed into jeans and a plaid shirt, her hair down and curling around her shoulders. He watched while she petted the roan gelding and whispered in the big horse's ear then handed Coco a nibble.

For just an instant, it felt as if he'd gone back in time to a good place where they were happy and in love. She'd turn and smile at him then run into his arms. They'd kiss and whisper things about their day. Then they'd go inside and have supper or spend some time together and then have a late supper.

Jackson held that memory close while he stared at the woman he'd loved and lost. And he reminded himself things were different now. He was a different man. Apparently, Riley had moved on, too. Running her own successful business, keeping this place in tiptop shape, living her life as if nothing had happened to break them apart.

He had to admire that, even while it rankled.

Then she turned and saw him, her eyes going wide in surprise. For one quick second, he saw the fear and confusion in her gaze and wished he could wipe it all away. Then she tossed her hair and came toward him, her arms swinging with determination.

"Jackson."

"Hello, darlin'. I don't think you're happy to see me."

"What are you doing here?"

He loved the breathlessness in her Southern drawl.

"I told you this morning we needed to talk."

"So, talk."

There it went. That nervousness again. Was she hiding something from him?

"Are you feeling better?"

"Much, thank you. I guess I…ate something that didn't agree with me."

"Are you sure?"

She pushed at her hair, adjusted her sleeves. "What else could it be?"

Okay, she was definitely hiding something. She wouldn't even look him in the eye. He'd find out, sooner or later.

"Riley, I only came by to tell you that I'm moving into the lodge and I'm running it from now on."

That brought her head up. "You know, Jackson, you can't just waltz back in here and announce any grand plans. You don't own this land anymore."

He got close, close enough to smell that flower garden that always followed her around. That scent he used to drown in when he held her close. Swallowing, he tilted his head to her eye level.

"I still own a percentage of the hunting lodge, sweetheart. Just enough for me to make an executive decision. And my decision is final. I'm taking my lodge back. And I'm managing it."

He saw the flare of a temper tantrum brightening her eyes. "But Uncle Floyd has been doing that. And he's good at it."

"Uncle Floyd can stay on and help me at his same salary. I don't have a problem with that. In fact, it'll save me having to hire someone."

She looked relieved at that. "Good. They lost everything a couple of years ago. I won't put them out on the street."

"Nobody's putting anybody out on the street, but I'm tired of being the odd man out. So I'll run the lodge and I won't bother you one bit unless it's to do with business. Deal?"

She looked skeptical and shocked. "I guess I don't have any choice. Does this mean you'll be around for a while?"

Why did he get the sense she was afraid of his answer.

"Yes, darlin', I told you I was home for a good long while. Like for the rest of my natural life. Hope you can live with that."

She stepped back, a soft gasp lifting out over the dusk. "I…I'll manage. I've managed *without* you for five years. Might as well learn to manage *with* you around."

Jackson should have felt some sort of satisfaction, but instead he just felt tired to the bone. Fighting with Riley was always a full-on assault. "Good. Then I'll be on my way."

"I'll tell Uncle Floyd. He stays here in the house unless there's a hunting party at the lodge. Then he and Aunt Verde stay there."

Jackson had to admit she'd gone right on without him. And that tore at him more than anything. "You've got a nice setup here, Riley. The old place looks good, real good."

"Yes, it's worked so far. We're out of the red at least."

Okay, so she'd managed to get in one jab at his lack of responsibility. And this was just the first day home. Deciding he was too tired to take the bait, Jackson nodded. "I'll see you around, I reckon."

"I suppose so. Good night."

Then he grinned and spun back around. "Oh, I forgot. Aunt Verde invited me for supper. I think I'll take her up on it. That way Floyd and I can go over everything, so we have a clear understanding."

"But—"

"You got a problem with that, Riley?"

She looked around then shook her head. "Of course not. I'm so tired, I might just eat supper in my room."

"Suit yourself." He held out his arm. "Can I escort you back to the house?"

"I can walk for myself," she replied, heat in each word as she pranced right by him. "Let's get in and wash up before Verde sends out a posse."

"Yes, ma'am."

Jackson followed her, enjoying the way she sashayed in those jeans. In spite of their differences, he decided it was good to be home.

And so good to be near Riley again.

Now if he could only figure what she had up her pretty little sleeve.

CHAPTER THREE

"RILEY SINCLAIR, YOU will not be rude to your guest."

Aunt Verde stood there with her hand on her ample hip and stared Riley down through her no-line bifocals.

"He's not a guest. It's Jackson, for Pete's sake. I don't care where he eats. I'm eating in my room."

"Coward."

"Aunt Verde!"

Her aunt pushed at her permed gray curls, her complexion clearly flushed. "Girl, I've never known you to back down from a good fight or to run when you're scared."

"I'm not scared," Riley replied, near tears. Which wasn't like her, either. She rarely cried on an everyday basis. She saved her tears for a good ole hissy fit. But the hormones were already kicking in so she'd become used to these mood swings and emotional highs and lows. "I've just had a long day and I'm exhausted."

Aunt Verde touched a hand to her arm, her expression turning compassionate. "And seeing Jackson again hasn't helped, right?"

"Right." Seeing her ex-husband on the same day she'd found out she was finally pregnant was just too weird to think about. Fate or…a warning?

Aunt Verde leaned close and whispered in her ear. "If you hide out in your room, he's gonna think he's gettin' to you, honey."

"He is," Riley said on a frustrated breath. In oh, so many ways.

"Of course, he is. But we don't want him to know that. He'll get a swollen head as it is. He probably thinks he can just waltz right back into your life."

Riley burst out laughing at the expression on her aunt's face. "Oh, okay. I'll have dinner with y'all. And Jackson. I'm starving anyway. And besides, I might miss out on the fun of you putting him in his proper place."

"That's my girl," Aunt Verde said. "I'll go call the men. They're talking football and farming. Could be all night."

"I hope not," Riley said under her breath. She just prayed she'd make it through dinner without hurling again.

JACKSON DIDN'T REALIZE how much he'd missed good home cooking. Nothing beat pot roast, field peas, corn bread and mashed potatoes. Unless it was blackberry cobbler, of course.

He pushed back from the table and groaned. "Aunt Verde, if I stay around here I'll gain ten pounds."

Aunt Verde laughed. "You and Riley both. Our gal's been eating up a storm lately."

Riley's frown didn't mar her oval face. But the look of dread and fear in her blue eyes sure spoke volumes.

"Well, I do love vegetables," she said with a little too much enthusiasm. "Those sliced tomatoes were so good I think I could just bite right into one."

Jackson laughed out loud. "Riley Sinclair, you know you'd never just bite into a tomato. No, ma'am. You have to have it sliced up all dainty with a scoop of low-fat cottage cheese on it. And some freshly ground black pepper all over it."

Aunt Verde cackled. "He sure knows you, Riley."

Riley shot Jackson a shrewd glance, her elegant eyebrows lifting. "He's been away awhile, though. I've changed a lot, even if I do still love tomatoes and cottage cheese."

Uncle Floyd had stayed quiet but he cleared his throat and grinned over at Jackson. "We talked about all the changes around here. I told him most of it was your idea. I think Jackson's impressed with you, Riley."

Riley held a hand over her stomach. "Didn't think I could hold on to the old home place, Jackson?"

"No, didn't think you'd *want* to hold on to this old place," he countered. "I figured you'd sell it off, piece by piece and turn the whole lot into some fancy subdivision."

"She'd never do that to Southern Hill," Verde said, slapping Jackson on the arm. "Riley loves this place."

Jackson gave his ex a long, measured look. "Does she now?"

Riley stared across the kitchen table at him. "You know I do. I've worked hard to keep it going. And let me tell you, it wasn't easy." She stopped, touched her stomach again. "I did what I had to do."

The room grew quiet, the unsaid things hovering in the air like the night chill hovering outside. Jackson wanted to ask a lot of questions but he'd get the details in time. Floyd would update him once they got on even footing with the lodge.

Verde got up and started clearing dishes. "There's still some coffee left. Anybody want another cup?"

"Not me," Jackson said, his eyes on Riley. She actually flinched at the mention of coffee. "You cutting back on caffeine, darlin'?"

"Who, me?" Her laugh was brittle and calculated. "Don't you think I should?"

Uncle Floyd shifted his gaze from Jackson to Riley. "Verde, weren't we gonna take a walk after supper?"

Verde stopped loading the dishwasher. "Not that I can recall—I mean, yes, I think we did discuss that earlier."

"I'm ready now," Floyd said, his poker face never changing.

"Okay, already. Let me finish here." Verde hurried so much, dishes shook when she slammed the dishwasher shut. "I guess these two will behave while we're gone."

"I think they will." Uncle Floyd got up and stood holding his hands to his high-backed chair. "Jackson, I appreciate our talk and I'm happy to take second fiddle to you. I think we'll make a good team. Long as

I got something to occupy me each day and I got my Verde to come home to, I'm as happy as a pig in mud."

Jackson stood and shook his hand. "I appreciate that, Floyd. And I do thank you for taking such good care of the lodge." He winked at Riley. "Thanks to all of you."

Riley pushed at her chair and got up before Jackson could come around the table and help her. "I should… I have work to do."

Floyd gave his wife a worried glance then smiled over at Riley. "Honey, why don't you rest? Take Jackson out into the sunroom and have a nice chat. He needs to get caught up on the operations around here."

"That's right—I sure do," Jackson said, chiming in only because he didn't want to leave just yet. He'd use any excuse but he really did want to find out more about what Riley had done with the place. She'd hold it against him, since when he'd left, things weren't nearly as neatly organized as now. Southern Hill seemed to be thriving again. It galled him that he should have been the one doing the organizing, but too late to get all hot and bothered about that now.

Riley crossed her arms. "Okay, all right. C'mon, Jackson. But only for a little while. I'm dead on my feet."

Jackson nodded to Floyd and thanked Verde for the meal. "I'll see y'all later."

It felt odd, being a guest in his own home. Memories of his mother in this same big kitchen made him smile and then made him sad all over again. Being an only child of two stoic parents had shaped him his whole life. After they'd died during the early years of his marriage, Jackson had floundered in grief. But Riley and her family had been there to support him and help him get through that horrible grief. He really did owe them a lot. He should be grateful that, even after the way he'd treated her, even after losing their baby, Riley had saved his home. He'd certainly been in no position to fix what was broken—on this farm or in his marriage.

He poured himself another cup of coffee and followed Riley down the two steps into the multiwindowed sunroom. The security lights in the backyard glowed over the pool, making it shimmer each time the pump pushed water around the big rectangle. That brought other, more intimate memories of swimming out there with Riley.

He stood at one of the big windows. "You must have hired a whole squad to redo this place."

Riley sank down on a deep wicker chair covered with a plush floral cushion. "I did it piece by piece, room by room, acre by acre. I needed something to occupy me after…"

She left it hanging there in the air.

"After we lost our baby and you asked me to leave."

She didn't speak. But she nodded.

Jackson sat down on the matching wicker settee and placed his coffee on the glass table. "Riley, I know a lot of water has passed under the bridge, but…I do want you to know I'm sorry for all the pain I caused you."

She didn't say anything. Just kept looking out at the yard.

The live oaks hummed and swayed in the night wind, the Spanish moss flowing over the trees like silver threads. Somewhere, an owl hooted. He could hear the train moving through town a few miles away, its powerful rumble matching the roar of regret running inside his head.

Jackson worked to control that roar. "It's still peaceful here, at least. I guess that'll never change."

"It might now," she said, her tone firm and sure, her smile bitter and sweet.

"You mean because of me, right? Because I'm back and I've messed up your peaceful existence and your lovely little empire?"

She stared over at him. "Yes. But I can't figure out why you came back, especially since you told me you never wanted to lay eyes on me or this land again."

Wow. He deserved that, he reckoned. How could he explain things to her in terms she'd understand? "I was mad and hurting, Riley. We both were."

She sat up, placed her hands on her lap. "So you're saying that's all different now? You're willing to forgive and forget?"

He leaned up, too, his gaze settling on her, his gut clenched in a tight hurt. She looked ethereal sitting there in the muted lamplight. Here with the darkness surrounding them, she was young and sweet and not so sure of herself. He wanted to lash out and take up the old fight. He also wanted to reach out and bring her home to his arms.

"I'm willing to forgive, Riley, but I can never forget," he said. "I need to go."

He stood, stared down at her, a whisper of hope moving through his heart. If she'd just say the word. Just say anything to make him think she still cared.

She stood, too. "Yes, it's been a long, eventful day. I can't remember ever being this tired."

Concern pushed away his hope. "Are you all right? You sure seem kind of puny."

"I'm just dandy," she replied, the tartness of that statement like a slap.

Jackson let out a breath. "I guess I've messed up your pretty little life, haven't I, sweetheart?"

She lifted her head and gave him a direct, blue-eyed stare. "Yes, you sure have. Or at least you think you have. But I've changed, Jackson. I gave myself a makeover right along with the one I gave this place." She put her hands on her hips and lifted her chin. "You thought I'd be helpless without you, thought I'd fall flat on my face. But I didn't do that. I pulled myself together and I got busy. I saved Southern Hill. But I sure didn't do it for you."

Anger coursed through his blood. "Oh, well, then why did you do it, Riley? Just so you could lord it over me if I did come home. So I'd be a laughingstock around Sinclair, Georgia?"

She wasn't laughing and neither was he.

They stood there glaring at each other across the glass coffee table. The wind picked up, causing the chimes hanging under the eaves to jingle and sway.

"I didn't want this to be about you at all. I hated to see everything your parents and grandparents had worked so hard for being destroyed because of our problems. I couldn't live with that on my conscience, too."

"Oh, and what's on your conscience now, suga'? What keeps you awake at night?"

"Not you, if that's what you're implying."

Jackson steeled himself against her verbal assault. This, this was familiar. This fighting and taunting and accusing. This blaming and circling and screaming. But even this was better than being alone across the world and wondering why everything you'd ever loved had somehow slipped through your fingers.

"I'm not implying anything," he finally said, dropping his hands. "I didn't come back to stir up old wounds. I...I just needed to come home. It was time. Way past time."

She kept her eyes on him, kept her hands tucked against her midsection. "As long as you understand things have changed," she said. "I can't go back. I'm in charge of Southern Hill now and I've done a passable job. I kept some of the people I trusted and hired others to replace the people I didn't like. Even with the drought and the economy, we've managed to hang on. The hunting lodge has helped a lot. Uncle Floyd seems to have a talent for that kind of thing. And he needs his job."

Jackson sensed the fear behind that self-righteous statement. "So you want me to step back and let you go on as if nothing's changed?"

Her bittersweet smile stalled out. "Well, you always were better at stepping back than stepping up."

That did it.

He was across the room in two steps, his hands dragging at her arms, his face an inch from hers. "You still blame me for everything, don't you?"

One whisper. "Yes."

She didn't even try to deny it. She wanted him to suffer. "Did it ever occur to you that I might have a few regrets, too?"

"I don't know what you regret, Jackson. You left in such a hurry, I didn't have time to think about that, let alone ask you what was on your mind."

"You kicked me out, remember?"

"I didn't kick you out. I let you go. You didn't want me anymore. Maybe you never really wanted me."

His whole body went numb with pain. Relaxing his hold on her, Jackson moved his hands down her arms and took her fingers in his. "Riley, listen. It's just me and you here, honey. Nobody to impress or mislead. Just us. We had so much when we were together, but we lost a lot when…our little baby died."

She tried to pull away. "Don't speak about him."

And that was part of the problem.

He refused to let her go. "Don't you want to remember him, to talk about him?"

"Of course. You were the one who refused to talk about him or your feelings." A crystal-blue wall of pain covered her eyes. "I remember him every day."

"Well, so do I. So do I."

She gave up trying to pull away. She went slack in his arms. Jackson didn't know if she was playing possum so he'd let her go, or if she was yielding just a tiny bit.

"Riley?"

"I…I need to go inside, Jackson. I don't feel so good."

She seemed to shrink as she fell against him. Jackson didn't stop to think. He lifted her up into his arms and carried her through the house and straight up the stairs to her room.

Their room.

"I'm fine," she said, seeing where they were. "Put me down."

"I will. Right here on the bed."

She balked at that. "No. I mean, you don't have to stay. I'll be all right. I told you I was tired."

"Yes, but I don't believe this is just from being tired. You've obviously worked yourself into a frenzy, either because of that infernal magazine thing or because I'm back and you don't want me back. Or maybe it's something else. Wanna tell me what?"

"It's nothing," she said, lifting on her elbows to stare up at him. "You don't need to stay."

"You aren't gonna tell me the truth, are you?"

"There's nothing much to tell."

She pushed up and found her footing. Or so she thought.

Jackson stepped back and saw her go pale, saw the shock and fear cresting in her eyes. "I have to—"

She scooted past him and ran to the bathroom, slamming the door after herself.

Okay, that was so *not* how Riley operated. He'd never seen her like this, sick and faint and pale. Except when…

His heart stopped. Except when she'd been pregnant.

"Riley?"

"Stop shouting at me. I'm fine."

He paced the floor, his gaze scanning the room he hardly recognized. Maybe he hadn't recognized the obvious, either. She really had moved on. With another man.

Jackson had never felt such a keen, overwhelming jealousy. He wanted to kill that man, whoever he was.

"Riley, I'm not leaving until you come out here so we can talk."

He heard the water running. Then he heard it shutting off.

Finally, the bathroom door opened and she walked out. "I'm okay."

"You're as pale as these sheers," he said, pointing toward the curtains across the big bay window. "Are you gonna level with me, or do I have to ask every available man in town to find out who did this?"

She opened her mouth to speak then shut it. Then she glared at him. "What are you talking about?"

"I think you're pregnant," he said. "And I want to know who the father is, so I can kill him with my bare hands."

She started laughing. Then she started crying. "You can't be serious."

"I am very serious," he said, not sure if he should scold her or comfort her. She had to be pregnant. Her emotions were all over the map. "C'mon, Riley. You didn't think I'd ever find out. You were hoping I'd just go away before I figured things out, but I know you. And the only other time you acted this way was when you were carrying our child."

She pushed at her hair, grabbed the back of a cream brocade-covered chair and leveled him with a look of disbelief. "Yes, that's right. The only time I ever got this way before was when I was carrying your child, Jackson. *Your* child." Then she came around the chair and stared up at him. "And guess what? I am pregnant again."

He thought he might faint. Just the thought of Riley with another man made him want to bust a hole through a wall. "Who's the father? I have a right to know."

She laughed again. Shook her head. Started crying again. "You do have a right to know. You sure do."

He bobbed his head, gritted his teeth. "Okay, so out

with it. Tell me who you've been fooling around with, Riley. I'm not leaving until I know the truth. Who's the father of this baby?"

She wiped at her eyes and held one hand to her stomach and the other to the chair, her face moving from sickly pale to a flush of anger. "This baby is yours, Jackson. I'm carrying *your* child. So there, now you know." Then she pointed to the door. "Now get out of my house."

CHAPTER FOUR

JACKSON HAD TO sit down. Did she think he was an idiot?

"You can't be serious." He scrubbed a hand down his face, slapped that same hand against his leg. "I mean, how could that even be possible?"

Riley sank onto a plush green ottoman, a look of surprise on her face. She pushed back the loose hair around her temples then slumped forward, holding her hands together. "We had extra embryos, remember?"

Jackson shot up off the chair. "You had yourself impregnated with our frozen...stuff?"

"Not stuff, Jackson." She sat up straight to glare at him. "Embryos—our embryos—that we planned to use a couple of years after...our first baby."

"And you just went ahead and used one of 'em without me?"

He remembered enough to know he'd contributed to the procedure before...and they'd saved some of his sperm, too.

"I used several. I wanted a baby. You weren't here. They don't last forever." She shrugged, her hands palms-up.

"Son of a—" He stopped, shuddered through a breath. "And if I hadn't come home?"

"I guess I would be doing what I'd planned on doing anyway. Become a single mother." She got up, her blush turning a bright pink now. "And that's exactly what I intend to do now that you are home—be a single mother. You are in no way obligated to me or the baby."

Jackson couldn't think of anything more mean and manipulative. "You're gonna have our child—my child—without me?"

"Yes," she said, gritting the word out. "You weren't here and my biological clock was ticking away. I took matters into my own hands the same way I had to do with this place and my boutique. I had to take care of myself."

"So you just went and got yourself pregnant?"

It shouldn't surprise Jackson that Riley didn't even need a man to make a baby. Heck, she'd always been strong-willed and independent, but this took the cake.

"It wasn't that simple," she replied, her hands gripping the chair again. "It took a lot of procedures and several tries."

He let that soak in, but shock still radiated all around him. "What'd you do, go back and forth to Atlanta?"

"Yes. The doctors there are very qualified."

"The same doctors we had before?"

"Yes, and a couple of new ones."

He lowered his head, memories of taking those drives with her moving through his mind with all the intensity of I-75 traffic. It made him sick to think of her doing that, taking that on, without even consulting him.

Made him sick. And then made him mad. But underneath all of that, he felt a sweet hope rising like a phoenix, winged and strong. He was going to be a father again. A second chance. The second chance he'd prayed about. Unless Riley denied him that chance.

He found his own chair to grip, so he wouldn't move toward her. "It's my baby, too, Riley."

She looked up at him, tossed her hair away. "Says who?"

"Says me," he retorted, unable to stand still. He cleared the space between them, his hands touching on her elbows. "I'm the father. I have rights."

Her wide-eyed stare pinned him. "Oh, really? You had rights while we were still married, remember? Only, once I got pregnant and even after we lost our baby, you didn't want any of those rights. Or have you forgotten all the nights I lay here alone while you went out hunting and drinking with your lodge buddies? Sounds as if you're gonna take right back up where you left off—without a thought for me."

"Oh, I'm thinking about you right now, suga'. And what I'm thinking can't be said in polite company."

"I don't care what you think," she retorted, her voice rising. "I told you to leave, so go."

"This is…should still be…my house," he said, shouting the words, all of his pent-up regrets turning to anger. "I tried, Riley. I really did. But you turned away from me one time too many. You never actually needed me for anything and this just goes to prove that."

She came around the chair, her eyes blazing. "I turned away because you refused to talk to me and you acted like you hated the sight of me."

Never hated, he wanted to say. Never that. He couldn't tell her that his own guilt was eating away at him. And that's why he couldn't face her, couldn't reach out to her. But now, now, she'd gone and done something that would never bring them any kind of peace or closure.

She'd gone and got herself pregnant with his child. Without him.

"I don't hate you," he said, meaning it. "I just hate that we've reached this point."

"*We* didn't reach anything," she replied. "I made this decision on my own. I wanted a baby."

"Good way to write me off forever," he said. "Perfect way to get even with ole Jackson. Twist those knives a little tighter in my back, why don't you?"

"I didn't think I'd ever see you again," she replied, turning toward the French doors. "Now just go, please."

But Jackson couldn't leave it at that. No sir. He stalked toward her, pulling her around and into his arms. "I'm not going anywhere, sweetheart. Starting here and now, I'm gonna be on you and that baby like a duck on a June bug. I told you I'm here to stay, Riley. And now, I have even more reason to be back here. I'm gonna be a daddy."

"No, you are not," she said, trying to pull away.

Jackson held her there, not too tight. He didn't want to harm the child. But he held her all the same, and…it felt good in spite of his anger and regret. She felt good. A little skinny, but good. He moved his hand down to her stomach, held it splayed there. And his whole system went soft as swamp mud. "A baby, Riley. Our baby. I wish—"

"I wish you'd leave," she said, but it was a weak plea. He saw the need in her pretty, scared eyes. A need she'd deny, no matter what. Because she hated him that much. Didn't she?

"No, you don't wish I'd leave. If you wanted me gone, you wouldn't have told me about the baby."

"I had to tell you," she said, her frown muted in the lamplight. "I'll be showing soon and you know how the rumors fly around here. I didn't want you to think—"

"That you'd been with another man," he finished, triumph cresting in that realization. At least she still had some class.

"I had to explain," she said, her eyes going wide.

"I got it," he replied. Riley was all about saving face, after all.

He leaned down and gave her a soft peck on the cheek, that swift stolen touch enough to kill him. "Congratulations, darlin'. Not only did you get your wish for a baby, but Jackson Sinclair is back in town. You got your husband back, too. That just about beats anything anybody could offer you."

"Ex-husband," she reminded him, pulling away. "You need to remember that."

"Maybe so," Jackson said, turning toward the door. "But being divorced doesn't mean a thing to that baby. I'm the daddy. And I'm giving you fair warning. That child will know me, whether you like it or not."

SHE DIDN'T LIKE IT. And she really hadn't meant to blurt the news out that way. But Jackson always did know which buttons to push. Tonight, he'd used all his brooding charm and all of her regrets to get her so flustered she'd told him the one thing he didn't need to know.

Now that he was gone and she was all alone, she had plenty of time to remember and ponder and wonder. What would she do now that Jackson was back?

"Well, at least it's out of the way, out there for all the world to know."

Except, she hadn't even told Aunt Verde or Uncle Floyd about the baby. Margie Sue was the only one who knew.

Besides Jackson.

"I'd better do some damage control," she said while she rubbed hand cream on her skin.

Then she stopped. This was a baby, not some publicity stunt or promotional event. A baby. Her baby.

Jackson's baby.

The only damage control Riley needed to do was in taking care of herself and this child. And she'd need to work on her feelings for Jackson—her love/hate feelings for the man she'd once planned on being with forever.

But forever was hard to reach.

Riley climbed into the big, empty bed and thought of Jackson. Thought of the way he'd touched her tonight, gentle but full of a burning rage, cool but filled with a heated need, bitter and cold but warm with the possibility of…hope.

If she'd turned, pressed against him, reached up to kiss him, would he have stayed with her?

Probably. But they were no longer married and her reputation was pretty much shot to begin with. Now she was pregnant and she was *not* married to Jackson anymore.

To ease that sticky situation, she thought instead about the baby. She really hadn't had a free moment to celebrate this newfound joy. Then she thought about that tiny grave a few miles up the road to town.

And her tiny son, buried there. They'd planned on calling him Jack Thomas. Not just Jack or Thomas. But Jack Thomas. A good, strong Southern name. A big name for such a tiny baby to live up to. He would have done it, though. He should have grown to be big and strong, to play baseball and soccer, to take his first girlfriend to the prom, to go off to college, preferably at the University of Georgia. Or maybe Valdosta State or Georgia Tech. It didn't matter. Her son would have conquered the world.

Would have.

Riley touched her stomach, a solid fear paralyzing

her joy. What if this one didn't make it? What if she lost this baby, too?

I won't let it happen, she said on a silent whisper. *Dear God, please don't let it happen,* she prayed on a silent plea.

Riley curled up and tried to sleep. She'd need her rest now. She'd get tired, really tired, more often. Her stomach would grow big and round. She'd be careful this time. She'd do everything right this time.

Because if she lost this child, there wouldn't be a next time.

JACKSON WATCHED THE sun come up over the piney woods surrounding the sparkling lake at the Southern Hill Hunting Lodge, his mind on one thing and one thing only.

He was going to be a father.

He sipped the always-strong coffee he remembered and let out a cross between a contented sigh and a disillusioned grunt.

He was going to be a father, if Riley let him.

He'd do it anyway, no letting about it. She might have run him out of town on a rail but he wouldn't let her keep him from his child. He could sue. After all, she couldn't have done this without him. Technically, even if she'd done it emotionally and physically without him. Even if she'd done it out of revenge against him.

He could sue for his parental rights. He'd probably signed them away right along with everything else, though. Riley could have easily sneaked some kind of document in with all the other divorce papers. Sign right here, Mr. Sinclair. This is to state that you are willingly giving up any rights to what might become a baby one day.

This could become very dicey.

And they'd be right back where they'd left off. In court. In a nasty battle yet again.

Jackson was tired of battling.

"What you thinking about so hard, son?"

Jackson turned from the wall of windows covering one side of the lodge's rustic gathering room to find Uncle Floyd standing there eating a sausage biscuit. Homemade biscuits and real Southern Hill sausage, at that. Verde made the best biscuits on earth.

"I'm wondering," Jackson said. He wasn't sure who all knew about the baby, so he didn't say anything about that. "You've done a great job with this place. I'm wondering if I should mess with that."

Uncle Floyd finished his biscuit and dusted off his hands. "You ain't exactly messing with anything. You own this place, and I ain't getting any younger. I was just keeping watch till you came home."

Jackson had to grin at that. Uncle Floyd had always been easygoing and laid back. "And what if I hadn't come home?"

"I knew you would, one day."

"Really?" Jackson wondered about that since he hadn't felt the same. He'd only decided to return about a month ago. Something about sitting alone on one of the world's most beautiful beaches could do that to a man. He loved this view of the lake and the trees better than anything he'd seen out in the big world. And on that particular night with the moon full and smiling down on him, he couldn't get Riley or this place out of his mind. He realized he was severely homesick.

"Really," Uncle Floyd replied with mannish confidence. "You had to go searching in order to find what you need right here."

"Are you sure?"

"Pretty sure. I did see the way you looked at Riley last night, son."

Jackson shook his head. "I wouldn't bet on that, Floyd. The woman told me to get out of her house."

Floyd kept his smile intact. "Which, in womanspeak, means 'Jackson, please don't go.'"

"Okay, when did you become Dr. Phil?"

Floyd adjusted his hunting cap. "Son, it don't take a therapist to see that you and Riley belong together. It just takes the two of you learning to compromise and forgive the way Verde and I have."

"Oh, I see," Jackson replied, amused and intrigued. "And how did you learn the fine art of compromise?"

"By always saying 'Yes, dear,'" Floyd replied with a wink.

Jackson waved his hand in the air. "You're still full of it, old man."

"Don't forget it," Uncle Floyd replied. "Now, you ready to get on with our day, boss-man?"

Jackson drained his coffee then turned to grab his own hat. "I reckon so. What's on the agenda?"

"Got one party coming in for the weekend. Some Atlanta fellows—a doctor and two lawyers. City folk, but they love to hunt deer and quail. They're all licensed up and permitted, too."

Jackson settled into the old familiar pattern, laughing at Uncle Floyd's strange terminology. But the man knew the hunting laws like the back of his hand. Floyd would abide by the licenses and the permits, or no hunters would enter the front gate. Even before Floyd had started managing this place, he'd been a regular fixture around here. Riley's daddy and brothers, too.

And Jackson. He loved this place. Back then, he'd spent more time here than he had at home with Riley. Part of the problem between them, but something he couldn't explain. But now, that didn't matter much. She didn't need him anymore. Maybe she'd never needed him. The lodge *did* need him. He wanted to keep the legacy his daddy had left for him. The hunting and fishing, the comfort of old friends laughing and having a good steak and a cold beer, those things brought him peace.

That had always been his excuse, until the night he'd learned that something had gone wrong with the baby boy they'd been expecting.

While his wife lay in the emergency room, waiting for him to come, Jackson had been out of cell range deep in the Georgia woods.

This time that has to be different, he told himself.

Whether Riley wanted him there or not, no matter how much he loved this lodge or not, he'd be present for the birth of this baby. He had better cell coverage now and…he had better sense, too. He just needed to make Riley see that.

In the meantime, he still had a job to do.

"Show me the deer management report first, Uncle Floyd. Then we'll talk about the drought and how that will affect the upcoming season. I'll be glad to help you with the fellows from Atlanta. I'm itching to get out there."

"Good," Uncle Floyd said, his dark eyes squinting toward the rising sun. "Good to have you back."

"Good to be back," Jackson said.

He could do this. He could manage the lodge and… be a good father. His daddy had done that and farmed this whole plantation, too. And Jack Junior, as they'd often called Jackson's daddy, had been a good father to his only son.

Hadn't he?

CHAPTER FIVE

"So, THE MAGAZINE people want to get a layout into the December issue," Riley explained to Margie Sue in her office three days later. "They're willing to hold production so they can get us in, so they're coming back at the end of this week. We have the holidays coming up and it will be good to be featured in the December issue, so we need to get cracking on sprucing this place up." She stopped, gasped. "I'll be a nervous wreck."

Margie Sue kept nodding and "Uh-huh-ing." She only did that when she really wanted to be the one doing the talking.

"Out with it," Riley said, dropping her hands down on her desk. She grabbed a saltine and nibbled at it then chased it with some lemon-lime soda while she tried to ignore the queasiness in her stomach.

"When's the last time you saw Jackson?" Margie Sue asked, her eyes sparkling as brightly as the retro jewelry dangling on a display out in the showroom.

"Who wants to know?" Riley asked back, her hormones going on full throttle. She'd tried not to think about Jackson, let alone see the man. She'd been purposely avoiding him since she'd broken the news about the baby. But then he'd obviously been avoiding her, too. Which meant he didn't really care all that much about her being pregnant. And that was just fine by her. Really.

But she couldn't get him off her mind. Why did he have to blow in on an ill wind looking even better than he did when he left? Why did she care? She needed to rest and focus on this shop and her baby.

"I want to know," Margie Sue said, her hand on her hips, bejeweled bangles dancing down her slender wrist. "I mean, is he part of the family again? Can we invite him to our annual fall barbecue this weekend?"

Riley jumped up so fast the pretty potted mum on her desk jiggled enough to rain down burnished blossoms onto her desk pad. "What makes you think he's part of the family again?"

Margie Sue looked confused. "Well, because of… well…"

She stopped, clamped her mouth closed. "I guess it's really none of my business."

Riley shook her head, disgusted with herself for even trying to be mean to Margie Sue. "It's not that. It's just…that Mama and Daddy have been calling asking the same thing. Bobby even called me and he never gets involved in anything, but my baby brother misses Jackson. They always were close."

Margie Sue did another "Uh-huh" then smacked her gum. "Delton's been wondering, too. But I told him to back off."

Riley had to smile at that. Margie Sue would protect her like a mama bear but she'd also bug her until she got answers. Right now however, Riley didn't have any answers.

"You're in a pickle, girl."

"Don't I know it," Riley said, getting up to test her queasiness. When her head didn't spin, she took a tentative step. "I haven't announced this pregnancy yet and I'm afraid if Jackson shows up anywhere, he'll be beaming and bragging and doing all that man stuff about being a father. But he's not going to be a father. At least not to this baby."

"You told him?"

Oops. "Yes, I blurted it out when he came by the house the other night."

"Uh-huh." Margie Sue couldn't seem to find words for a reply.

"I hadn't planned on telling him, but you know how I am when I've got my back against the wall."

"I sure do," Margie Sue said, her expression one part sympathy and one part stunned. "How'd he take the news?"

"I'm not sure," Riley admitted. "He wasn't too happy that I'd gone and done this without him. But it was kind of cute how angry he seemed when he thought I'd been with someone else."

Margie Sue put a hand to her heart. "He still cares, I reckon."

Riley didn't want to think that. Or did she? "He wants to be a part of the baby's life."

Another sympathetic look. "Well, it is something to consider if he's planning to stay."

They heard the shop bell jingle. Her sister-in-law glanced toward the open door then lowered her voice. "When exactly are you going to announce it to everyone, honey? And why can't Jackson be a father to his baby? If he's gonna be around—"

"We can't count on that," Riley said, sitting back down while waves of dizziness crashed inside her head. "I won't count on Jackson, ever again."

Margie Sue gave her a concerned look. "Ever again is a long time."

"So is never," Riley retorted. "I appreciate your concern but I need to let this settle. I'm pregnant and Jackson is hovering around. That sure wasn't in the plan, so I have a lot to get used to."

"But you're going back for your checkup Friday, right?"

"Yes. I'll ride up there Friday morning and be back before we close for the day, I hope."

"Okay." Margie turned to go back out onto the floor. She made it to the office door then pivoted. "Riley, Allison just came in."

Riley let out a little moan. Her other sister-in-law. The gossipy stuck-up one, married to her middle brother, Curtis. Riley and Allison tolerated each other for the sake of their families, but some days it was hard work. "Great, just great. She only comes around when she either has a scoop or wants to get in on one. You don't think—"

"She's probably dying to know how you feel about Jackson being back. Don't give her any ammunition."

"I won't. Can you run interference until I go freshen up? I don't want to look green when she sees me. She's so good at guessing this kind of stuff."

Margie Sue backed out of the room. "I'll keep her occupied."

Riley hurried to her private bathroom connected to the office. This shop had once been a quaint little cottage located at the end of Railroad Street. She'd bought it cheap and renovated it to suit her needs. The various "rooms" had been turned into different retail zones but with open walls between them so the customers could stroll through. This also provided Riley and her staff a good view of the whole place.

She'd wanted the boutique to look like a big closet full of everything a woman could possibly want, maybe because she had those things and longed for the one thing most of her friends already had—a child.

This shop—The Life of Riley—had become her baby and she'd spoiled it with enough enticing girlie-girl things to keep her and a lot of other women happy. At least for the past few years.

But now, finally, her wish had come true. And like the princess her parents had raised her to be, Riley wanted this heir to have the best of life. Riley already had the keys to the kingdom with Southern Hill Plantation and her shop.

Now she wanted her own little prince or princess to carry on. And yes, she intended to spoil this baby, but with love, lots of love.

She thought about Jackson. Court jester or return-

ing Black Prince? Did he deserve to be a part of that
love she so longed to pass around? Wouldn't he also
want to spoil his child? Then she thought about tiny
Jack Thomas. He'd never had a chance to be spoiled.
That thought ripped through any feelings she might
have for Jackson.

Torn between duty to her ex-husband and the need
to protect herself and this baby, Riley pushed the tur-
moil out of her head and armed herself for a chat with
Allison. Yes, right now, she'd rather face her infuriating sister-in-law than think about Jackson.

HE WAS THINKING about Riley.

Jackson hit a hand on the sunrise/sunset charts lying
on his desk. Seeing these twelve-month charts only
made him think of all the sunrises and sunsets he'd
had to endure out there all alone over the past five
years. And the next nine months to come.

Being alone could change a man.

Hearing he was going to be a father could do the
same.

In his case, being alone had forced him to grow
up. He'd seen a lot of things, sailing around the world
in the yacht. Contrary to all the rumors, the woman
hadn't completely wiped him out. She'd taken Southern Hill—the main house, the land, livestock and the
pecan groves, but she'd insisted he take the revenues
from the lodge.

It had not been a grand gesture.

Riley wanted him to remember what she'd told him

the night she'd asked him for a divorce. "You can stay at the lodge, since that's your home away from home anyway. And you can keep all the income earned from the lodge. I don't want that money. Ever."

Ever. Because the lodge represented her bitterness and scorn. And reminded her of the night she'd lost their child.

So giving him control over that place also made him remember where they'd gone wrong. And he did remember, every single day since he'd walked away from her.

So why had he come back to run the lodge? To torment himself even more?

Because it was all he had left.

When he'd decided to return to Sinclair, he figured it wouldn't be easy. He couldn't just move back in with Riley. But he could move into the lodge and lose himself in all the outdoor activities he'd enjoyed growing up.

Sitting here now in the big paneled office that used to belong to his father, Jackson saw the truth staring at him with the same starkness as the deer head over the buttery leather sofa. This place had been safe for him. A hiding place when things went bad on him. A haven when he didn't want to deal with reality. An escape when he didn't want to man up.

And, he had to admit, he hadn't been much of a man in the first few years of their marriage. He'd played at it, but he'd never actually stepped up. Maybe because in his mind, he could never *live up* to his daddy's demands or…to his wife's demands.

He'd missed his parents. He'd wished they'd been closer. They held a pretty, contrived facade for the world, but when they were all three alone together, the quietness settled over them like an old blanket. Jackson had always felt he'd let his folks down for some reason. Never mind that he'd been a star on the football team yet still managed to maintain his grades. Never mind that he'd worked hard on the land and at the lodge, but rarely got a smile or a compliment.

He'd married Riley because he loved her. But…he'd needed to leave her so he could escape all the guilt of not understanding what he'd done wrong. Too late to talk to his parents and ask them about that. But it wasn't too late to make things right with Riley.

Did he come back here to hide out from Riley? Or had he insisted on running the lodge to show her he actually could?

Either way, he was here now and he wasn't the easygoing, carefree man he'd once been. He'd never take things for granted again. He was going to be a daddy himself. Again. A second chance to make things right. Now he understood so much more about what being a father really meant. That brought about a whole new understanding of things. And a new determination to make things right, once and for all.

Jackson's formidable, demanding daddy and quiet, shy mother had died a year after Jackson and Riley's wedding. So Jackson and Riley had taken the big master suite on the second floor and Jackson had taken over the responsibilities of being the sole heir to Southern Hill. Life had gone on, the same but different.

Jackson knew losing both of his parents had messed with his head. In his quest to keep Southern Hill running, and in his need to enjoy being a newly married man, he'd forgotten to grieve. He'd forgotten to feel, to want, to live.

Then, a few years later he'd lost his son. A trip around the world couldn't cure that kind of hurt.

"You can run, but you can't hide," he said now, saluting the solemn stare of the deer head. "Sooner or later, it'll all catch up with you."

He would stand up to Riley and he'd show her he'd changed.

The old desk phone rang. Jackson stared at it then realized he needed to answer it. They didn't have secretaries around this lodge.

"Hello?"

"Jackson, old buddy, heard you'd sneaked back into town!"

"Delton?"

"The one and only."

Jackson grinned. One of his ex-brothers-in-law. He'd loved each of them like brothers, too. He'd been an only child, but hanging with the Buckingham boys had taught him a lot of things, both good and bad. Boy, how he'd missed Riley's big family when he'd traveled around.

"How you doing, Delton?"

"Finer than frog hair," Delton said on a lazy drawl. "I'm calling to invite you to our little First Hunt barbecue this Saturday. You available?"

For some of the best barbecue in the world? Yeah, he was available. That little family barbecue was a hundred-year-old tradition and all the hunters from this part of the state attended with their families. It was part fallfest to celebrate the harvest and part Boy Scout campout to celebrate the beginning of hunting season.

But it was so much more than that. Being invited to the Buckingham barbecue had always meant family to Jackson. Especially when his parents had been alive and they'd all shared those special times with the surrounding community.

He remembered being with Riley at most of the barbecues, remembered long walks in the woods and times cuddled together on the hayride around the Buckingham property. He remembered eating s'mores and kissing her with the taste of marshmallows and chocolate between them. He remembered her mother making hot chocolate for them. No wonder he'd been so touched when one night during his travels, a little Hispanic girl had offered him that particular drink. And had shown him what true love and forgiveness was all about.

Jackson closed his eyes and for just a minute, he was back in that safe, warm place.

"Hey, you still there?"

"Uh, let me check my busy social itinerary," Jackson quipped to loosen the memories. "Yes, I just happen to be free Saturday. I wouldn't want to miss the famous Buckingham Farm First Hunt Barbecue, but I am helping Floyd with a day-hunt Saturday. I might have to bring those Atlanta boys with me for some good eatin'. One doctor and two lawyers."

"Bring 'em on," Delton said, chuckling. "Never hurts to glad-hand a paying customer and you never know when you might need a doctor or lawyer as a friend. We'll make 'em want to come back next year or maybe even next week."

"We need that," Jackson said, thinking of the baby. "I'm helping Floyd run the lodge now."

"I heard," Delton said. "That's a good fit for you since you used to hang out there so much."

Jackson didn't miss the implications of that innocent remark. "I guess so. Didn't have much of a choice."

"Riley givin' you the cold shoulder?"

Jackson wanted to say, "Yes, but she's having my baby so I'm planning on finding her warm side."

But he didn't. Instead, he said, "She has her reasons for being that way. I...wasn't exactly Husband of the Year."

Delton grunted. "Well, you should at least get a conciliatory trophy for putting up with my wildfire little sister."

Jackson wanted to laugh, but it hurt too much. "I loved putting up with her, most days."

Delton cleared his throat. "We all know that. Maybe something good will happen for y'all now that you're back. It's never too late."

"I made a big mistake," Jackson admitted, glad to have a buddy to talk to. Which sounded sappy and silly, but there it was. He'd been out there alone for so long, he was rusty, his feelings faded and corroded. But still brittle.

Delton chuckled. "We all make mistakes. But, Jackson, you know what they say about making the same mistake twice? The first time *is* a mistake, the second time is a choice. We're all hoping you and Riley make the right choice this time."

Delton Buckingham never failed to surprise him. "I can't believe y'all even want me back."

"Oh, we all do," Delton retorted. "Except maybe Riley. But she'll come around."

Jackson doubted that. "Regardless, I'll be there Saturday. Thanks for inviting me, Delton."

"Good, good," Delton replied. "Now, I have to let you in on a little secret, okay?"

"I'm listening," Jackson said, falling right back into the old pattern of playing straight man to Delton's jokes.

"I'm not telling Riley you're coming and you'd be wise to not tell her, either, know what I mean?"

"I do," Jackson answered, his hand taking a nervous pass over his hair. "Do you think that's wise, though?"

"It is if you want some barbecue," Delton said on a chuckle. "She won't make a scene if you happen to show up, but if she knows you're coming, she won't even make an appearance and I just can't have my baby sister missing out on the barbecue. My mama would tan my hide on that one."

"Good point," Jackson said, memories of Delton's slightly twisted logic making him smile. "Okay, I guess I can live with that. But if she isn't happy, I'll have to leave."

"Fair enough. And I'll send a big plate home with you for your trouble."

"Can't beat a deal like that. I'll take you up on the to-go plate."

Jackson hung up, wondering if he should just stay home.

Or rather, stay here in his rustic suite at the lodge.

He got up and walked to the big window across from his daddy's desk. He missed his parents. He missed Riley more.

He wondered how she was feeling today.

Then he wondered when she'd be heading back to Atlanta for her baby checkup. Whenever it was, he planned on being there with her.

But first, he'd have to make her tell him what time and where. Or he'd just have to do a little snooping then follow her all the sixty miles to Atlanta.

CHAPTER SIX

RILEY HEADED OUT the back door to her car. She was
going to be late for her first checkup since she'd found
out she was pregnant if she didn't hurry. It was a good
hour and a half drive to Atlanta with traffic.

"Bye, bye, honey," Aunt Verde called from the sunroom. "Be careful now."

"I will," Riley replied. Aunt Verde knew she had a
doctor's appointment in Atlanta, but thankfully hadn't
asked anything more when Riley had told her she was
going in for a checkup.

Riley planned to sit her whole family down this
weekend and tell them the truth. Her parents had called
to see her reaction to Jackson being back, and she'd
assured them she was handling it okay.

"I don't believe that for one minute," her mother—
Verde's sister Bettye—had told Riley the other night.
"I remember you and Jackson being happy once. I
pray for that again."

"Pray away, Mama," Riley had retorted. "Just pray
that I don't buy that lodge right out from under him
and send him packing again."

"You're all bark and no bite," her Southern-to-the-
core mother had answered. "You just need to get this

mess straightened out and get right again. Divorce is not becoming, Riley."

And didn't she know that. Her mother had been mortified when Riley had asked Jackson for a divorce, but in true Bettye Buckingham fashion, she'd stood up for her only girl, too. Bettye didn't let anyone at the country club or the garden club bad-mouth her children. She'd take care of that herself, thank you very much.

Riley loved her family, but hated how they smothered her. She knew they loved her and the smothering came from that love. But being the only girl amongst three brothers, she'd had to prove to everyone, including her family, that she did have a brain in her blond head. They all thought Jackson Sinclair had hung the moon. Riley had to show them she could make the sun shine.

So to speak.

Now she had the task of telling her conservative, traditional-values-type family that she was going to have a baby through artificial insemination and eSET—elective single embryo transfer—from an embryo that had been frozen for five years.

Her mama would faint.

Her daddy might cuss.

Then her mama would tell her daddy to hush up that ugly talk in her house.

Then her three brothers would start shouting their own thoughts and give out sage advice while they placed bets on how much the baby would weigh and what the kid would be named.

Margie Sue would hug Riley. Allison would grin and start texting her friends—and she'd start bossing Riley around. And Bobby's college cheerleader girlfriend would post it all on Facebook to her sorority sisters.

"I have to do it," Riley told herself as she backed out of the garage and turned to head up the driveway to the road. No way to hide this from her family the way she'd tried to hide all of her marriage problems.

A car sat parked in the driveway. A shiny red sports car.

"Jackson!" She hissed the name through clenched teeth. What was he doing parked crooked in her drive? Now she really would be late.

She pulled up and got out of her car. "What are you doing?"

He stood there, leaning back against the car in a good-looking pose in jeans and boots, his white button-up shirt as crisp as the autumn air. "And good morning to you, too."

"I can't be late, Jackson. You need to move that car."

He pushed off the convertible. "Where you headed?"

"Uh...to Atlanta. I have things to do up there."

"I'm sure you do, suga'. Things like maybe going to the baby doctor. I'm going with you."

Riley's heart did a little flip. "No, you are not."

He lost the devastating smile and pounced a little

closer. "You're going for a checkup and I'm going with you."

No way. She couldn't let him do that. She'd be a nervous wreck. "What makes you think I'm going to the doctor?" Or rather, who had told him?

"No thinking about it, Riley. I know. I have ways of finding out things."

She didn't want to know those ways, but if Margie Sue or Delton had blabbed this, she'd let them both have it. "You have the wrong information. I'm going to Atlanta for other purposes."

"Don't lie to me," he said, getting in front of her. "If you want to make that appointment, you'd better level with me. 'Cause I'm not moving my car until you do."

Riley wanted to scream. She couldn't be late. This was too important. But she didn't want Jackson there, either. She glanced around, thinking she could saddle up and ride the fence line into town then find another car. But he'd only follow her. And she couldn't risk being on a horse right now.

"I'm waiting," Jackson said, his tone easy and slow, his striking blue eyes gleaming.

"Get that car out of my driveway," she said, hoping he'd have a little compassion.

But that didn't work, either. "Riley, I don't want you driving to Atlanta alone."

Oh, so now he was trying the he-man tactic.

Which made her try the I-am-woman tactic. "I do it all the time."

"You're pregnant now, though."

"Maybe so, but I don't need you to be my chaperone."

He pulled her close then stared down at her, his eyes snapping fire. "I'm not your chaperone, but I am that baby's daddy. And I'm going with you to the doctor."

She wanted to cry but she wouldn't give him that satisfaction. She only wanted to get to the doctor. "Move the car. We have to hurry."

His triumphant expression rankled her like barbed wire, but she didn't care right now. She intended to take care of herself and this baby. And if Jackson did anything to upset her or cause her to have problems with this pregnancy, she'd never forgive him.

But then, she'd never forgiven him already.

THE DRIVE TO the Reproductive Center was awkward to say the least. Riley stared at the countryside and tried to let the turning of the leaves soothe her flustered soul.

"This might go better if you'd talk to me," Jackson said, his expert control of *her* car rattling her as much as his presence.

"What do you want to talk about?" she said on a snap. The I-75 traffic flowed by with the same speed as the thoughts running through her head.

"Our baby."

That statement brought her head around. "My baby."

"Our baby," he said again, glancing toward her for a fraction of a minute, his eyes shuttered and hard to read. "Whether you like it or not, you yourself told me I'm the father. And I believe you."

"Well, good. I was so very worried about that."

He grunted and passed several cars. "Same old Riley. Hiding behind that witty sarcasm."

She huffed and held on. "Same old Jackson, hiding behind that good ole boy attitude."

"You know how the song goes, darlin'." He quoted the lyrics from a favorite country song.

"Very funny, Toby Keith."

He turned the radio to a country station. Johnny Cash filled the air with prison woes. And she felt like a prisoner in her own car.

"I see your taste in music hasn't changed, either," she said, memories of other twangy songs playing in her mind.

"Nope. Not too much about me has changed but *I* have changed. A little older, maybe a little wiser."

"Wiser?" Now that was interesting. He'd always been smart and capable, but he'd just never seemed to care all that much about what anyone thought. Especially her. "How did you become wise, Jackson?"

He sped past a semitruck then shot her a glance. "Being alone with myself on that boat, I read a lot, thought about everything. I sailed from port to port and did a lot of things I'd never thought about doing here. Caught a shark off the coast of Florida, went parasailing there, too. Helped rebuild houses after a hurricane in Alabama."

"Okay, now you sound like a Jimmy Buffett–Alan Jackson duet."

"Well, I did try to live like I was dying." He grinned then turned serious. "But wait, that was Tim McGraw."

She inhaled a breath. While she'd been here, alone and grieving for her lost baby and her lost marriage, he'd been out there parasailing? And fishing? And re-building houses?

"I can't picture you doing charity work. You always told me to just write a big check for anyone in need."

He shook his head and gave her a wry smile. "I couldn't picture that, either, but I did it. For about a month. We rebuilt twenty houses in Alabama *and* Mississippi. I learned a lot. You ever need something fixed, call me, babe."

Babe. He used to call her that. It had slipped out so easily through his sweet-talking lips. He probably didn't even realize he'd said it. But suddenly, she wanted to hear about every minute he'd been away. Just to torment herself. Or maybe just to pick at him.

"Where did you live?"

"Mostly on the boat."

The *Riley.* He'd named the darn boat after her the day they'd bought it together in Savannah, back when things were good. They certainly christened it that night out in the waters just off of Tybee Island, too. Kind of ironic that he'd had to see her name each time he set sail.

"Where is that precious boat of yours now?"

"Somewhere up north. I sold her."

Shocked, she turned in the seat. "You sold your boat?"

"Sure did. I won't need that boat anymore. I'm a landlubber now, darlin'."

"But you loved that boat!"

He gave her a mock-frown. "And you hated it."

"I hated that you went to Savannah and sailed away for days at a time," she reminded him. Then because that reminder sounded so whiny, she threw up her hands. "But whatever. No skin off my back."

"And it's a pretty back."

That drawled-out compliment made her blush. She pushed at her hair and continued on. "So you sold the yacht and now you're back to torment me?"

He stopped smiling. "I'm not into torment, Riley. Believe it or not, I also talked to some very smart people while I was out there roaming around."

"I know, I know," she said, giving him a fake smile. "Bartenders are always so wise."

"I don't drink anymore," he replied, his expression tinged with anger. "I talked to professionals— you know, therapists who help people deal with stuff."

That floored her. "You're kidding. You never wanted to go to therapy with me."

"No, I sure didn't. I guess it took you throwing me out to see I needed help."

"I guess so."

She couldn't help but be hurt that he'd gone through that without her. She'd had a good support system after…they lost little Jack Thomas and after Jackson had left, but she'd often wished they could have ironed things out together. She'd tried to comfort him after his parents died, but he always brushed her off with a smile and a kiss. Things had become better when she'd talked him into having a baby, no matter the means. But he'd hated all the tests and the timelines and the clinical aspects of the treatments. But then after months of being disappointed, they'd found out she was pregnant. At first, they were both happy, but soon Jackson began to shut down even more.

It just seemed to Riley that if he'd loved her, he would have fought for her and that meant doing whatever it would take to save their marriage. But then, she had given up, too. What was the point?

Instead, he'd sailed away like a pirate tired of his booty. Or in this case, a man who no longer loved his wife.

Sullen now, Riley stayed close to her side of the car. Why had she let him come with her? And who had ratted her out?

"Who told you about my appointment?" she asked, to change the subject.

He kept his eyes on the road.

"Jackson?"

"I never reveal my sources, suga'."

"So you haven't changed all that much, after all?"

He glared across at her. "You can believe what you want, honey. You can give me that pretty pout all day long. You can try to keep me away from you, keep secrets about what's happening with that baby. But it won't work, Riley."

He whirled the car through the downtown Atlanta traffic then turned onto Pine Street and headed toward Peachtree.

"I don't need you in my life," she retorted. "I wish you'd stayed at home."

He parked the car and turned off the engine. "That's just it. I don't actually have a home. But I have a baby on the way. And that's important to me, whether you believe me or not."

She didn't believe him. She wasn't used to this new, more formidable Jackson. He'd always been assertive and persuasive, but he'd never been dependable or responsible concerning her first pregnancy.

What had changed him?

Therapy?

Sailing around the world?

Building houses for less fortunate people?

Or not having a home of his own anymore?

She didn't know. Wasn't sure how to handle this.

When he came around the car, she honestly expected him to throw her over his shoulder and march her into that medical center.

Instead, he opened the door and held out his hand. "Let me help you, Riley. Let me show you how much I've changed."

Did she dare?

Right now, in spite of how he made her pulse beat too fast and her blood pressure do zips and turns, she didn't have any choice. She had to see the doctor, to be reassured that she was truly going to have a baby, to hear words of comfort and confirmation that this time, things would go so much better.

And now, Jackson wanted to see her through it?

Or…did he just want to remind her of how badly she'd failed the first time?

CHAPTER SEVEN

"HOW ABOUT SOME lunch?" Jackson asked two hours later. "It's already past two o'clock."

"I am starved," Riley admitted, her stomach agreeing. "I didn't have much breakfast. Mornings are the worst now."

They were in the lobby near the exit doors. Jackson breathed a sigh of relief that she'd even allowed him to talk to the doctor with her. But she hadn't wanted him in the examination room.

He could tell she was fading fast, so he tried to be agreeable. "Okay, then. You stay right here and I'll bring the car around. We'll find some place nearby."

She nodded. "They have cafés all over the place here, but it might be nice to get away from the medical center."

Concerned at her pale skin, Jackson grabbed her arm. "Hey, you okay?"

"I'm tired," she said, giving him a weary smile. "All the blood work and testing, the poking and examining, it's draining." She lifted her chin then. "But, it's worth it. Even when I had to give myself the hormone injections." She stopped, blinked back what looked like tears. "I'm sorry, Jackson. I just want things to work this time."

Jackson swallowed back his own fears. "Here, honey. Sit right here and I'll hurry. We should have gotten you a snack."

She allowed him to take her to a chair. Once he had her settled there, he said, "I'll be right back. The parking garage isn't that far." He whirled to leave then turned around. "Do you want some water?"

She had her phone out, scrolling for messages. "No. I'm okay. It's the hormones and I get cranky when I don't eat. Go ahead."

Jackson hurried out the door then after he was out of her sight, he sprinted to the garage. He was in the car and back by the pickup doors in record time. He rushed inside only to find Riley sitting there with her eyes closed.

"Riley?"

"Hmm?"

"I've got the car right out front."

She opened her eyes and blinked. "What is wrong with me? I nearly took a nap sitting straight up."

Jackson bent down in front of her and pushed at a strain of golden-blond hair. "You're pregnant, suga'. Remember when you used to fall asleep with your head on my shoulder while we watched television?"

She came awake then stared at him as if he'd grown two heads. "We need to get going. I wanted to be back before the shop closes."

Jackson let her slide past him then stood to follow

her. So much for going down memory lane. Once they were in the car, he stayed quiet, stewing in his own lost memories. Finally, back out in traffic, he didn't dare suggest any of their old hangouts in Atlanta.

"What would you like to eat?"

"Let's just go home."

"No." He maneuvered through an intersection then glanced over at her. "Riley, you need to eat, for the baby's sake."

She looked angry but her features finally softened in defeat. "Oh, all right. But you need to understand something. Just because I let you come with me—or rather you forced me to let you come with me—and talk to the doctor doesn't mean I'm letting you run the show. I'm fine on my own. I've read books about babies and more books about having babies. I know what this type of pregnancy involves already. I don't need you hovering or reminding me of the way things used to be." She took a breath then charged right back in. "This time I'm in control. This time things will be different. Do you understand?"

He understood all right. He understood that she wasn't in a forgiving mood to the father of her baby. "Yeah, I got it loud and clear. But right now, I'm only concerned with feeding you. Then I'll get you home and things will be different. You can count on that for sure."

WHAT DID HE mean by that? Riley wondered thirty minutes later as she washed her hands in the bathroom of a popular deli. Her shaking hands. She needed to eat, but her appetite was not cooperating. She felt weak and tired, but she wouldn't give Jackson the satisfaction of seeing her that way. Looking at herself in the mirror now, she saw the fatigue and the worry right there on her face. Having him back in her life was taking its toll on her. She couldn't let his presence mess up things with this pregnancy.

Then she remembered the pride in his eyes when the doctor had gone through the protocol, remembered him asking knowledgeable questions. She'd seen a real look of concern in his expression. For a little while, they'd truly been a couple talking to a doctor about their unborn child. Then he'd asked to go into the exam room with her and Riley had said no. Even the doctor, who knew they were divorced, had lifted an eyebrow at that refusal.

Had she been too demanding and harsh with Jackson?

"Why do you have to be so mean?" she whispered at her reflection. "He's only trying to help."

No, he's trying to get back in your good graces so he can spend more time with you. So you'll relent and let him be a part of your baby's life, dummy.

She needed to remember how charming her ex-husband could be. But when the charm wore off, he could stonewall with the best of them. She needed to remember how hard she'd fought for their home and land, the lodge and her boutique. How she'd stayed and kept everything intact—for him.

Without him.

She'd learned to take care of herself and everyone else, too. While her husband had tucked tail and run away. Or rather sailed away without a care in the world. How could she be sure he'd really changed?

Riley gathered her wits and went back out to their table. Jackson stood when he saw her, ever the gentleman at least. But he didn't help her with her chair.

"Your soup's on the way," he said, passing her some bread to eat while they waited.

Riley tore off a piece of the crusty bread and tapped some butter on it. The bread was hot and good, but it seemed to stick in her throat. She grabbed her iced tea and took a big gulp.

Jackson stared out the window then glanced back to her. "I'm sorry if I overstepped the boundaries, Riley."

Boundaries? Was that what she'd put up around herself? More like protective walls.

"It's okay. I just can't allow you to think—"

"That we might have a chance? That we'll just pick right back up where we left off? I'm not thinking that, darlin'." He shrugged then put his elbows on the table. "Look, I blew it. I know that. I didn't handle things the way I should have. But we both had a lot to deal with back then."

"Yes, we did," she said, bobbing her head while she tried to ignore the dusting of dark hair on his arms just underneath his rolled-up shirtsleeves. "That was then. This is a new reality for me. I've been planning on this for a long time now but I didn't plan on you being around when it happened. I'm all set to raise this baby alone."

He took his elbows off the table and leaned in. "Even if I show you I'll stick around this time?"

She honestly didn't know how she felt about that. "How can I be sure?" she asked. She took another bite of bread. "How can I even hope?"

The waitress brought their food—her vegetable soup and his hamburger and fries. "Anything else?" the perky girl asked.

"We're good," Jackson said. Then he glanced at Riley. "Aren't we?"

"Yes." She waited for the girl to walk away. "I just need time to adjust. And I can't do that if you hover and plot and stalk me at every turn."

"I'm not stalking you," he said, his gaze on his food. "I just wanted to be there with you today, to show you I support you, whether you want to include me or not." He nabbed a French fry. "I needed to hear the doctor talk about how all of this happened. I feel like…I'm still out in the ocean, drifting around."

She wanted to tell him he should have stayed there, but she'd berated him enough for one day. He *had* come up here with her and she had to admit, his presence during the initial visit with the doctor had reassured Riley and brought her comfort. But she couldn't count on that comfort.

She couldn't count on her ex-husband.

So she ate her soup to give her baby nourishment and she steeled herself against the emotions roiling over her like a tidal wave. Riley glanced around the busy restaurant, seeing other couples laughing and holding hands. Seeing mothers with young children, smiling and chatting.

While she sat here, silent and worried, with the only man she'd ever loved, and realized she was shutting him out of her life on purpose because he'd hurt her so very badly.

And yet, she couldn't wait to hold his baby in her arms and pour out all the love she still had inside her on that precious child.

How would she ever get through this?

Riley lifted her gaze to meet Jackson's. And she could have sworn he was wondering the very same thing.

He'd get through this somehow.

But he wouldn't leave this time. He'd show Riley and everyone else in this town that his ancestors had built, that he had staying power, too. Sure he'd been confused and maybe a little immature when he'd left, but he'd grown up overnight out there on his own. He'd been forced outside his comfort zone, forced to live as a stranger in a strange land. Up until the day he'd left Sinclair, he believed he was secure in his little world—his domain. He'd had friends, family, work he loved, a home he loved and a woman he planned to spend the rest of his life with.

But due to his stupidity and his bitterness, all of that had ended in the blink of an eye.

So, yes, he'd been forced to step back and take a

good, long look at himself and why his life had come crashing down around him. And he didn't like what he'd seen.

Jackson turned the car into the long driveway to the house and felt the hurt of a hundred memories hitting at him. The big white house looked like the perfect country home with its wide front porch and green-shuttered windows. The upstairs turret room used to be his parents' bedroom. Then it had been his and Riley's. Jackson ached to lay his tired head on that big brass bed, longed to get a good night's sleep, knowing he was truly back home.

But it wasn't to be.

He parked the car in the garage and turned to Riley. "Thanks for letting me go today. I'll see you inside then I'll be on my way."

She nodded, quiet now. "I'm so tired, I don't think I have the energy to run by the shop."

He got out and came around the car. "I think Margie Sue and the other sales associates can take care of things for one day."

She smiled at that. "I do have a good staff, but we're having the fall festival—new things for the next season. I love being there when my customers come in to try on sweaters and coats. And boots—we got in the cutest boots the other day."

He grinned at her. "You still are a clotheshorse, aren't you?"

"Yes, but I need to order a whole maternity line."

When her hand automatically went to her still-flat

stomach, his gaze followed. He itched to touch that place where their child was growing inside her, ached to make it all right for her and this baby.

"You'll look beautiful in anything, Riley. You know that."

She backed away, obviously not comfortable with the intimate words he'd just spoken. "I need to go inside. I'm gonna take a long nap before dinner."

He thought of asking to come in with her, but Jackson knew she didn't want him there. "Okay. Guess I'll see you…around."

He'd almost said tomorrow. But her big brother Delton was right. Best Riley didn't know Jackson was attending the barbecue. He'd have to see how she reacted when he got there tomorrow and decide whether he should stay or not.

He wanted to stay, tomorrow and every day.

He wanted to be near his wife and his baby.

His ex-wife, he reminded himself.

"Good night," she said, turning to go into the house. But she did whirl back around. "And, Jackson, thanks for going with me. It did help with some of my worries."

He didn't dare move. "Good. If you ever need me again—"

"I'll let you know."

Then she was gone, the scent of honeysuckle and vanilla lingering in the air while the memory of her lingered in his head.

"I'll see you tomorrow," he whispered toward the

turret room. Then he walked to where he'd left his car and got inside and drove away.

UPSTAIRS IN THAT very room, Riley sat on the bed and stared at the bag of prenatal vitamins and information pamphlets the nurses at the center had given her. Here alone in her room, she felt overwhelmed by everything that was about to change in her life. It didn't help that with this pregnancy she was remembering each and every step with the last one.

At first, they'd been so happy to hear she was going to have a baby. When Jackson found out it was a boy, he was over the moon. He teased that he'd wanted another little Riley, but she knew he was happy with having a son to carry on the Sinclair name. She took care of herself, worked hard to eat right and follow the doctor's advice.

Worked too hard.

In all her worries over the baby, she'd made one big mistake. She'd neglected her husband.

She hadn't meant to do it, but trying to get pregnant had already put a strain on their marriage. The first few years had been great. They'd laughed and loved each other, taken care of the land and the lodge and Riley had started plans to have a baby. Then came the discovery that they were different from most of their friends. They had a problem conceiving. The next couple of years had been a series of experts and doctors, of hormone injections and trying to hit the mark with temperature charts and times of the month.

After trying everything, they'd finally decided to try in vitro and the embryo transfer. And even though Riley had finally gotten pregnant, something had died inside their marriage.

The spark was gone. Jackson stayed at the lodge more than he stayed with her. Often he would drive to Savannah and take the boat out for a whole weekend while she sat at home, determined to take care of the child she carried.

Why had he left her alone so much when she'd needed him the most?

It had never been about another woman. She knew that. No, it had been more about the tremendous responsibilities he suddenly faced, as a father, as a farmer and landowner, as the sole heir to a vast legacy. Riley thought he was doing okay in the months after his parents died, but now she knew better. He'd held all his worries and fears inside until everything came crashing down around him and…caused him to turn away from Riley during a time when they should have been celebrating their joy.

On the night she'd gone into labor, they'd had a horrible fight. He'd left for a hunting and fishing weekend with some of his fraternity brothers. Out of reach, both physically and emotionally.

The baby came early. Too early. And Jackson was nowhere to be found.

She'd lost the baby, alone and afraid. Even though her family had been there with her, Riley had cried out for her husband.

He'd come home the next day to find out he wasn't going to be a father after all.

And that had ended the marriage.

Riley held a hand to her lips, tears rolling down her face. "I can't go through that again, Jackson. I just can't."

She knew she'd hurt him, pushed him away because she was so afraid she'd already lost his love. But he'd been drifting away since the day they decided to go the fertility route. He didn't like all the protocol necessary to bear a child. Did it make him feel less than a man? Or did he blame her because she couldn't conceive? She didn't know, and back then, she didn't care. She only wanted to have a baby. So she'd worked on not losing her child instead of trying to understand her husband. And in the end, the worst had happened anyway. Not only had she lost her child, she'd lost her marriage.

Riley lay back against the pillows and pulled a chenille blanket up around her chin. Wiping at her eyes, she told herself to snap out it. She'd be okay. She could do this. She'd already planned on doing this alone.

Why did he have to come home in the middle of all of this?

And could she trust him to be the father this baby needed?

Riley didn't know the answers to those questions. But she wouldn't do anything to harm this child. And if that meant avoiding Jackson Sinclair, then that's what she'd have to do. No matter how much it hurt.

CHAPTER EIGHT

RILEY WAVED AT Aunt Verde and Uncle Floyd and gave Killer a final pat on the head. "I'll see y'all at the barbecue. I'm shutting the store down early today, so I should be there by one o'clock."

Aunt Verde smiled and called out, "Okay. Don't work too hard. It's such a pretty day."

"Yes, it is," Riley said, after cranking her car and heading toward town.

She felt better today. In spite of all the emotions pouring through her, she'd managed to get a fairly good night's sleep. No dreams about a dark-haired man in a red sports car.

He haunted her every waking hour so she was really glad Jackson had stayed out of her nighttime dreams. And today, she intended to have a nice morning at the shop then shut things down for the barbecue.

They always shut down early on the Buckingham First Hunt Barbecue Day.

Her parents wouldn't allow her to work while they all played. They'd have tents set up in the big back-yard that led down to a nice quiet pond. Her brothers would be manning the grills full of everything from chicken and brisket to ham and venison. Her mother and the other women would bring out loads of side dishes and desserts, including potato salad and cheesy potato casseroles, all sorts of vegetables and salads and homemade biscuits and breads.

But Riley was craving dessert. Apple pie or maybe a good hunk of pound cake with strawberries on the side. What they didn't have fresh, they had canned or frozen. No one ever starved around here.

She hummed herself right into the store and worked the morning away selling pretty things to fun-loving women. She sold a darling yard ornament featuring a hummingbird to picky Cynthia Hudson. Then she talked Gena Norman into trying on the cutest leggings and matching heavy cotton tunic. Gena loved the outfit so much, she kept it on, and after Riley had removed the tags, decided to wear it to the barbecue.

Riley stayed out on the floor, working till the last customer was out the door. Then she announced, "Time to go."

Everyone dropped what they were doing and got ready to shut down. The sales associates giggled and gossiped their way out the door.

"Why, with this nice fall weather everyone in town will be there, I reckon," Margie Sue declared as she headed home to get her famous coleslaw and a batch of homemade cream cheese brownies. "I'll see you soon."

"I'm right behind you," Riley called.

It didn't occur to Riley until she walked around the corner of her parents' rambling ranch house an hour later that "everyone" would include the one person she didn't need to see today.

Jackson Sinclair.

He turned to see why everyone had suddenly gone quiet.

Jackson caught Delton's fear-filled expression then spotted the reason Delton seemed so worried.

Riley came traipsing around the corner, carrying a covered dish and wearing a bright outfit and a happy smile.

Until she looked up and saw him.

"Busted," Delton said on a grunt. Then her brother gave Jackson a thumbs-up and promptly disappeared behind a grill.

Jackson saw the shock, followed by despair, on her pretty face. In spite of her surprise at finding him here, she maintained that famous Riley trick of saving face. She only stumbled slightly in her brown boots.

Glancing around as if she was searching for a place to hide, she grinned and called out, "Riley's here now, folks. The party can begin."

She looked pretty even if she did look mad. She wore a blue cashmere V-neck sweater over a colorful plaid blouse, her hair caught back in a loose ponytail. Her jeans were fitted and slender. She had them tucked into her sleek boots.

She appeared carefree and young, even if she was pregnant and worried—and not so happy to see him. It occurred to him that not everyone knew she was expecting. He had to wonder who did, besides him?

He wanted to go to her and help her with her dish, but before he could muster up the courage, Fred Marshall hurried to her side.

The know-it-all divorced accountant had always rubbed Jackson the wrong way. Back in high school, Fred had carried a torch for Riley. Apparently that torch had rekindled itself since Jackson had left. He didn't like the proprietary way the man rushed toward *his* wife. It didn't matter that the world considered them divorced.

Riley would always belong to him.

"RILEY, LET ME help you."

Riley's pasted-on grin relaxed at the sight of Fred Marshall coming toward her. The lanky man with the dirty blond receding hairline was a far cry from Jackson Sinclair.

But right now, he'd do. "Hello, Fred. You didn't tell me you'd be here today."

And neither did my ex-husband, she thought with a perfectly controlled fuming. Jackson had failed to mention anything about the barbecue the whole time they were together yesterday.

Wonder why that was?

"Oh, you know I wouldn't miss the barbecue," Fred replied, glancing over toward where Jackson stood with a frown on his face. "I noticed we have extra company this year."

Riley lifted her chin and laughed, refusing to take

the bait. "Yeah, the crowd gets bigger every year. Seems more and more riffraff manages to sneak in."

She allowed Fred to take her food to the big table underneath one of the tents and then before he could latch on to the subject of Jackson, she turned to hurry into the house to stash her purse.

JACKSON WATCHED THE whole encounter between Riley and Fred with an amused smile on his face and a seething frown inside his heart. He thought about running after Riley, but all of her brothers and her daddy, too, were watching him like hawks out scouting for vermin. He'd have to tread lightly around here. Just until he was back in everyone's good graces.

Delton magically reappeared, holding a glass of iced tea. "So…I think she took it pretty well, don't you?"

Jackson grabbed the tea and drank it down. He needed something stronger, but his days of getting drunk and making a spectacle of himself were over. "Yeah, she took it just fine. That's why she went right straight inside the house."

Delton's chuckle shook with nervousness. "Oh, she's just in there chatting away with all the other women. You know how they like to have their hen parties."

Jackson wondered about that term. More like a posse roundup. And there was nothing more dangerous than a posse of women out on the hunt. Especially if Riley was the leader of the pack.

Delton carried on with fortitude and a cold beer.

"C'mon, Jackson. The Bulldogs are playing. We got a betting pool going. Georgia has to win big."

Jackson glanced to where Delton and the boys had rigged a big-screen television underneath one of the tents. The sight of red-and-white jerseys filled the screen. "I guess watching the game is one way to pass my time left here on earth."

"Ah, you can't believe Riley would do anything foolish like that. She won't embarrass herself or anyone else, not today. Mama would have her hide."

"Or mine," Jackson replied. He had yet to venture into the house to speak to any of the ladies. He was brave but even a brave man knew to stay out of dangerous territory.

He'd find Riley later and have a private talk with her.

"You should call him out, make him suffer, embarrass him," Allison said, her brown eyes going beady as she grabbed another drink and chased it with a big chip full of guacamole.

Riley cringed at the chewing sounds going on with her sister-in-law. Allison must be hungry. She'd been nibbling since Riley found her in the kitchen earlier.

Bettye Buckingham tapped Allison on the shoulder. "Dear, you know how I feel about you gossiping and chewing at the same time. Swallow that guacamole, please."

Her mother winked at Riley behind Allison's back. "Riley, honey, you want a drink? Eat one of those stuffed shrimp. Your daddy worked on those things all morning."

"I'm not that hungry, Mama," Riley said. "I've got my mineral water right here."

Allison slurped on her drink. "Riley, did you give up the good stuff? Mineral water, seriously?"

Margie Sue came by, frowning. "Allison, aren't you drinking a nonalcoholic margarita yourself?"

Allison swallowed too fast and started coughing. "Uh, yeah. Uh, I forgot. I promised Curtis I wouldn't get tipsy too early."

Shaking her head at Allison's never-ending theatrics, Riley followed Margie Sue into the dining room where even more food was spread out on the long oak table. "I feel sick," she whispered.

"Throw-up sick?" Margie Sue asked, giving Riley a sharp glance.

"No, just sick of all of this. You know, watching over my shoulder, wondering when I'll run into Jackson. He's stolen the thunder of this pregnancy right out from under me."

"Only if you let him," Margie Sue replied.

Riley grabbed a cracker and nibbled at it. "He's kind of hard to ignore." She lowered her head. "Did you know he was coming today?"

"No," Margie Sue said. "But I've got a sneaking suspicion that my dear husband did. In fact, I wouldn't put it past Delton inviting him. I think he grieved almost as much as you when his buddy Jackson left."

"They were always close," Riley conceded. "Maybe they should move in together."

Margie Sue snorted then covered her giggles. "Now there's an image."

"What y'all laughing about," Allison said from the door, her dark eyes full of amusement and questions. Allison did not like to be left out of any conversation. She also did not like how close Riley and Margie Sue had always been.

"Oh, just talking about men and how they operate," Margie Sue replied. "Y'all about ready to go out and announce that the food is ready?"

Allison practically leaped into the air. "I know I am." Her smile held something secretive and triumphant.

"What's up with her today?" Riley asked Margie Sue before they went through the house, gathering clusters of women together to go outside. It would be just like Allison to squeal her guts about Riley's pregnancy. But there was no way the woman could have figured things out. Riley hoped. She planned on telling everyone her news in her own time.

"Beats me," Margie Sue replied. "Can't blame it on tequila since she's not really drinking today."

Allison loved her mixed drinks, Riley thought. Maybe she was trying to cut back. After all, she did have three little boys who kept her running. Or maybe Curtis frowned on how Allison acted when she'd had too much to drink. Whatever.

Riley wanted to stay inside, so she held back. But

her mother, ever the alert one, grabbed her by the sleeve. "C'mon now, Riley Priscilla. Head up, shoulders back. Smile in place. This is your family, honey. Show some Buckingham backbone."

Riley moaned in protest, but she did as her mother asked. Her mama was right. She couldn't show fear. Jackson would pounce on that like a bull seeing red.

She reached for her mother's hand. "Mama, later… I need some time alone with you and Daddy. I have something I need to tell y'all."

Bettye looked worried. "Is everything all right?"

"Fine, just fine," Riley replied. "It's nothing bad."

She wanted to tell her parents about the baby.

JACKSON WAITED, HOLDING his breath as all the guests gathered around the big yard. Riley's daddy always had a few words to say before he said grace over the food. Then they'd get on with the eating and partying.

And he'd find Riley and smooth things over. If her whole dang family could be polite to him, surely his ex-wife could, too. When he saw her walking out the door with her mother, he breathed a sigh of relief. At least she hadn't left.

He maneuvered his way around until he was nearby but not so close to her as to be obvious. Then he listened along with the growing crowd as Charles Buckingham talked about the blessing of family and the bounty of the earth.

"We've had some tough times lately," Charles, cleaned up and wearing a polo shirt after the early-morning hunt, said to the crowd. "Drought's been tough this summer, but fall is here now. We'll be okay. We've got each other and our town."

Riley's father smiled at several people in the crowd then rubbed his hands together. "Let's get this food blessed so we can eat and watch some football."

He lowered his head, but his son Curtis called out before Charles could start the prayer. "Uh, Daddy, can I say something before you bless the food?"

Charles glanced at Bettye then back to his middle son. "Sure, Curtis. What's on your mind?"

Curtis grinned then tugged Allison under his arm. "We've got an announcement."

Allison giggled and grinned. "We're having a baby. And this time we sure hope it's a girl."

Everyone started hooting and hollering and clapping. Bettye and Charles hugged each other then grabbed Curtis and Allison in hugs.

Jackson searched the crowd for Riley, his eyes meeting hers as the roar of congratulations surrounded them.

She gave him a sad little smile then turned and headed away from the crowd.

CHAPTER NINE

HE FOUND HER down by the pond.

Carrying two plates of food, one in each hand, and two bottles of water, one in each of his jean pockets, Jackson walked through the crowd and searched for Riley.

He should have known she'd find a quiet spot and pout a little bit after hearing the news that Allison was pregnant for the fourth time. Riley had always loved being the center of attention, but today, she'd shied away from all of that. And as usual, Allison had made sure she was the center of attention. Bad timing or did her brother's conniving wife know about Riley's pregnancy already?

Now to gauge Riley's reaction and her mood. Was she upset about Allison's announcement or was she mad because he was here? Or was she was just worried about their baby? Probably all of the above.

And it was so like uppity Allison Buckingham to want to take some of the shine off of Riley's tiara, pregnancy or not. Those two had been rivals in high school and beyond, but Riley held her dislike of her overbearing sister-in-law in check for her brother's sake. Curtis loved the woman and that was good enough for Riley even if she only tolerated Allison. But each time Allison had another fine strapping boy and held that over Riley's head, the fractured relationship became a little more strained.

This time, Riley should have been the one announcing her pregnancy. They should have been the happy couple—Riley and Jackson. But that "together" name didn't work anymore.

Still, Jackson couldn't help wanting to reach out to her.

Riley was sitting on an old wooden bench, staring out at the only ducks in Sinclair, Georgia, that couldn't be hunted—per Bettye Buckingham's strict orders that these were her pet ducks and therefore off-limits.

"I brought you a plate," he said by way of a greeting.

She didn't even look up. Her gaze followed the ducks. "I'm not hungry."

Jackson sat down beside her. "I have potato salad and broccoli salad and asparagus and chicken. And some fruit salad, too. All those healthy things you used to love."

"Potato salad isn't exactly healthy."

"But you love it. It won't hurt you to eat a little."

She looked at the plate then looked up at him, her expression grateful if not a bit dispassionate. "Thank you."

He watched as she took a bite out of a fresh-baked yeast roll then he started in on his own brisket and grilled sausage. "Mmm. I have sure missed the Buckingham barbecue."

"Is that why you crashed it today?"

He saw the hint of a smile in her eyes. "Your brother invited me, but he's quaking in his boots, hoping you don't find that out."

"And he should be," she said, nibbling on the potato salad in a dainty Riley fashion, chewing tiny little bits and doing it with impeccable manners. Even pouting mad, Riley always used proper decorum. "I bet he knew all about the new baby in the family, too."

"Our baby? I didn't say a word."

She shook her head then chewed on her grilled chicken. "No. Not this baby. Allison and Curtis, of course. Another one. Can you believe that?"

He heard the little catch in her words. Heard it and felt her pain all the way to his heart. "We don't need to worry about that, darlin'. I'm gonna take care of you and our baby."

She whirled to glare at him, her blue eyes full of a burning hurt. "Don't talk like that, Jackson. I've told you I can't let you back into my life. I'm not ready—"

"But you might be one day, maybe?" He hoped, he prayed.

Riley got up and put her plate down on the bench. "I can't predict that, but right now I can say that I don't see it happening. I'm not sure why you came back, but I feel like there has to be a catch. There's always a catch."

His appetite gone, Jackson stood, too. "Riley, quit being so stubborn for once. What do I have to do to prove to you that I care, that I'm here?"

She stared up at him, her eyes reflecting the sky. "You don't need to do anything. That's what I'm saying. This isn't your burden to bear, your joy to experience. I'm doing this on my own, my way this time."

He tugged her close. "And what's that supposed to mean anyway?"

Riley gave him one look of longing then brought her guard up again. "It means I intend to go through this without any help from you. It means I want to raise this baby by myself. I've told you that already, so you need to start listening."

"Why?" he asked, wondering how he could convince her that he wanted to be a part of the baby's life. Wanting to convince her that he'd made a big mistake but that mistake had actually made him a better man.

"Why?" She crossed her arms in a protective mode and stared out at the pond. Then she looked back up at him, her eyes wide and telling. "So neither I nor the baby will be hurt when you walk away again."

She turned to leave, but Jackson was right there. "What makes you think I'll do that this time?"

"Past experience," she retorted, an angry frown marring her face. "I have to remember the past so I won't make the same mistake again. I mean, would you be pursuing me so heavily if I wasn't pregnant?"

He hesitated a fraction of a second in replying.

"See," she said, her hand lifting in frustration. "It's not about us, Jackson. You just want this baby, maybe to appease yourself, maybe to prove something. But don't kid yourself about wanting to be back with me.

You made it very clear all those years ago that you *don't* care."

He held her, his heart crashing into pieces. "Don't you want to talk about all of that, Riley? About how *you* pushed me away until I got tired of fighting."

"You were already walking away," she shot back. "I could feel it, Jackson. You refused to *talk* about anything back then. You didn't seem to want this baby as much as I did. And because I wanted a family, I was losing you." She stopped, looked down. "And then, I lost our baby, too. I'm sorry, Jackson, but I can't go through that again."

"What if you don't have to go through that again?"

She stared out at the lake then glanced back toward the house. "You can't make that promise."

No, he couldn't. But he wanted to, so badly. He wanted the same thing she wanted—a family. Maybe she was right about before. He'd halfheartedly agreed to all the procedures and the tests and the hormones and the waiting. Always the waiting. And each time they'd failed, he'd felt less and less of a man. He'd felt as if he'd failed her somehow. He needed to prove himself to her, but she wasn't ready to believe in him. Maybe she never would believe in him again. But pushing her now wouldn't win points. He knew how Riley's mind worked. She didn't like being forced into anything. She'd resist him on principle alone.

"Okay," he said, backing away to gather up their unfinished meals. "I'll give you some time and space.

If you don't want me in this baby's life, I'll just have to learn to live with that."

She looked skeptical and surprised. "Do you promise?"

"I can't promise anything, remember," he replied, glad to be able to give her a comeback line. "I might want to go with you to the doctor every now and then."

Her expression bordered on fear. "But that will only make things worse."

"You need somebody, Riley. What about the birthing classes? Who'll help with that?"

"My mama and Margie Sue, if I ask."

"You need me there," he told her, lowering his voice when some of her nieces and nephews ran by. Then he tried to tease her into agreeing. "Margie Sue is scrawny, suga'. You need somebody with muscle to help you get through all that."

"No, I don't. You sure weren't there the night I—" She stopped, looked back at the ducks. "Never mind."

Before he could argue more, a curly-headed kid around ten came running up, giggling. "Hey, Aunt Riley, my mama says you and Uncle Jackson should just get married again and get it over with. Is that gonna happen?"

Riley's skin went pink. She shot Jackson a mortified look then turned to her nephew. "Dewey, you tell your mama to mind her own business."

"Okay, I'll do that." The boy ran off, hooting and hollering, without a care in the world.

Jackson suppressed the chuckle clogging his throat.

She was still in there somewhere, his Riley. The fighter, the scrapper, the beauty queen. "I guess you told him," he said, shaking his head.

She glared at him then gave him a twisted smile. "I shouldn't have said that. He'll go back and tell Allison what I said, word for word."

"Good," Jackson said, grinning. "'Cause we wouldn't want to spread any false rumors."

She nodded. "Nor any false promises, either."

Then she pranced back toward the house, leaving him to throw the remnants of their meal in the trash.

RILEY STOOD IN the dining room by the row of big, paned windows that overlooked the backyard. Long ago she'd stand here eating a waffle with cream cheese and jelly before school while she waited for Jackson to pick her up. She'd dream of watching the sunrise with him after they were married and living at Southern Hill. Because back then, there had never been any doubt that they would be married and that they would live in Jackson's ancestral home. She'd stand here and dream of her wedding—the long white dress, the bridesmaids and flower girls, the ring bearer. Then she'd blush while thinking of the honeymoon and being with Jackson forever. Now she ached with regret and longing but her heart burst with a new joy and a new hope in spite of that. She might have lost the dream, but now at least she would have a child. If she could just make it through this pregnancy.

Remembering their earlier conversation, she watched

as Jackson shook Delton's hand and headed to his truck. He glanced back once, his gaze moving toward the house, then he got into his vehicle and headed out.

Had she ruined her marriage by forcing Jackson into having a baby? Riley had always been forceful whenever she wanted something. And she'd wanted a child. But had she used that want for all the wrong reasons—to hold on to her restless husband, to save her marriage, or to have someone to love in case Jackson left her? He'd never talked to her about any of it. Never once told her how he felt about all the doctors and procedures. But she'd watched him pulling away with each step toward having a child.

And why hadn't her handsome husband wanted a child as much as she did? Why did the realization that he'd only been going through the motions for her— that he really wasn't as invested in her pregnancy as she'd been—still hurt her so much? She couldn't let him back into her life for that reason. Jackson wanted to pretend again. But this was real.

Riley watched the people roaming around her parents' big backyard, people she'd known most of her life mingling with new friends and newcomers to Sinclair. She'd looked forward to this day for weeks now, but even more so when she'd found out she was pregnant again at last. She'd planned to tell her immediate family after everyone else had left.

But with Jackson spending the day here and with Allison still beaming and bragging, she didn't think she had the stomach to announce anything. It wouldn't hurt to wait a little while longer, just in case.

She whirled to go home and found her formidable mother standing there blocking her path.

"Hello, Mama." Riley started around the big kitchen island.

"Where you headed, Riley Priscilla?"

Uh-oh. Whenever Bettye Buckingham called her that, Riley was usually in for a long lecture.

"Home," Riley said, breezy and sure.

"It's early," Bettye replied, her hands on her hips. "What's going on with you today, anyway?"

Suddenly tired and wanting desperately to fall into her mother's arms and bawl like a baby, Riley steeled herself by standing tall. Planting a big smile on her face, she said, "Besides the obvious, nothing much."

"And you mean the obvious being that good-looking, slow-talking ex-son-in-law of mine?"

"That would be the one," Riley said, shrugging. "I feel uncomfortable around Jackson and I'm really ticked that Delton invited him."

"Jackson—no matter his faults—is always welcome in my house," Bettye said, shaking her head. "Or at least as far as the darn backyard. I told your daddy to keep him out there so I wouldn't sit him down and give him the talking-to he needed five years ago."

"Mighty thoughtful of you, Mama."

"I try to be polite to my guests. Even the one who broke my baby girl's heart."

"So you get why I'm a tad uncomfortable?"

Bettye shook her head again. "No, ma'am, I don't get that at all. Riley, I've known you to be mean around Jackson. I've seen you pull that drama queen act with the man and I've seen you crushed to pieces when he hurt you. And I've seen the two of you making up, all goofy and starry-eyed. But I've never seen you uncomfortable with him. You've been quiet and moody all day long and that's not like you. Something is up and you're not leaving here until I know what it is."

"I can tell you what's ailing her," Allison said as she breezed into the room, her big brown eyes focusing on Riley. "She told my son to tell me to mind my own business."

Bettye glanced from Allison to Riley. "Is this true?"

Riley didn't care one way or another. "I might have said something like that, yes." Then she got in Allison's face. "Your son told *me* that you said Jackson and I should just get married again and be done with it."

Allison's faced turned splotchy with embarrassment. "That little imp. I've told those boys not to repeat what they hear at the dinner table."

Riley's smile caused Allison to realize she'd just confessed to gossiping. "I didn't mean it the way it sounds, Riley. I was actually *hoping* you two would get back together and I guess I voiced that out loud and Dewey misinterpreted it."

"So you did say it?" Bettye asked, pinning Allison with a mother-in-law look.

Allison actually squirmed. "I reckon I said something like that, but—"

"And Riley, did you tell Dewey to tell his mama to mind her own business?"

"I did, yes."

Bettye took Allison by the arm and guided her toward the door to the patio. "Of course you were only speaking out of love and concern, darlin'. 'Cause you're so very thoughtful that way. Now go on and find a comfortable chair and rest your feet. You have to take it easy, remember. I'm so excited about another grandbaby so I'm only gonna say this once. You don't need to be bothered by Riley's troubles. You need to… well, mind your own business."

Allison didn't know how to respond. But her open mouth said it all for Riley. Lord love a duck, but her mama could sound so sweet when she was telling someone off, she'd put a rattlesnake in its place and the snake would kiss her for doing it.

"You are priceless, Mama," Riley said after Allison blustered out, still red-faced. "I love you."

"I love you, too, darlin'. Now spill it. What's going on with you? Is poor Allison right? Are you still in love with Jackson Sinclair?"

CHAPTER TEN

RILEY STARED AT her mother, shocked that Bettye would even suggest she was still in love with Jackson.

"Well, I'm waiting," Bettye said, her diamonds flashing even though she held her hands on her hips. "Your daddy thinks you're pining away for Jackson now that he's back in town. You've been acting funny for days now."

Riley let out a sigh. "Get Daddy in here then and I'll tell y'all everything."

Bettye looked shocked then worried. "Honey, you're scaring me. You never agree on the first try."

That was true. Riley had always been defiant. Usually they'd argue for a bit before she confessed or gave in. But she didn't have the energy to do that today. Her spitfire energy had burned down to a little wick of puny warmth. She really needed a long nap.

"I am fine," she said, pointing to the backyard. "But I do need to talk to you and Daddy."

Bettye opened her mouth to speak and then closed it shut. "I'll be right back."

Riley poured herself a glass of water, her stomach churning and bubbling. Praying she wouldn't lose what little bit of lunch she'd eaten, she spotted the dessert table and suddenly had to have a piece of buttermilk pound cake.

When her parents walked in together about five minutes later, she was standing at the sink biting big chunks out of the thick, buttery slice she'd taken.

"Girl, you still hungry?" her daddy asked, grinning at her. "I've never seen you eating over the sink."

"Charles, don't tease her. You remember how I used to do the same thing when I was—"

"Pregnant," Riley said through a chunk of pound cake. Then she started coughing.

Her daddy got her a glass of water and handed it to Riley. "Did you say *pregnant,* honey?"

Bettye Buckingham's eyes went wide with joy and concern. "Oh, my, my. You and Jackson…sure didn't waste any time. How did that happen so quick?"

Riley regained her voice, her eyes watering. "We didn't. I mean, I haven't been with Jackson…in that way."

Yet.

Her daddy's face went from pale with shock to red with rage. "Then somebody around here better step up and be a man about this."

"Daddy, please," Riley said, motioning to the table. "Can we sit down? I'll explain."

Her parents rushed to the table and almost collided as they pulled out chairs and then gave each other strange glances. Riley composed herself, wiped her eyes and took another drink of water. "Yes, I am pregnant," she said. "And yes, Jackson is the father. But he won't be in the baby's life on a day-to-day basis. This is my baby. It was my decision."

"I'll kill him," Charles Buckingham said on a loud shout, one fist hitting the table. "How in the world did y'all let this happen?"

Riley's mother put a hand to her mouth, her blush showing the agitation of explaining this uncomfortable turn of events to the Garden Club. "We'll make do," she finally managed to whisper. "We'll be okay. We'll make do."

"Nobody has to make do," Riley said, giving both her parents a steadying look. "I used a frozen embryo from…the last time. We saved some just in case. So I did in vitro with a transferred embryo and…well… it took."

Her daddy looked confused and then let out a grunt. "You mean, Jackson…didn't…I mean…"

"No, nobody did anything together," Riley replied. "I went back to my doctors in Atlanta and they fixed me up with tests, blood work and lots of hormones. I was primed and pumped and ready to reproduce and we…uh…we'd saved some sperm and some eggs." She stopped, her eyes misting. "And so, I'm going to have a baby. I wanted to tell y'all earlier but—"

Her mother put her hand over Riley's. "But Allison beat you to it, right, honey?"

Riley nodded. "I didn't want to try to one-up her or play second fiddle." She shrugged. "It was just too hard to explain and then Jackson came home and I never thought I'd have to deal with him and this, too.

And now Allison's all giddy and glowing and pregnant again. And I'm a blubbering mess and Jackson wants to be back my life."

Charles got up and reached for Riley. She stood and fell into her daddy's arms.

"You could never be second fiddle to anyone, suga'."

"Thank you, Daddy." She stepped back to wipe her eyes.

Her mother wrapped Riley in her arms. "Oh, honey. You're so brave to do this. How far along are you? And why didn't you tell me all about this before now?"

Riley let go of her mother. "I'm about six weeks. I didn't want to say anything until I was sure. It's been months now but this was the second try. I couldn't believe it when the doctors told me."

"And then Jackson showed up," her mother said, nodding. "That explains so much."

"Does he know?" Charles asked.

"I sure do."

They all turned to find Jackson standing in the open doorway out to the patio. "She told me when I first got home."

Her daddy glanced from her to Jackson, caught between bliss and murder. "And how do you feel about this?"

"I don't know," Jackson said. "I honestly don't know what to think since I wasn't exactly in on the decision."

Riley's heart skipped a few beats. What did he mean by that? Didn't he want this baby? Or was he going to do a repeat of the last time? It would be so like him to promise her he'd be around then turn tail and leave again.

He came into the room, his eyes on her. "I want to be a part of this baby's life, but your daughter insists she can do this on her own. We'll have to see about that."

Riley wanted to throttle him. "I thought you'd left."

"I did," he said. "But then I thought about you and how you wanted to tell your parents about the baby. I came back so I could defend myself."

"Why would you need defending?" she asked, anger coloring the question. "I haven't bad-mouthed you to anyone. I don't have to."

"Because I've done enough damage already? Is that what you were gonna say?"

"We all know how things went between you two," her daddy said. "But having said that, this is between you two. Just remember the child, Jackson. And you, too, Riley. Remember the child needs two parents."

"That's the most important thing," her mother said on a low breath. Then she turned to Riley. "We will support you in anything you decide, honey."

"Amen to that." Her daddy looked at his wife. "We'd better go check on the rest of our guests. You two have a lot to discuss, I imagine."

"I think we've covered everything," Riley said. "And I'm really tired. I'm going home."

Jackson shook his head. "I came back to talk to you."

Riley watched her parents making a beeline to the

door and willed them to come back. "Not now, Jackson. I've had enough for one day."

"I'll follow you to Southern Hill then. You can rest while we talk."

"If you follow me, I won't get any rest."

"I promise I won't stay long."

She didn't want to argue with the man but she sure wasn't going to stand here in the kitchen with him and let the whole town gossip, either. They'd already caused quite a scandal just being here together and talking to each other. She could only imagine the rumors once word got out about her pregnancy. The town of Sinclair wasn't exactly all caught up on cutting-edge birth technology. People would think she'd lost her mind, trying to have a baby from a frozen embryo and a test tube.

"I don't know."

Jackson let out a deep breath. "Riley, we need to talk and I'm going to follow you home so we can have some privacy."

"Okay. But I can't fathom what else we have to talk about."

He didn't respond to that. "I'll see you at your place."

She heard the inflection in that comment. He resented that she lived in what should have been his home. Only, he never acted like he wanted that home. Or her.

Where had they gone wrong? she wondered all over

again after she was in her car and moving down the long country road. Where had she gone wrong?

And why did Jackson want to keep rehashing the past when she'd made it clear they didn't have a future?

HE'D NEVER UNDERSTAND why she thought she could have his baby without him even knowing about it or caring. Jackson was fuming with anger and resentment now that the initial shock of hearing he was going to be a father had settled over him. Now he was mad that Riley had decided to get herself pregnant without his knowledge and that she had planned to raise their child on her own.

And in this town, of all places?

How would she have handled the snickers and the scorn, the condemnation and the gossip?

Well, this was Riley, after all. She'd probably flaunt the baby in bows and buttons and tell everyone to mind their own business. Yes, knowing Riley, she'd land on her feet and keep right on going, baby stroller and diaper bag in tow.

And maybe that was what made him the maddest. And the saddest. She'd never really needed him that much.

His Riley had always been independent and self-sufficient and smart and way ahead of her time. At times, it had been hard to keep up with her. Or understand her need to always be going at full throttle. She'd decided they needed a baby and that was that. He'd gone along, not wanting to disappoint her. He'd wanted children, but he'd never felt like true father material. And he'd never voiced that to Riley.

It didn't matter now. Riley wanted what Riley wanted.

She'd been that way all through their dating days, always thinking ahead, always planning their agendas. Never just enjoying a regular date, a spontaneous outing. No, sir. They didn't just go on a date. They went on a highly choreographed, fully planned event. This practice had continued on through their elaborate wedding and into their carefully controlled marriage. And she'd enticed him into having a baby by railroading him straight up to Atlanta to see a fertility doctor.

Things started going sour after they'd both realized it wasn't going to happen on Riley's carefully planned timeline. Jackson felt like one big failure.

How could he ever explain that to her?

In her mind, she'd done everything right.

In his mind, he'd done everything wrong. And he'd decided he'd never make her happy.

Only now, he wanted more than anything in the world to do that very thing—make Riley Priscilla Buckingham Sinclair happy.

But he hadn't factored in a baby.

Jackson pulled in beside her then got out and gazed out over the burnished woods and fields. "This place is still just as beautiful as I remembered."

Riley held on to her purse and let her own gaze wander. "Yep. Thankfully, some things don't ever change." Playing with the buckled strap, she glanced over at him then back out at the pond. "This place means a lot to me, Jackson. I didn't take it out of spite. I needed to be here…after I lost the baby. I needed to feel loved and not so lonely."

He moved around the car. "So you didn't take my home away from me just for revenge?"

She shook her head and dropped her purse on the hood of her car. "No. I mean, I know that's what everybody thought. And I was angry and bitter and maybe I wanted to hit you where it hurt, but if I'd really wanted to make you suffer I would have gone after the lodge, too."

She went silent and then picked up her purse and headed into the sunroom and on into the kitchen.

Jackson followed, thinking about how she let him keep the lodge. He'd always believed that had been part of her conniving divorce settlement, giving him the one place that only reminded him of his failings. She'd screamed that he loved hunting and fishing much more than he'd loved her or their baby.

Hurtful, bitter words. Words that even now, still stung.

He followed her in. "Go sit on the porch. I'll bring you some hot tea. Or would you rather have hot chocolate?"

She gave him a surprised look then scooped up that ridiculous rag of a dog. "Hot chocolate would be nice. But you don't know how to make that."

"Yes, I do," he said. "I've learned how to make a lot of things since I've been gone."

She actually smiled while Killer gave Jackson a low growl of disapproval. "Maybe you can tell me what you did while you were away."

"I will. Want marshmallows?"

"Yes, lots."

Jackson grinned at that. "I'll be right back with the best cup of hot chocolate you've ever had in your life."

"Don't make promises you can't keep, Jackson Sinclair."

He settled her onto the wicker love seat then leaned down and placed Killer on the floor. The dog yapped, but Jackson kept his gaze on Riley. "Anything I promise you from here on out is for keeps."

And he meant that. His pregnant ex-wife might not realize it yet but…he had changed a lot since she'd last seen him.

He'd finally realized that everything he'd ever wanted was right here with her.

CHAPTER ELEVEN

"I HAVE TO admit this is pretty good hot chocolate. How'd you learn to make it this way?"

Jackson grinned at her, causing Riley's breath to hitch in her throat. The warmth of the creamy chocolate couldn't match the heat of that grin. He must have put some magic ingredient in this stuff. She'd have to hold herself in check or she'd regret letting him follow her home.

Jackson finished off his drink and then held the cup upside down until the last of the melted marshmallows slid slowly down into his open mouth.

His terribly adorable, sexy mouth.

Stop that, she told herself while she gulped her own drink.

She couldn't let him back in. Not into her life or this baby's life or…she shouldn't even have let him into her house. Not while Aunt Verde and Uncle Floyd were still at her parents' house enjoying their own campfire with the rest of their friends and family. She'd been tired before, but now Riley wished she'd chosen that option. She should have stayed there where there was safety in numbers. Being alone with her ex-husband was both torment and temptation.

Jackson finally put his empty cup down and wiped his mouth. "Well, I was down in South America—"

Riley sat up straight. "You were where?"

"South America. You know that big continent just below North America."

"I know where that is, silly. But how'd you wind up down there?"

He leaned forward and cupped his hands together. "I sailed around the world. I really did it, Riley."

She had heard about his excursion, but hearing him speak about it with such pride was hard. She couldn't believe it. After they'd lost their baby and she'd lain curled in a ball for days, crying her heart out, after they'd gone through the ordeal of the divorce, after everything they'd been through, he'd gone away and sailed around the world.

"That must have been some adventure," she said, her tone strained from the lump in her throat. "I'm glad you finally checked that off your bucket list."

He obviously sensed some of her torment. "It wasn't like that," he said. "I…I was miserable on most of the trip."

"Of course you were. But being out on the ocean without anything to worry you but the vast horizon made that all better, I'm sure."

He sank back against the floral cushions. "I thought you wanted to hear all about it?"

She got up so fast she almost knocked over the table. "I did want to hear about it but I've got the picture. I mean, I knew from the get-go that you'd gone off on that darn boat, but I guess I thought you'd holed up in some deserted cove and licked your wounds the same way I did. Now you tell me you sailed around the world and found a way to make a mean hot chocolate that's almost addictive. That must have been so nice for you."

He got up, too, his eyes blazing fire. "You don't have to be mean about it, you know. You weren't the only one who lost a child, Riley. You need to remember that."

Mad now and hurting, she pointed her finger at him. "Oh, I remember, all right. I remember that I was all alone during his birth and…after the doctors told me my baby was dead. I remember how I cried out for my husband but he wasn't there. Maybe you never really were there at all. Maybe you really didn't want to be married or have a family with me. And this is why I can't have you here now."

She moved toward the door to the kitchen. "You need to go."

He blocked her, his hands reaching for her. "No. I won't let you do this."

He stared down at her, the hurt in his eyes blinding her and making her even angrier. She didn't want to see his hurt. She still had enough of her own, thank you very much.

"Do what?" she asked, tearing her gaze from his. "Tell you how much I suffered, tell you how much you hurt me?"

"I know how much I hurt you," he replied. "I thought about it enough while I was out on that boat."

"Did you think about it when you were sitting on some tropical island drinking hot chocolate and forgetting everything by drinking something stronger?"

He brought her hands down and then tugged her close. "Yes, I sure did. I drank enough to cure anything, but I still hurt, I still blamed myself for not being there when I should have been. When I was down in South America I woke up one morning, hung over and groggy and I watched a woman go into labor on the street of some dinky little run-down village. Watched her and ran to help her. I carried her to the nearest clinic but there wasn't enough equipment or medicine to save her baby. Or her. She bled to death after the baby was stillborn."

Riley's stomach twisted and she stepped back. "Stop it."

"No, I won't stop it," he said, advancing toward her. "I'm just beginning. I didn't see paradise out there, Riley. I saw life. Real life. Life the way you and I have never seen it."

She wanted to bruise him a bit and make him hurt the way she'd hurt. "And so now you've become all noble and compassionate and you think that gives you the right to be back in my life? That gives you the right to be a good father, finally?"

"No. I don't have any rights where you're concerned. I know that. And maybe I don't really have any rights as far as this baby is concerned. But that day, after watching that poor woman die and seeing that still little baby, well, that brought it all back to me and…I think I had some sort of breakdown. Or more like a breakthrough. I'd held everything back and denied myself any time to grieve. But I cried, bawled like a baby. Did that curling up in a ball thing. And finally accepted my responsibility, my part in all the things that went wrong with us." He stopped, dropped his hands away. Then he stepped back and turned his face away.

Riley felt the cold air around her. Felt the pain she'd witnessed in his eyes before he tried to hide it. Felt her anger disappearing with each remembered tear. "So what happened after that?"

He relaxed a little bit and then turned to face her again, the frown on his face softening. "After the woman and the baby died, I went back to my room and lay down on the bed. Then a little girl came to my room with a steaming cup of hot chocolate. She spoke to me in Spanish and I didn't understand a word she said. But the look on her face and the meaning in her eyes told me she wanted to make me feel better."

He ran a hand down his beard stubble. "Her grandmother ran the inn and cooked. I figured she'd sent me the drink, maybe to cure my hangover with a little hair of the dog. After I drank the chocolate, the little girl took my hand and brought me into the kitchen. She smiled at her grandmother and pointed to my empty cup." He swallowed, looked away. "And she said 'More.' She knew that much English."

More.

Riley found herself caught up in the story. "She wanted you to drink more?"

He nodded. She showed me how to shave the chocolate, the cocoa, and mix it with whole milk and cream and sugar. She mixed cinnamon in there and even a hint of chili pepper. We made that second cup together. Then she took my hand and we walked to another room in the inn." He stopped again, touched a finger to Riley's hair. "It was a tiny chapel," he said. "The little girl sat me down and pointed up to the mural on the wall. And again, she said 'More.'"

Riley put a hand to her mouth. Jackson had never been very religious but she saw something shining there in his eyes now. Something that made him look incredibly young and vulnerable. "Did you drink the chocolate?"

"I did. And I cried some more. And I said a few angry prayers and then asked for forgiveness."

He reached for Riley again, his eyes full of hope and regret. "I found out from the grandmother that the woman who'd died during childbirth had been the mother of that sweet little girl. The innkeeper's daughter had died. But she and her granddaughter only wanted to comfort me."

Riley didn't try to hold back. She stepped toward him, her hand out. "Oh, Jackson."

"Don't," he said, stepping back. "Don't feel sorry for me or her. That little girl was stronger than the both of us. She knew what I needed, and even in her grief, she knew where I needed to turn." He wiped at his nose and stepped away. "I won't ever forget that day or what I learned. Yeah, I learned how to make hot chocolate, but I also learned something about myself. I want more, Riley. I want more."

Then he turned and went out to his car and left.

While Riley stood there, wanting more herself.

SHE COULDN'T SLEEP.

Riley got up and went to the window. The moon was high in the midnight sky, its soft grayish-white rays shining down on the yard and pasture. The pond glowed from that light, its shimmering dark waters doing a sleepy lap toward the shore.

She remembered other such nights when Jackson would wake up and find her here. He'd tug her back against him and wrap her in his warm, secure arms. Then he'd pull her back to bed.

She held herself now, all alone and cold. At times such as this, she would ache with the physical need to feel his arms around her again. Tonight was no exception. Especially after he'd told her that unbelievable story.

But she did believe him.

She believed he'd seen a woman and a baby die, believed he'd talked to that little girl and her grandmother. But had he really changed, even after going into that little chapel?

Had her ex-husband, the happy-go-lucky good ole boy, actually had an epiphany?

Had he really changed enough to have sticking power?

Riley didn't dare hope. And she didn't dare give him the chance to prove that. He'd never been serious about anything in his life. Their marriage had been part of the fun for him. When it came to doing the hard work, he checked out.

Jackson had often told her that Southern Hill ran itself. That he hired the best people to take care of things after his parents had died. Yes, he hired people all right. But the lone heir to this vast spread had rarely gotten his own hands dirty. And it had been that way with their marriage, too. Jackson just played at being a husband while he played with all the toys that his world and his money allowed him to have.

Riley had felt like a toy herself. Like his wind-up Barbie, always there with a smile, her pearls and her pumps, playing the part of the happy homemaker and the good wife. She wasn't sure when exactly she'd discovered that she was miserable, but she did remember when she'd first mentioned she'd like to open a shop.

"Now, Riley, honey, you'd get bored with that after the first week. You've got more than enough here to keep you busy."

"What is this, Jackson? The 1950s, where women were kept on a pedestal and treated like dirt on a man's boot?"

"Do I treat you that way, darlin'?"

No, he'd treated her with respect and he'd loved her.

She knew that. But he'd also envisioned her a certain way. So she'd decided she'd live up to that image.

Later, after toying with the idea of a women's clothing and accessories store, she'd come up with an even better idea. An idea that would obviously please her husband.

"I want a baby, Jackson."

"Whoa, where did that come from?"

"From me roaming around in this house all day, from me going to Junior League meetings and hearing about all the babies being born, hearing about all my friends having children."

"Is that what y'all discuss at those meetings?"

After several more discussions and several weekends of being alone while he hunted and fished and hung out with *his* buddies, the rebel in Riley had gone on high alert.

And she'd gone after getting herself pregnant.

She'd truly wanted a child. But looking back on it now, she could see that she'd used the excuse of having a child to hide her loneliness and her fears. If she had someone to pour out all her love on, someone to spend time with, she'd have a purpose. Even before they'd married, she'd hinted at doing her own thing, at maybe opening a small business. She even had a degree in business, for goodness' sake.

"I have a good head for business," she'd reminded Jackson many, many times.

"You have an adorable head, honey. And you're doing a great job of running this place."

Yes, she'd taken over a lot of the day-to-day duties, the paperwork, the constant balance of money coming in and money going out, the stock options, the banking needs. This place was a big business, with farming and livestock, with the pecan trees and the pond and with the hunting lodge that brought in so much revenue. And kept her husband away from her.

They'd argued more, fought more. Finally, Jackson had given in to the idea of having a baby. Just to shut her up, she was sure.

But he'd never truly wanted the baby as much as she had.

She stared up at the moon now and held her hands to her tummy. "I want you. I do. I will love you and I'll show you that you can be anything, do anything you want. As long as you have love in your heart, you'll be just fine. No silver spoon, darlin'. Just good hardheaded Buckingham and Sinclair blood in your veins. We'll do this together."

She whirled, some of her old spunk coming back.

"I'll raise this baby and keep my business intact and I'll make sure I keep Southern Hill Plantation intact. For you," she said to her stomach. "Only for you."

And Jackson Sinclair could just stew in his own regrets.

Because she wouldn't give in to him. She couldn't. She was glad he'd seen the light, but as far as loving her and raising this child, Jackson Sinclair was still in the dark. He might want more, but Riley remembered how once, long ago, she'd wanted it all. She still wanted it all. Even if it meant not having the one man she'd always love.

CHAPTER TWELVE

RILEY STARED AT her desk pad, her gaze moving over all the commitments she had between now and Christmas. The shop had to go from a quick fall motif to an all-out Christmas extravaganza for the magazine shoot. Then she had holiday party invitations that would keep her busy from Thanksgiving through Christmas. Sinclair was noted as a gracious town full of Southern hospitality, and being a shopkeeper, Riley tried to make the rounds to each holiday event. She wanted to keep her customers happy all year long.

And she had to shop for some maternity clothes next trip to Atlanta. She'd be showing in a few more weeks. She smiled at that one then closed her eyes, dreaming about the nursery she needed to get in order.

"You sure look pretty. What are you dreaming about?"

At the sound of Jackson's voice, Riley opened her eyes and sat straight up in her chair, her heart thumping against her blue cashmere tunic. "What are you doing here?"

He cowboyed his way into her office then leaned over her desk, his hands pressing into her carefully planned calendar. "Good to see you, too."

Riley sat back to give herself a quick minute to take in the sight of him. She hadn't seen Jackson in three days. It seemed like three forevers. Mentally slapping herself, she breathed deep the scents of leather and spice. His worn leather jacket—the one she'd given him for Christmas a long time ago—looked even better with age. And so did the man.

"You through taking inventory, honey?"

Riley pulled her eyes back inside her head and looked up to find Jackson giving her a smug smile.

She touched a hand to her hair then pushed her chair back and stood up. "I'm just wondering what you're doing standing over my desk like you own the place."

He stood up straight…and still filled the room, his muscle and heat pushing at the delicate colors and fluffy sofa cushions. And her heart.

He whistled toward Killer and the little mutt came running. "I came to see about your next checkup."

Riley restacked some already-stacked papers then glared at her traitor of a dog. "You don't need to worry about that."

"I'm not worried. I intend to be there. I intend to drive you to your appointment."

Why couldn't the man take a hint?

She tidied her already-tidy desk. "Jackson, I've explained this over and over. You can't be a part of this pregnancy. After the baby is born, and if you're still around, we'll discuss visitations."

He put his hands in the pockets of his jeans and gave her a look of disbelief. "Visitations? That sounds so formal. How about we talk about me being the donor at least. Do I need to get proof of that before I can be a daddy to this baby?"

His tone sounded familiar. As in, how-they-used-to-fight familiar. He'd told her more than once that he didn't feel like a husband. He was just her daddy donor.

Had she really made him feel that way?

"Are you threatening me, Jackson?"

He put down her hyper dog. "No, baby. I'm telling you I'm tired of your grandstanding and pushing me away. We're in this together, Riley. Whether you like it or not."

He had a point, but she wasn't ready to concede yet. "You weren't invited to this pregnancy, so don't think you can muscle your way in."

Frustration poured over him, followed by a stark frown of anger. "This doesn't have to be this way. It took both of us to produce this baby, even if one of us wasn't around."

She got up then and placed her hands down on the desk, mocking his earlier stance. "A lot of things didn't have to turn out this way, but they did. You checked out on the first try so I can't trust you to be here on the second."

His anger turned to what looked a lot like hurt. "I guess you're never gonna forgive me."

"Nothing to forgive anymore. I just can't forget."

"Yeah, well, there is that, too. You know how to hold a grudge…I'll give you that."

"I think you should go." She turned away for a minute to compose herself then pivoted back around. "Why are you still here?"

"I'm beginning to ask myself that same thing. You know, I want a second chance but if you keep acting like this, I might just give up. I don't take to being treated like a stray dog."

"There's the Jackson I remember," she said, her own rage hidden behind a serene smile. "I didn't plan on you being a part of this so don't worry about trying, okay. Just…leave me alone so I can take care of this baby."

His anger turned to concern. "Are you doing that?"

All of her bluster went away in a puff of steam. "Of course I am."

"I mean, are you feeling okay? Nothing out of the ordinary, right?"

Great. Now she felt bad for even letting him think something was wrong. "I'm fine, Jackson. But having you around has thrown me for a loop. I'm sorry if I seem severe in my requests."

"I get it," he said, relaxing back on his boots. "You don't want me here. You don't trust me. You don't love me anymore. I came home at the worst possible time."

"Yes, all of the above." She pulled at her tunic and lifted her shoulders, thinking she should have said three out of four instead of agreeing with him. She would always love him, but that didn't help matters. "Now if you'll excuse me, I have a lot to do before the magazine people come next week."

"You got the magazine gig?" he asked, following her around the office. "That's great, but you don't need to overwork yourself with that camera crew."

"Thanks for the advice. I'll be sure to keep that in mind." She wouldn't say anything more. He didn't need the details of her life and he certainly didn't need to be giving her unsolicited advice. "How's the lodge going?" she asked, hoping to give him a big hint that he needed to leave.

"Good." He followed her out onto the floor and stood watching while she straightened a rack of sweaters. "I used some of the contacts I made in my travels to reel in some newcomers. We're booked solid for the whole season. And we've got a big fishing tournament lined up for this spring. Should bring a lot of spending revenue to the whole county."

"That sounds promising," Riley replied, thinking she probably wouldn't have to see him very much anyway. He'd be up to his good-looking eyeballs in man stuff. Probably would forget about her and the baby altogether. And that would be for the best. She'd rather not have him in her life at all, than to have just a part of him.

That was the problem that had pushed them apart. She wanted too much, way too much. But Jackson wasn't ready to give his all. She didn't think he'd ever be ready for that kind of commitment even if he did pretend to want more.

"Don't let any of that fool you, sweetheart. I'm making sure I carve out time for our baby."

Drat, could he read her mind?

"Shhh." Riley whirled to glare at him and ran smack into his arms. Using the intimate contact to whisper in his ear, she said, "I haven't exactly announced it to everyone. So don't talk about it out loud."

"Or ever?" he asked, holding on to her shoulders.

"That'd be even better."

"You'd like that, huh?" He held her when she tried to move away. "How long are you planning on keeping this a secret from everyone? Are you embarrassed because I'm the father?"

Riley's face burned hot from all his questions. Hurrying back to her office, she said, "People are staring. You need to leave."

But he didn't leave. He was right behind her. "Let 'em stare. They know we have a history. And we'll soon have a future, if I have any say in the matter."

She couldn't think along those lines. Too dangerous. "Let me go, Jackson."

He finally stood back and dropped his hands, but his gaze held her, moved over her face and her lips. "For now, darlin'. But this isn't over." He stomped around the desk and hit a finger on her desk pad. "I will be going to the next appointment with you come Tuesday. Count on it."

He'd read her appointment calendar. Before Riley could protest, he was out the door.

But that masculine scent of leather and spice and the outdoors lingered long after he was gone.

And so did the ache in her heart.

"LET'S GO TO lunch."

Riley frowned up at her mother's suggestion. "I can't, Mama. I've got things to do. We're getting ready for the big day—the magazine shoot. I'll just grab an apple and some crackers or something."

"No, ma'am, you will not," Bettye said while she crooked her finger and motioned for Riley to come with her. "We are going to the Hamhock so you can get a good, nourishing meal in your stomach, understand?"

Riley's stomach growled loudly at that suggestion. "I told you, I'm busy well into next week getting things in order."

"So you need to eat between now and then," Bettye replied. Then she lowered her voice. "Riley, think of the baby."

Okay, that stopped her cold. Riley dropped the armful of scarves she'd been hanging and pranced to her office to get her purse. Giving her mother another frown, she came back and called out, "Margie Sue, my mama's making me eat my lunch. I'll be back in thirty minutes."

"She'll be back in an hour," Bettye corrected.

Margie Sue waltzed over to the accessories wall, her black pants and colorful fall motif jacket making her look ready for an elegant pumpkin gathering. "Take your time, Riley. You know, we're all highly qualified to get this store prettied up for the magazine layout. You trained us that way." Turning to Riley's mother, she added, "Make her rest. We'll be just fine."

"I know that," Bettye said, hooking Riley's arm with hers. "But apparently she doesn't."

Riley put a finger to her lips. "Hush up, both of you. Remember, I haven't announced anything yet."

Margie Sue shot Bettye a tight-lipped glance. "Okay, okay. It's gonna be all right."

But Riley wasn't sure it would be all right. She'd done everything possible the first time to make sure it would be all right and she'd lost her little boy. What if something happened this time, too? How could she ever come back from that dark place again?

"Stop worrying," Bettye said, smiling over at Riley as they walked down the street. "Take a deep breath, honey. Smell that cool, crisp fall air. Thanksgiving is just days away. Don't let the good stuff pass you by."

Riley had to agree it was a beautiful day. She gave her mom a quick peck on the cheek. "You always know the right thing to say, don't you?"

Bettye's smile showed off her dimples. "I only know that I love my girl and I want you to be happy."

"I'm happy," Riley said. "Why wouldn't I be?"

Bettye patted her arm. "Jackson, honey. I'm sure he's like a burr in your bonnet. He always did know how to make a grand entrance."

"His timing is lousy," Riley said, glad her mother understood. "I can't let him back into my life, Mama. And I can't worry about him. I have to focus on this baby."

They'd reached the Hamhock, so Bettye pulled the door open and turned back. "Better get used to him,

Riley. He's inside eating lunch with two of your brothers and your uncle."

"Mercy, get on in here," Dorothy Lyn Harmon called from behind the long counter. "Riley, it's so good to see you and your mama." She shot a meaningful glance toward the traitors in the family. Curtis and Bobby both looked sheepish and then waved. Jackson lifted his chin in a nod of acknowledgment.

"Hey, boys," Bettye called out. "My, you sure are busy today, Dorothy Lyn."

Riley cringed inside but hid her embarrassment behind a prom queen smile. The smell of hamburgers on the griddle merged with the scent of baked bread and fried chicken. She prayed she didn't heave right there. She'd managed to avoid Jackson all week and now here he sat, looking good enough to eat with a spoon.

She mustered up enough calm to speak to her friend. "How you doing?"

Dorothy Lyn chuckled and pulled her red bifocals down on her nose, her green eyes dancing between Riley and Jackson. She loved to dress in bright colors so Riley made sure she picked out things for Dorothy Lyn every time she went to market. Today, the restaurant owner had on a bright green sweater with orange leaves floating across the front. "If I was any better, suga', you'd have to slap the silly right off my face."

Dorothy Lyn loved to smile and shoot the breeze with her customers. And she had such a loud voice usually everyone in the place could hear every word she shouted.

Such as, "Looky here, boys. Riley just walked in with her mama. How 'bout that?" The "boys" she'd called out to sat there grinning. Or at least Riley's two turncoat brothers were grinning. Jackson kept his eyes on Riley.

"Don't be shy," Dorothy Lyn said to Bettye and Riley. "C'mon in and find a seat. We got plenty for everybody."

To Dorothy Lyn, this was a natural means of carrying on a conversation. She meant no harm. She was just pointing out the obvious.

Jackson did his own cringe and finally spoke. "Hello."

"Hi, Jackson," Bettye called out, her smile as fresh as a daisy.

The whole place seemed to go into a freeze-frame. Everyone stopped to see if Riley would speak to her ex-husband. Forks stopped clinking against plates, coffeepots went still, the ice dispenser spurted to a halt, and the drone of people talking and laughing ended on a hiss of feeble conversational steam. Riley felt everyone's eyes on her. Especially, she felt Jackson's eyes on her. Just one more reason she should have stayed at work and nibbled on a pack of crackers. She shifted back toward the door.

But Bettye wasn't having any of that. Gripping Riley's arm with an ironfisted strength, she whispered, "Stand up straight, sugar, and hold your head high. You got nothing to be embarrassed about."

Her mama was right. Riley took a deep breath and

smiled again, meaning it this time. She shouldn't be annoyed or embarrassed about Jackson being back in Sinclair. She had her little domain here, after all. All the fashionable ladies shopped in her store. She had a full membership to the country club and in the Junior League. She attended all the best parties and gave to several worthy causes. She even had men who wanted to date her, and sometimes, she actually took them up on that. She was fine, just fine. And she did not need to speak to Jackson to make that fact known.

"I'm fine, Mama," she said to remind herself and everyone else, and loud enough for everyone to get the message. "And I'm starving for some corn bread and collard greens. With roast beef and rice and gravy. Sweet tea to drink."

"You get all of that, Dorothy Lyn? I'll have the same."

"And sweet potato pie, too," Riley said, her smile beaming.

"That's my girl," Bettye said, grinning. "Let's go find a table."

Jackson watched Riley and hid his own grin. She'd done the Riley thing right there at the front door of the restaurant. It was a sight to behold, the way she'd gone from embarrassed and afraid to defiant and fearless. He'd seen her do that so many times through the years, so many times. She always managed to pull it off with class and flair, her head going up, a little dare in her blue eyes.

He'd sure like to see her do that over and over again,

but he mostly wanted her to just be Riley all the time. She'd somehow fallen into this pattern of trying to be a rebel with all sorts of causes. But Jackson liked the real rebel in her, the woman without any restraints. Riley had a good heart, but that heart had steered her in the wrong direction too many times.

That heart had been broken, too. By him and the death of their baby. It was his fault that Riley had lost some of her beautiful fire. He knew it but he was determined to fix things between them. If he couldn't have her back, maybe he could be a father to this child, at least.

If Riley would let him. That would be his biggest challenge. To get back into Riley's good graces—at least enough to be able to see his own child. She'd warned him it wouldn't happen but…he wasn't the same ole Jackson. He'd show Riley he could be a better man, a stronger man, for their child.

But the look she gave him as she passed his table didn't bode well for his plan. She barely acknowledged him with just a tiny little nod. Even after he'd said a loud hello, everyone in the place had seen her deliberate cut.

Now he was the one who'd been embarrassed. So she got points for snubbing him. He could handle Riley. Later and in private. But he had a feeling things would go from bad to worse before they got better.

CHAPTER THIRTEEN

DELTON SLUMPED OVER the side of his big pickup, his hands hanging in front of him. "Something's up, Jackson. Riley invited the whole dang family over to Southern Hill for Sunday dinner."

Jackson figured she was about to do the big reveal.

Maybe he should be there, muscle his way in since Riley had accused him of doing that already.

"Are you and Margie Sue going?"

"I reckon so. I can't turn down anything Aunt Verde cooks. And I can't tell Margie Sue I don't want to go. 'Cause I do. I'm curious. I don't mind as long as Riley stays out of the kitchen."

Jackson laughed at that. "So you know for sure Riley isn't cooking, huh?"

Delton lifted his dark ball cap and settled it back on his head, the tractor company motif running across the cap a little sideways. "Are you kidding? I mean, my sister can cook when she's in the mood. But a full Sunday dinner? I don't think so." He shrugged and lifted away. "Must be something mighty important. Probably gonna give all of us a lecture about hanging around with riffraff."

"You mean me?" Jackson asked, looking pained.

"I don't see any other riffraff around here."

"Very funny." He followed Delton around to the driver's side of the truck. "You'll have to let me know what's going on."

More like, he'd be in big trouble when Delton found out about Riley being pregnant. Awkward didn't begin to cover this situation. In a place like Sinclair, people didn't divulge such personal things. At least not in mixed company. Everyone loved to gossip behind closed doors but they preferred to keep the intimate details of their own lives behind closed doors, too.

This kind of powder-keg event would keep tongues wagging for months, maybe even years. Leave it to Riley to be the trailblazer on getting pregnant without a man around.

"I sure will," Delton said, bringing Jackson out of his thoughts. "Unless my lovely sister puts a gag order on all of us. You know she's been known to do that."

"I know her well," Jackson replied, waving goodbye to Delton. "See you Saturday for the hunt."

"I'm ready." Delton floored the Chevy and headed off to oversee his own holdings.

"Not sure I am," Jackson said as he turned to walk back toward the lodge. Hunting and fishing and overseeing the timber tracts, he could handle. Having to explain all of this to the world, not so much.

He stopped, taking in a breath as he surveyed the big lodge. Built in the early part of the last century, the two-storied log structure would last at least another century or two. The wide windows were tall and inviting, the long hallways full of comfortable guest rooms. The great room had a looming A-frame ceiling that reached beyond the rugged staircase and open landings to the second floor. A great antlered chandelier was centered in the top of the ceiling. And the massive stone fireplace could keep most the whole bottom floor—which included the great room, kitchen and dining room—toasty warm. His suite and the main office and a bath were located out of sight down a hallway on the first floor, but he had his own fireplace.

Why did he love this place so much?

Had he put the lodge above all else in his life?

Or had he used it as a hiding place, the way he'd done during his childhood? Jackson had always found comfort and solace deep in the walls of this old building. It breathed to life his ancestors and his heritage. Why had he abandoned all of that?

And how in the world had he managed to leave Riley?

He turned and looked out the other way, toward Southern Hill. The big white house sparkled like a diamond set amongst the great oaks and tall pines. So many memories, growing up and, later, being there with Riley.

But the lodge had always suited him better. As far back as he could remember, he'd loved this old place. He'd learned to hunt with his grandfather and his daddy and he knew every inch of these woods and pastures, thanks to the time he'd had with them. He watched both of them conduct business here with a handshake and a grin. And…he'd returned here the night his son had died. Returned to the roaring fire and the warmth of a place where he felt safe.

He thought of Riley and how hard she was fighting to keep him at a distance. Maybe he deserved that. Maybe he needed to leave and stay gone. Because he'd certainly kept her at a distance once she got pregnant. After she lost the baby, it was way too late to see the error of his ways. She wanted no part of him then. He hated himself then.

He'd vowed to stay away.

But his heart was here—with Riley and their sweet little boy. And with this new baby, too. How could he prove that to her and the town that only tolerated him because his name was Sinclair and because he gave them something to chew on and talk about?

Jackson pushed away the distant memories of never measuring up. Instead, he focused on the here and now. He was back. He'd come home because it was time. He wouldn't spend the rest of his life lonely and miserable.

And he wouldn't give up on Riley, either. Just seeing her made his pulse sharpen and race. Touching her broke his heart because she no longer wanted his touch. Even arguing with her was better than the stony silence they'd settled into right before the divorce.

He glanced back at the house once more then headed toward the wooden steps of the lodge. He made it to the big porch when his cell buzzed.

"Riley?"

"I need you to come to the house Sunday after church. I'm having a family meeting."

He didn't dare tell her he already knew that. "Oh, really? So why do you want me there?"

"I'm going to tell the whole family about the baby…and I thought you might as well be there so you wouldn't get a lot of questions later. We can get it over with and out in the open. Then I'll be able to get on with things."

"Perfect plan," he said. She always had a plan. And she'd obviously thought about this one long and hard. "I'll be there."

"Okay. I'll see you then."

"No, you'll see me tomorrow. Remember I'm driving you to your appointment."

"Jackson, you don't have to do that."

"I want to, and yes, I have to." He swallowed a lump of pride. "I need to, Riley."

She went quiet on him. Then she replied, "Oh, all right. Pick me up at nine. I don't want to be late."

"See you then."

He disconnected then turned to stare back across the big lake, toward the house, thankful that Riley had thought to include him in the family meeting. And for the first time since he'd come home, he felt hopeful.

"I HOPE YOU don't take this the wrong way," Riley told Jackson the next morning. "I'm only letting you come along to shut you up."

"What if I have something else to say?" he asked, his hands gripping the steering wheel of his sports car.

Thankful that the car rode as well as hers, Riley tried to settle back and relax. She'd be mortified if she hurled in Jackson's car. "We can talk about anything at all, as long as you understand this does not mean I'm giving in."

She didn't tell him that she'd had a long night of wide-eyed thinking. That she was having second thoughts about shutting him out. That she was kind of glad he'd demanded to come with her to the doctor. She had some pride left, after all. She wasn't ready to concede on anything, especially her heart.

"Okay." He pointed toward a big field. "Look at those hay bales. Looks like the drought didn't hurt that field too much." Then he saw a billboard. "Wow, Kenny Rogers is on tour. Coming to Atlanta for a Christmas show."

"Very funny." She wanted to laugh but she hadn't slept very well and…being this close to him was torture. Maybe she should have insisted they take her car. It wasn't such a tight squeeze.

"What did you tell Aunt Verde?" he asked, his gaze on the traffic, his profile so nice to look at.

"I told her the truth," Riley replied. "I sat her and Uncle Floyd down last night and told them I'm pregnant. And before she could faint and he could get the shotgun, I explained how I got this way."

"How'd they take it?"

Riley let out a sigh. "Aunt Verde had already figured it out but she was afraid to ask. She jumped to the same conclusion as you did. Thought I'd been fooling around. She actually asked me if Fred Marshall was the daddy. I set her straight right away on that. Can you imagine?"

"I'd rather not," he quipped. "And I mean that."

Riley's heart did a little sputter at the possessive tone in his voice. "You're not jealous of Fred now, are you?"

"Jealous, no. But if he lays a hand on you, I'll break his teeth."

"Jackson, he's my accountant. He takes care of the money and keeps me out of jail by helping me file my taxes."

"Just so that's the only thing that pompous dandy files, or he'll be in jail. And me right beside him for assault."

She slapped at his arm. "You are so bad." But she couldn't hide her smile. "And so jealous."

"Okay, so I'm jealous, yes. Just how many men have you dated since I left?"

She wouldn't tell him slim to none. Well, maybe a few. "That's none of your business."

He glanced over at her. "C'mon, Riley. I want to know."

"You first," she said, her playful tone gone now. "How many women did you get to know when you were trolling around the world in your precious yacht?"

He didn't answer. Just shook his head and let out a sigh.

Her pulse hit triple time. "Jackson? Is there something you need to tell me?"

He passed a slow-moving pickup truck. "Just seeing if you'd react."

She gave him a sweet smile. "This is me, reacting."

But her pulse was still running through a jealous haze.

"I didn't find anyone special, if that's what you're asking. I met a lot of people, but no one—" He stopped, checked the mirrors. "No one I'd want to bring home."

Riley held on with both hands. Was he telling her the truth to save her any pain or embarrassment? Or had he been about to say no one compared to her?

Before she could question him, he put his hand over hers. "I only want to bring one woman home. And that's you, babe."

Riley didn't pull away. Instead, she took a deep breath. She was tired of fighting him, but she wasn't ready to let him back in completely. "I've decided something after talking to Aunt Verde this morning and I'd like to talk to you about it."

He gave her a quick stare, his eyebrows lifting. "Oh, yeah. What's that?"

"I've been thinking," she began.

"Oh, that can't be good. When you put on that thinking cap all sorts of things begin to happen."

"I've been thinking," she said again, lifting her hand away. "Maybe you do have a right to be a father to this baby."

"You think?" She saw the relief flooding over his face. "Do I?"

"Yes." She swallowed, hoped she'd made the right decision. "Both Margie Sue and Aunt Verde think I'm being too harsh, not letting you have parental rights."

"I agree with those two very wise women. And we both know it's not a matter of *not letting me*. Legally, I could take you to court on all accounts. You did use my little swimmers to have a party with your tiny eggs."

"You have such a way with words," she said. "And yes, legally, you do have certain rights. I don't want to go through another court battle. This baby doesn't need that added stress."

"And neither do you," he replied. "So Aunt Verde and Margie Sue both told you to play nice?"

She nodded, her hands together on her lap. "Well, they made valid points. And I got to thinking. We both were blessed with great parents. I'd hate to keep this little one from knowing you. I just want to focus on having this baby and giving him—or her—a good life. With a mama and a daddy, the way I'd always dreamed it would be."

He shot her a gentle glance. "I agree with that, too."

She swallowed a bit more pride. "If I can't have the perfect dream, I can at least give my child a solid foundation."

"A good plan. I can help with that."

"And if you really are going to be around for a while, I can't deny you time with your own child."

"That sounds reasonable."

"Okay, then. We'll go to our lawyers and draw up the documents to give you joint custody. That means we'd share the responsibility of raising this child equally. And since you'll be living so close—at the lodge—that shouldn't be so difficult. We're neighbors so this baby will have a strong support system, between the two of us, and with my extended family."

She halted, gulped in air. Riley had thought about this all night, especially after she'd talked to Aunt Verde and Uncle Floyd. They both thought Jackson deserved a second chance.

"He's working hard, honey," Uncle Floyd had told her. "He's changed. He's more responsible now and more centered. He ain't drinking anything stronger than coffee, I promise. I don't know where all he went while he was out there, but he's a full-fledged man now. He'll make a good daddy, too."

She found the courage to tell him the rest. "But Jackson, I mean this—if you up and leave again, don't bother coming back. You can't do that to our child or to me. It won't be fair and I won't stand for it. You get one chance, just one. Next time, I will hire a lawyer and I'll make sure I get full custody."

He didn't say anything for a few minutes. Riley sat there, so close to him she could reach out and put her hand on his cheek if she dared. So close, she could reach over and kiss him or lean close and almost lay her head on his shoulder.

But she didn't do any of those things.

"Jackson?"

He pulled the car into the parking garage next to the medical building. Then he got out and came around to help her out. And when he had her out and standing, he shut the door then gently pushed her back against it.

"There's only one thing wrong with your oh-so-carefully-thought-out plan, darlin'."

Riley felt the full power of his gaze on her, burning her to her spot. "What are you talking about?"

"This," he said. Then he tugged her close and lowered his mouth to hers. The kiss was almost harsh but it turned soft, so soft, and so sweet with longing and intention. Riley lifted to meet him, drinking him in as if she'd been lost in a desert. Oh, how she'd missed Jackson's kisses.

And just when she was letting go and giving in, he pulled back and said, "You see, sweetheart, I don't intend to stay in that lodge across the lake forever. If I have my way, we will have joint custody, all right. But it'll be together, in our own home. 'Cause I'm here to stay and I don't plan on signing away my rights again ever. I lost the right to be your husband and maybe I don't deserve the right to be this baby's father."

He leaned toward her again. "But that won't happen this time. Because before that baby is born, I plan to be your husband again. Now, let's go see how *our* baby is doing."

CHAPTER FOURTEEN

"THERE YOU GO." Dr. Reynolds pointed to the tiny pea-shaped object on the ultrasound screen. "That's your baby."

Riley smiled, tears streaming down her face. "My baby." She reached out and Jackson took her hand. "Do you see it, Jackson?"

He nodded, his eyes a misty blue. "I do. So tiny, but a Sinclair for sure."

Riley could only nod. "A fighter."

"Everything looks good," the doctor said. "We'll print you out a couple of pictures."

"Good," Jackson replied. "The family will want to see this."

Riley glanced over at him. Hearing the joy in his words touched her, but he wasn't supposed to be part of her family anymore. "They'll all be so tickled," she managed to say through a sniff.

"Just keep doing what you're doing," the doctor said. "Take your prenatal vitamins, eat healthy food and get as much exercise as you can. Stay in touch with us and with your local doctor. I'll see you in a few weeks."

He helped Riley to sit up, shook Jackson's hand, then left.

Jackson helped her stand. "I'll wait outside so you can get cleaned up and dressed."

Riley let the warmth of his touch seep through her. Why were doctors' offices always so cold? She didn't want to let go of that strong, secure hand. But she had to do just that.

"Thanks. I'll be out in a minute."

Jackson smiled over at her. "You look…radiant. Being pregnant suits you."

Riley swallowed and nodded. "You might not think that when I'm in the ninth month. By then I'm sure I'll have dark circles under my eyes and fifty more pounds around my tummy."

"You'd still be radiant to me."

She watched him leave then turned to steady herself against the exam table. Why had she allowed him to come anyway?

Because you still care.

Yes, and it was nice to have him here. Before, Jackson hadn't had time to come with her to her checkups. He'd wanted a child, no doubt about that. He'd bragged and planned like any expectant father. Maybe that had been an act, nothing more. Maybe he hadn't really been ready to be a father to that child. He'd mainly left it all up to her as long as she and the baby were both healthy. Everyone had believed that they were. But something had gone wrong. So wrong.

Riley dressed and turned to put a hand over the tiny bump under her blouse. "We're gonna be careful this time, aren't we?" She needed to remember that holding Jackson at a distance had to be part of that regimen. Bringing him along for a checkup was one thing; letting him be there every day for her was quite another. But how could she stop these feelings she'd tried to hide for so long?

Checking herself in the dressing-room mirror, she made sure she did look "radiant." If Jackson thought she was under any kind of stress, he'd start making demands. He was already that involved in this pregnancy. It was sweet but it also confused her. Maybe he had changed. Maybe this time he was truly ready to be a real father.

Steeling herself against that lethal charm he carried around, she made her way to the checkout desk. Jackson was sitting near the reception window. "Almost ready," she called to him.

He lifted a chin in acknowledgment.

"Your husband is so nice," the cute blonde behind the desk said. "He sure was proud when I handed him those ultrasound pictures."

"We're not—"

"Going to have time for lunch," Jackson said from behind her. He flashed Riley a thoughtful look. "I'm starving."

"Me, too." She didn't try to correct the perky girl at the window. "Thank you," she said when the woman cleared her bill and gave her the next appointment schedule.

Outside, the autumn day shone brightly. The breeze

was cool, but the sun was out. It did a dappled dance through the trees and chased the falling leaves.

"Let's go get a Varsity hot dog and have a picnic somewhere," Jackson suggested, his mood shining right along with the sun.

Her stomach rumbled rudely at that suggestion. "I'm not so sure that's the healthiest thing for the baby, but that does sound good."

"Then we'll do it. I don't think one chili dog will hurt."

"We'll find out," she said, before sliding into the car seat.

The hot dog from the famous restaurant might not hurt, but allowing him to get close certainly could. Torn between sticking to her plan of keeping him at a distance and wanting to bring him into her heart, she fastened her seat belt and wondered if she'd made the right decision. Because if she let him get under her skin, it could be that much harder to watch him walk away again. It would also be difficult to raise this child alone when in her heart, she wanted Jackson to be there with her.

AN HOUR LATER, Jackson pulled the car out of the interstate traffic and found a quiet park near a school. "How's this?"

"Great," Riley replied. "I've sniffed those chili dogs all the way from downtown Atlanta. I need mine and I need it soon."

He laughed at that. "I see a table. Maybe it'll work."

The little roadside park was clean and the wooden table with attached benches looked passable. Jackson unloaded the bag of hot dogs, onion rings and French fries then handed Riley her orange drink.

"I haven't had Varsity food in a long time," she said before diving in to take a bite of her chili dog. "Hmm, this is so good."

He enjoyed watching her eat. Riley wasn't shy or picky about her food. She had a big appetite and she loved good Southern cooking. And yet, she managed to stay slender and in shape. Wondering how she'd fare during this pregnancy, he decided he'd help her along.

"So…do you get a lot of exercise?" he asked, hoping to make polite conversation and find out some things at the same time.

She held her hot dog in midair. "I try. Why?"

"Oh, no reason. I mean, you look great."

"But if I eat like this I won't, right?"

Women always jumped to the wrong conclusion. "I was trying to compliment you, darlin'."

She nibbled on her chili dog then turned to him. "I exercise, yes. I swim and I walk and used to be, I'd ride my horse. You should remember that since you never wanted to go jogging with me. I guess you still prefer weight lifting to taking a long walk."

"I'll walk with you. Can you run, though, being pregnant?"

"Yes, as long as I'm careful."

"So when do you want to take a long walk with me?" he asked, couching it in words he hoped she'd see as a challenge rather than an attempt to make time with her.

Her expression held surprise and…disbelief. "I like to walk in the morning when it's quiet, before I go to work."

"Good, I'll be waiting for you in the yard tomorrow morning at dawn. We can walk around the lake."

She looked perplexed and embarrassed. "I didn't mean you had to be there with me, Jackson."

Of course she didn't mean that. But that's exactly what he wanted—to be there with her. "I want to, so I can make sure you're following doctor's orders. Besides, I could use the exercise, too."

"What about the lodge and strength-training?"

"I'll put in a full day at the lodge and I can go into the gym there and lift weights after work. No problem."

She mulled that over, probably trying to find a way to squirm out of this. "Well, we could walk the perimeter of the lake. I'll catch you up on the farm. Uncle Floyd monitors things, but my brother Curtis took over management after—"

"After I left. He told me as much at the barbecue."

"Does that bother you?" she asked, giving him a look that dared him to complain. "I've given most of my relatives a job on Southern Hill."

"Why should it? You're the one with the big family. I'm just along for the ride."

"That about sums it up," she said, a definite chill settling around them.

"What does that mean?"

"You," she said, sending him a piercing glance. "You—the other you—always went along for the ride, but you never stayed for the cleanup."

"That's how you see me? Even now?"

"Yes." She settled back on the rickety bench then nabbed an onion ring. "Jackson, you were an only child and spoiled to the bone. Your parents hired people to do the dirty work. Your daddy made you do chores and follow him around, but I don't think your heart was in Southern Hill."

She'd hit too close to home on that one. But she didn't know the half of it. "Oh, and where was my heart, honey?"

She put down the crispy half-eaten onion ring. "I don't know. I thought it was in our marriage, but maybe you just went along for the ride on that, too."

"That's not fair, Riley," he said, wondering why he'd let that little shard of hope fill his mind, and wondering how he'd stepped right into a sticky situation with this subject. "I worked hard on both the farm and at the lodge." Dropping the last of his hot dog bun, he wiped his hands on a paper napkin. "You know how my daddy was. He demanded the best. And when he didn't get it—"

"He turned mean," she finished. "But you two were so close. You always stood up to him and I think he respected you for that."

He got up to pace, his boots hitting the dirt. "Are

you sure about that? Do you believe he really did respect me?"

"He seemed to. I never heard him complain."

Jackson turned, a burning shame covering him. "That's because he never showed his bad side in public. He only saved that for me—so he could berate me and lecture me and make me feel as if I was the dumbest jock on earth."

Riley held a hand on her paper cup. "Jackson, I've never heard you talk about your daddy like that."

"That's because I never did talk to you or anyone else about him and his ways. He was a tough, hardhearted man, Riley. So…yes, I rebelled. When I'd try to do something, he'd only chastise me or tell me I didn't have a lick of sense. So I let other people take care of the land I loved and I let other people do the work he didn't think I could do. I gave up trying to please that man."

She put a hand to her mouth. "And did you do the same with me? Is that why you left?"

He looked down at her, wishing he could explain. "I wanted our marriage, our life, to be different. He was a good man. Went to church on Sunday and got up with the sun on Monday. But he was never really happy." He shrugged, wished he hadn't opened this can of worms. "I think he wanted more children and when my mama couldn't produce them, he turned bitter. He hid it well, but most of the time he treated her about the same way he treated me."

Riley shook her head, the disbelief on her face causing her to frown. "No. They loved each other. Anyone could tell."

"Yes, honey, they did love each other. But that didn't make it right, the way he treated her, the way he treated me. He wanted you and me to get married so he could have a connection with your family. Because you have brothers, Riley. You have the family I never had. He loved it when I'd bring home a Buckingham. But you were the main Buckingham prize."

"So you only married me to please your daddy?"

He ran a hand down his face. Why did he have to go and open his big mouth on this? And why now? Maybe because he had changed and he did want a second chance. That meant laying it all bare, opening old wounds and being honest.

"I married you because I wanted you to be my wife. Don't ever doubt that. I…loved you. And I also loved your big, crazy family. I wanted to be a part of that, because I felt comfortable with you and with your family." Looking away through the trees, he said, "I missed that, being gone all these years."

She looked shocked but her eyes held sympathy. "Did you want that for us—a big family?"

"Of course I did. I loved hanging out at your house. Your house was alive. My house was like this dark tomb. We were all civil at my house, but we didn't have the kind of energy and chaos I always found around your folks."

"We are a wild bunch."

He grinned at that. "Yep, a wild bunch but even

now, Riley.Even after all that happened between you and me, your family still accepts me. Heck, you're even making an effort." He let out a sigh. "I guarantee you that if my daddy were alive today, he'd turn me away. He'd be ashamed and embarrassed because I created a scandal."

She got up and leaned back against the old table. "Why didn't you ever tell me about this?"

"What, and ruin it for everyone? After we got engaged, he was happy for a while. He got kind of mellow in his old age. You never saw the worst of him. And I guess I didn't even realize how he had influenced me until…until we started talking about having children."

"What are you saying, Jackson?"

Hearing the hurt in her question, he couldn't tell her. He didn't want to get into this anymore. He'd tried for years to push it aside, the resentment, the pain. He had to be a man about things, didn't he?

"I'm not saying anything. Nothing at all." He started gathering their trash. "It's getting late. We need to head back."

"No, you can't just blurt this out to me and then clam up. I need to know. Is this why you…didn't seem to want a child? Or at least didn't seem that interested when I was pregnant before? Is it?"

He tossed their bag into an open trash can by the table. "I wanted a baby, Riley. More than you'll ever know."

She followed him to the car, her eyes blazing. "But

you pulled away. You checked out long before you left. I have to know why."

"I can't tell you why," he said, stomping to the car. "I don't understand it myself."

He opened her door and watched her get in and then came around to crank the car. "I'm sorry I brought all that up. It's something inside of me that I've had to deal with. I don't like to talk about it. Nothing for you to worry about."

"Nothing for me to worry about? It's everything, Jackson. Everything. And the fact that you didn't even bother to tell me any of this speaks volumes."

He didn't reply. He kept thinking over and over that she'd never bothered to notice how he was feeling. Riley was adorable and beautiful and caring and complicated. But she'd been so wrapped up in being married and producing children that she'd neglected the one person in her life who truly did want to go along on that ride with her. Her husband.

"Just forget I brought it up," he said.

She didn't say anything else. She was quiet the whole way home.

But when he pulled into the driveway by the sunporch and came around to open her door, she got out and stood, waiting for him, determination coloring her eyes. "Nothing for me to worry about, huh? I'd say there is a lot for me to worry about, a lot for me to think about, too. Jackson, if you'd told me some of this, if I'd had an inkling, I might have understood a little better."

"Understood what?" he asked, wishing he'd kept his secrets imbedded in his head. But he'd somehow managed to open that long-ago buried secret inside his heart. Now Riley would analyze him to death. "Understood what?" he asked again, dreading her answer.

"Why you were afraid to be a father," she said.

"I wasn't afraid. That's crazy."

"I think you were, Jackson. And…I think that, no matter how hard you try to prove otherwise, you're still afraid."

Then she turned and walked into the house.

CHAPTER FIFTEEN

RILEY DREADED SUNDAY.

Which only made her realize that having Jackson back in her life was not working in her favor. She loved going to church and seeing everyone she knew and loved. She enjoyed having a big Sunday dinner with her family, usually at her parents' house since Riley wasn't known for her cooking.

So why, oh why, had she offered to cook for everyone so she could announce her pregnancy to the entire family, including her obviously repressed ex-husband?

And why had that same ex-husband managed to somehow grace the doors of the church this morning?

Jackson, in church, and looking better than any deacon she'd ever seen. Jackson, in a nice suit and white shirt and tie, his shaggy hair all inky and smooth, his cowboy boots shined so pretty they'd almost blinded her when he swaggered by.

Remembering his lips on hers, Riley found it hard to concentrate. Each time he turned to smile at her, her heart did a little nervous dance. While her head told her she was crazy.

He'd sat a couple of rows ahead of Riley and her family.

Alone. He'd been all alone. No family to hug, no cousins, or aunts or uncles to laugh and chat with. No parents.

Sitting there in church, it had hit Riley that her ex-husband was hiding a lot of pain behind that charming smile. And maybe that pain had caught up with him when she'd insisted they have a baby. Maybe that pain had floored him when he'd lost his son and later… his wife.

So why hadn't she ever considered his pain before? Or even seen it for that matter?

Am I that self-centered and petty?

Riley checked the roast and then looked at the clock. Her guests were supposed to arrive around one o'clock. With Aunt Verde's gentle coaching, she'd cooked the roast last night so she'd only have to warm it up today. It smelled pretty good. How could she go wrong with her mother's recipe and Aunt Verde helping out? Her aunt and uncle had gone to visit a sick friend, but they'd promised they'd be back in time for Sunday dinner.

Riley was on her own in the kitchen until then, however.

A knock at the back door caused her to jump. Telling herself to get over this fit of nervousness, Riley hurried to the door and glanced through the glass panes.

Jackson. Thirty minutes early. What'd he do? Leave church and come straight here?

"You're early," she said, not even bothering with a proper greeting.

He looked sheepish and unsure. "I thought I'd get here before the others so we could talk."

"About what?" And why had she thought this was a good idea—inviting him?

He glanced around then lowered his voice. "About those things I said the other day…can you just let that slide?"

Riley straightened her big apron and put her hands on her hips. "You'd like that, right? Let's just sweep things back under the rug and get on with it."

"There's nothing to get on with," he said, pacing in front of her. "I shouldn't have told you any of that. It's over now, anyway."

"You think?" She whirled to get back to preparing the meal. Verde would be here any minute to help, but Riley needed to stay busy. "Me, I think those things needed to be said. In fact, I think we should sit down sometime and have us a long heart-to-heart talk. Maybe even go to a marriage counselor."

When he didn't respond, she turned around to glare at him. "I always thought you were the most fearless man I'd ever met. Even when we were young, you always led the charge, always met any obstacles head-on. That's what made you such a good football player. That's why you could make anyone follow you into a raging creek or over a muddy hill. That's one of the reasons I was so attracted to you." She shrugged, put her hands on the counter. "I also felt safe with you."

He took off his suit coat and laid it across a chair. "And now?"

She stirred sugar into the tea pitcher. "You're still that way on the surface, but inside you're scared silly of what really counts in life. And that makes me scared, too."

His frown lifted like a fence across his face. "You don't know what you're talking about."

Riley leaned over the big center island. "I didn't, until you told me those things the other day. Now I wonder if I ever really knew you at all."

JACKSON DIDN'T KNOW what to do. He didn't like being so vulnerable, being seen in such a bad light. He'd learned how to hide all of that angst so no one, not even Riley, would see it.

"You knew the good parts of me," he said, standing across from her on the other side of the kitchen island. "You always knew."

"Did I?" She went back to chopping vegetables for the salad. "Did I really, Jackson?" She tossed carrots and cucumbers into the lettuce bowl. "I knew I loved you. I wanted to spend the rest of my life with you. But there was always something, a feeling that I couldn't pinpoint, that made me think I was somehow lacking."

"You were perfect," he said, dropping his head down. "Too perfect."

Her eyebrows shot up. "What's that supposed to mean?"

He wouldn't lie to her anymore. If he wanted to

win her back, he had to be honest. Completely honest. "I never thought I was good enough for you, Riley. I still don't."

"What?"

They stood there, staring each other down across the counter. Jackson wanted to go to her, grab her to him and ask her to give him another chance. He should tell her that he did a lot of soul-searching out there away from the angst of his memories. He should tell her that he tried to run from the truth, tried to hide from their love and their issues, but he wasn't ready to open his raw heart to that kind of scrutiny.

"Jackson, how can you even think that?"

Too late to answer that now. He heard cars pulling into the driveway, heard voices echoing out over the yard.

"Your company is here," he said. "I can leave if you want me to."

"Stay," she said, the command low and gentle. "Don't keep running away, Jackson."

He didn't know how to answer that so he stood and watched as everyone piled in amid greetings and covered dishes and talk of the ball game on television. They laughed and talked and teased and annoyed each other with a good-natured curiosity and contentment that was welcoming and comfortable.

"Jackson, you ole hound dog," Delton called out. "C'mon in here with the menfolks. Game's about to start."

Jackson looked at Riley. She stood with her aunt and

her mother, going over the menu and the seating arrangements. Wearing that cute apron that stated Will Work For Shoes.

He wanted to work on getting her back. He wanted to have his wife and child and their life together. But for the first time, it occurred to Jackson that maybe, just maybe, he did need to open up to his ex-wife. So instead of seeing the man she thought he was, she'd finally see the man he'd become. She thought he was fearless, while he felt like a coward for leaving her.

He was so intent on watching Riley, so caught up in the windstorm of emotions whirling through his mind, he didn't even notice the smoke coming out of the oven behind her.

"Riley!" Her daddy motioned to the stove. "Something's burning, honey."

Riley turned and gasped. "My roast." She threw open the door of the oven and moaned. "That's just classic. Me, burning dinner. I mean, really!"

Curtis and Bobby rushed into the kitchen and grabbed two pot holders. Jackson went into action and pulled Riley out of the way while her brothers double-handed the smoking roast.

"Are you all right?" he asked, holding her away from the ruckus.

"I burned dinner." She looked at the big, charred roast.

"It's my fault," he whispered. "I got you all riled up."

She pulled away but stood near him while the whole family piled in to see the damage.

"Can we order a pizza?" Little Curtis asked, his big eyes on the ruined roast.

Margie Sue stepped forward. "I think we can salvage most of it, Riley. We can make chipped beef with it. That'll work with your mashed potatoes."

"I'm supposed to mash the potatoes?" Riley asked, her expression bordering on despair. "I forgot to mash the potatoes."

"Do we have bread?" Little Curtis's brother Lucas asked. "And peanut butter?"

"Yes, we have bread, but we are not having peanut-butter-and-jelly sandwiches," Bettye replied, her gaze on her daughter. "I tell you what, you boys go in and watch the game. We'll bring in some chips and dip to hold y'all off so we can work on getting this roast right, okay?"

"Okay, Granny," Little Curtis said, running off with his brother.

But Jackson didn't miss Little Curtis's response. The little boy whispered to his brother, "We should use that one for target practice."

Riley heard it, too. She glanced from her mother to Allison to Jackson. Was she going to burst into tears?

No. Instead of doing the predictable thing, Riley started laughing. She glanced at him then looked at her shocked mother. "Target practice. Allison, your boys are too cute for words."

"Well, thanks," Allison said, caught between a frown and a tight smile. "What's so funny about this, though? We need to decide what to do about dinner."

Aunt Verde walked in, sniffed the air and turned to Uncle Floyd. "We should have gotten here a little sooner, I think."

Riley burst out in another round of laughter, causing her mother to smile and even Allison to loosen up a tad.

Jackson wasn't sure if Riley's laughter was hysterical or if she'd just decided to go with it on the target practice roast.

When everyone kept looking at her, she wiped at her eyes and laughed some more. Then Bettye, Margie Sue and Allison started laughing. Pretty soon Verde was laughing, too.

Uncle Floyd just shook his head and went into the den.

"What's so funny?" Charles asked from his place in the recliner.

"This roast," Riley shouted. "I think I've created a new dish—blackened pot roast. Little Curtis is right. We need to order pizza."

Jackson grabbed a knife. "Not necessarily. I learned a neat trick when I was camping on the Appalachian Trail."

"You went camping on the trail?" Allison asked, clearly shocked. "I thought you were out on your sailboat."

"I was out everywhere and anywhere," Jackson replied. "But right now, we need to eat. So back up, ladies, and let me work my magic on this hunk of meat."

CHARLES PUSHED BACK from the dining table and rubbed his round belly. "I have to say, I think blackened pot roast is my new favorite dish. That was a mighty fine spread, Riley. That thick dark gravy over the roast was just right for biscuit sopping."

Riley had long ago stopped laughing. But she kept her smile intact. She was exhausted and frustrated and confused and embarrassed and…scared. But she had to tell her entire family about the baby. During dessert, she decided. Verde had cooked that. Pumpkin spice cake. Maybe Riley could serve it without doing any damage.

"Thanks, Daddy," she said. "Sorry about the lumpy potatoes."

"I didn't notice any lumps," Delton said. "But I did like the cheese in those tators."

Riley glanced at Margie Sue and caught her sister-in-law's wink. "Jackson…uh…fixed those, too."

"You might oughta keep him around for emergencies," her daddy replied, his gaze level with Riley to show her he was teasing, nothing more.

"I'll go get dessert," Riley said, hopping up.

"And then maybe you can tell us why you wanted all of us here," Bobby said, patting Riley on the arm as she walked by.

"I'll help," Jackson offered.

She could feel him right behind her. Riley wanted to scream, "Go away." She wanted to turn and shout to him, "Why are you doing this to me? Why are you making me care again? And how did you learn to make such a good gravy to cover burned roast while camping on the Appalachian Trail, for Pete's sake?"

But she didn't scream. At all. She remained quiet.

"You did a good job with all of this," he said, his voice low.

"Don't patronize me," she replied, equally low. "I ruined everything and now I'm so tired I don't even care about telling them today. Maybe I should wait."

"No, don't," he said. He got the dessert plates and the whipped cream while she sliced the moist Bundt cake. "Get it over with so you'll quit worrying."

"My mama's already asked me twice if I'm okay. She's good at keeping secrets but I think she's ready for this one to be out in the open."

"Then you go ahead as planned," he said. He took two plates and headed back toward the dining room. "I can leave if I need to."

"No, I want you here." She stepped back, wishing she hadn't blurted that out. "It's just easier this way. I don't want them hounding you with questions."

He walked back a few paces. "You want to be in charge of damage control. I get it."

"Damage control? This isn't a PR event, Jackson. This is my life. And having you here has complicated things way more than I ever dreamed. But like it or not, you are this baby's father. So I need you here when I explain everything to my family." She motioned toward the dining room. "Aunt Verde is gonna take the kids on a nature walk while I talk to the adults."

"Got it." He whirled with the two dessert plates

and passed them out then came back for more. But he didn't say a word to her.

She'd made him mad. Good. She was too tired to fight about it, but yes, she was still in control here. She might not be able to control burning a roast, but she sure could control her own life.

She hoped.

CHAPTER SIXTEEN

THE DINING ROOM had gone quiet.

Everyone was staring at Riley, waiting for her big announcement. Jackson felt for her. He also felt the sweat gathering at his collar and working its way down his spine. What if his ex-in-laws didn't want him to be a part of this child's upbringing? Could he blame them?

This should have been a happy day, a day where they'd both be grinning ear to ear. But Riley looked spent and fatigued. He willed her to hurry it up so he could make her go upstairs and rest. She was older now, not that she looked it. But he knew the risks of miscarriage and other problems increased with age. He'd read up on it last night on the internet.

Riley glanced at him then held on to her coffee cup. "I know y'all are wondering why I wanted to have this get-together right before Thanksgiving when we'd all be together anyway. But I have something important to tell y'all and I wanted it over and done with by the holidays. Mama and Daddy and Aunt Verde and Uncle Floyd and a few others know this already. And so does Jackson."

Delton grunted on that. "Well, I'll be danged."

Giving her three brothers a smile, she sat up straight and touched a hand to her upswept hair. "This is hard to explain so please bear with me. I'll answer your questions when I'm finished."

"Sounds like you're about to announce running for the state senate or something," Bobby drawled with a sly wink. "Or maybe you're getting back with Jackson?"

"It's not that, I can assure you," Riley said. But she cast Jackson a smile, all the same.

While everyone else in the room shot him arrows of part sympathy and part relief.

"Are you sick?" Allison asked, her brown eyes bright. "I've wondered. You look sick to me. And you've been acting strange lately. What's up?"

"Allison, hush," Curtis said on a gentle growl. "Let her talk."

Jackson sent a frown toward Allison and Curtis. Curtis put a hand on his wife's skinny arm. "Go ahead, Riley."

"I'm not sick," Riley began. "But I haven't been feeling all that great lately—"

"I knew it," Allison spurted. "I told you something was wrong, Curtis. Didn't I tell you that just the other day?"

Jackson hit a hand on the table. "Let her finish and then you'll understand."

Allison looked embarrassed but she shut up.

"I'm pregnant," Riley said in a rush.

The silence was sharp and glaring.

And then, everyone started talking at once.

"Pregnant? How can *you* be pregnant?" Allison asked, indignant that she didn't know this already.

"Pregnant." Delton turned to Margie Sue. "Did you know about this?"

Margie Sue nodded and put a finger to her lips. "We'll talk later, honey."

Bobby sat there staring at his older sister as if she'd turned into a statue. "How'd that happen?" he finally asked.

Then they all three turned to Jackson, their expression changing from shocked to angry to murderous.

"Did you—?"

"How'd you do that?"

"Are y'all back together?"

Riley stood up. "Listen to me," she said, her tone calm in spite of how pale she looked. "I told you I'd explain everything. I'm close to two months along now."

"So, explain," Curtis said, his hand on his wife's arm.

"Did you just find out? Why didn't you say something at the barbecue?"

Riley looked at Allison. "I didn't want to rain on Allison's parade."

"So that's why you were acting so weird," Allison retorted. "I told Curtis you were being mighty stand-offish that day. I thought it was because Jackson was back."

Curtis pinned his wife with a stern look. "Let's let Riley give us the details, suga'."

"Whatever," Allison said, shrugging.

Jackson seriously wanted to strangle her.

But Riley didn't seem to mind. In fact, she had a soft smile on her face. "I told Margie Sue right away since we work together. And I told Mama and Daddy the day of the barbecue. I told Jackson right after he arrived in town."

Everybody started up again.

"Who's the daddy then?"

"What did Jackson say?"

"Jackson, are you gonna shoot him?"

Riley hit the table hard enough to make the china cups rattle. "Nobody is going to shoot anybody," she shouted, her calm shattered. "I did what's called an eSET. It's an elective single embryo transfer."

"What in the world is that?" Delton asked, shaking his head.

"And who did it with you?" Bobby asked in an indignant growl.

Jackson finally spoke. "Riley used one of the frozen embryos from the…last time. From when she and I were married and started the whole fertilization process."

Delton glanced at Margie Sue. "What's he trying to tell us?"

Margie Sue looked at Riley. Riley nodded. Margie Sue cleared her throat. "Riley is pregnant with Jackson's baby."

The room erupted again. Some shouted for joy. Some sat silent and shocked. Some cried.

Riley sat back down and propped her chin on her hands.

Her daddy winked at her.

Her mother smiled at her.

Allison glared at her, but it was with grudging admiration and a bit of feminine awe.

Margie Sue gave her a nod of approval.

Riley sat silent as her three brothers went back over the details of the conversation until they'd finally figured it out.

"So y'all did the thing with the thing, but you didn't use all the eggs from that thing," Delton said, emphasizing each *thing,* his face becoming bright red as he talked. "So then Riley decided to do the thing on her own and it…it stuck."

"Yes, that explains it perfectly," Bettye said with another of her soft smiles.

Curtis nodded. "I reckon I can live with that."

Bobby kept glancing from Riley to Jackson and back. "This doesn't make a bit of sense to me."

"It'll be okay, honey," his mother said, patting his hand. "I'll explain later. But as a point of reference, think about how you help your daddy get cows pregnant—without the bull even there."

Bobby made a face. "I think I got it, Mama."

"All y'all need to know," Charles said, his voice deep and commanding, "is that our Riley is gonna be a mama. And while we might not necessarily understand or agree with her methods, we're gonna help her and take care of her and celebrate with her."

"I'm gonna be an uncle again," Bobby said. He gave Riley a thumbs-up.

"We all are, dummy," Curtis said.

Allison pouted and looked worried, some of her precious thunder stolen. So Curtis kissed her and whispered assurances in her ear.

Delton slapped Jackson on the arm. "So you been holding out on me, huh?"

Jackson nodded. "Yep. Wasn't my place to announce this."

"But you did have a say in it, right?"

"Not really. I'd already signed the papers for it years ago, so technically she didn't have to ask my permission." He tapped his fingers on the white linen tablecloth. "It's complicated."

"I guess so," Delton replied. "Last time I checked, people were still having babies the old-fashioned way."

"Delton, honey, you know Riley and Jackson had some issues in that area," Margie Sue said, her tone firm. "Let it rest, okay."

"But—" Delton glanced at his sister. "I'm happy for you, Riley. Truly."

"Thanks," Riley said. "Now that's that. Y'all can go back to the football game. And please, eat some more cake." She stood, gave Jackson a panicked look and promptly passed out on her feet.

Jackson and her daddy both jumped up as she slumped into a heap. Jackson caught her before she hit the floor.

And without a word to the people shouting and asking questions, he lifted her and carried her up to her room.

RILEY OPENED HER eyes and looked around, her head still spinning. Jackson was holding her, no, carrying her up the stairs.

"Let me go," she said, the feel of Jackson's arms around her too close and way too intimate. "I'm fine."

"Fine, my foot. You fainted right there at the dining table. This dinner was too much for you."

"It's not the dinner," she insisted, twisting to see his face. "I've just been going nonstop getting ready for that magazine shoot and...I still have bouts of dizziness and morning sickness. But I'm fine, for goodness' sake. Now let me go."

"You are going to rest," Jackson said. He pushed open the door to her room and carried her to the bed. Settling her gently against the pillows, he said, "Don't get up. I mean it, Riley."

She sent him a smoldering look. "You can't come in here and tell me what to do."

Apparently, he could and he would. "You have to be careful, suga'. I'm doing this for the baby, okay?"

Riley swallowed back a retort. What if something was wrong? What if she'd done too much, worried too much?

"I think I'm okay," she said on a meek whimper. But she couldn't help but be afraid. "Jackson?"

He ignored her and instead started hitting numbers on his cell. "I need to speak to Dr. Reynolds as soon as possible. Yes, my…my wife is pregnant and she just fainted. Eight weeks," he said. Glancing over at Riley, he lifted his hand to her. "Stay there, Riley."

A knock at the door caused Riley to lie back on the pillows. She was still dizzy and now, after all that food and excitement, she felt nauseated, too.

"It's Mama, baby," Bettye said, ignoring Jackson's frown. "Are you all right, Riley?"

Riley nodded. "I'm fine. Just got dizzy. No need for such a fuss." She closed her eyes and willed it to be so.

Bettye found a chenille blanket and pulled it up over Riley. "You do need to rest. You're a busy bee, but you have to be careful now. We're here to make sure you take care of yourself and that little one."

Riley tried to ignore her mother's concerned look. If she thought about it too much, she'd go into a panic and never leave her bed. She had to be strong for her baby. She couldn't worry about what might happen. She could only hope that this time things would be better. "I'm not that fragile, Mama. And I don't like being coddled. Jackson just needs to go."

"I'm not leaving until I hear from the doctor," Jackson said. He sent both of them a daring look, his eyes flashing fire.

Bettye took the hint. "I'll go help Verde with the kitchen. But I'm gonna check on you before we leave, okay?"

"Fine," Riley said, her eyes getting heavy. "I'm okay, Mama, really."

Bettye leaned down to kiss her forehead. "I'll feel better knowing Jackson is here with you."

Riley became pouty and belligerent. Jackson this and Jackson that. They all still thought the man had hung the moon. They'd all seemed so thrilled after they finally figured out what she was telling them. While she was resigned to having Jackson as the father of her child, technically, Riley still wished he'd stayed away until…until the baby was at least eighteen.

"Nothing for that now," she said out loud.

"What'd you say, honey?"

He still had his phone to his ear.

"You might as well put the phone down. Dr. Reynolds's service will have to page him. He won't be happy when he hears I'm fine, just fine."

"You are not fine," Jackson said, glaring at the phone. Finally, he put it down and came to sit on the bed. "Take a nap. You'll feel better."

"I'm okay," she said. "It's just part of being pregnant."

He rubbed his chin. "I don't like it."

"You don't have to deal with it. I don't expect you to deal with it."

"I'm not leaving," he said. "I'm calling that service again."

"The doctor will call once he's been contacted," she said, smiling even as she started to doze off. "Go home, Jackson."

He didn't go home.

When Riley woke up two hours later, Jackson was asleep in her dainty chaise lounge, his big sock feet dangling over the brocade ruffles. She almost called out to him, but instead she curled up tighter underneath the warm chenille fabric and took her time staring at her ex-husband.

His hair fell across his forehead in a disheveled frame, as if he'd run his hand through it over and over. His fancy boots were sitting by the chaise, neat and tidy. But his shirt was rumpled and his dress pants were drooping.

He looked adorable.

For just a minute, she allowed herself to dream of their marriage and this being a happy time. Only if that were the case, Jackson wouldn't be across the room in that chair. He'd be here with her, holding her body against his, his hand splayed across her growing belly.

A tear made its way down the side of her face. She used the soft blanket to wipe it away. Her baby was okay. She was okay. So why did she feel so sad?

Riley let out a sigh and closed her eyes for a second.

Jackson shot up, groaning in protest, a hand on his neck. "Did I wake you?" he asked.

"No, I've been awake a few minutes. Does your neck hurt?"

"I think I have a kink." He grabbed his phone and stared at it. "The doctor did call back. I had my phone on silent so it wouldn't wake you, but he said to let you rest and if you had any bleeding or cramps to get you to the emergency room. Do you?"

The little catch of fear in that question tore at her heart. "No. I actually feel refreshed and rested now. I guess I was just tired."

He stood up and stretched. "Good, good. I told him I'd call back if anything changed."

"I appreciate you doing that, but you didn't have to stay with me. Aunt Verde would have checked on me."

"I wanted to stay. I sent them all home and told her and Floyd to go in the den and watch the game."

Riley smiled at that. "They like to snooze in the recliners."

He went about tidying himself. "You have a good support system, but you scared me. I didn't want to leave until I knew you were okay."

She sat up and wiped at her eyes. "I'm good, really. You don't have to worry."

He came to the bed and sat beside her then took her hand and held it tight. "We have to work this out, Riley. For better or worse, we're in this together. And even though you didn't deem it necessary to consult me on this, I'm happy for you and I want to do things right this time. I want to be there every minute. At the doctor's office for all the checkups, then when you start the birthing classes, and when you go to the hospital to have the baby. Please don't make me stay away."

Riley wasn't sure how to respond to that plea. Her

heart tore open as bitter memories clashed with new-found longing.

But Jackson didn't give her time to think about it.

He leaned in and lifted her to him, his mouth hitting hers in a sweet assault. Riley tried to think straight, tried to breathe, but it was impossible. This was her Jackson, back in her arms.

She didn't stop the kiss. She didn't want to stop the kiss.

Maybe she was still lethargic from her nap but this felt right. She fit so perfectly in his arms. She longed so much to stay there. But did she dare?

He pulled away to stare down at her. "Just let me in, Riley. Let me be the man I should have been all along."

"I don't know," she replied. "I just don't know what to do." She pushed at her hair. "You've got me all messed up and confused. I can't be confused. I have things to do. I have to keep things straight in my head. And I will protect this baby, no matter what."

"Think about it," he said. "I don't want to do anything to hurt you or the baby. Just don't shut me out."

Riley nodded, still groggy but feeling better. When she tried to get up, he held her back. "Rest a little longer."

"Jackson, I need to go to the bathroom and then I'm going downstairs to get something to drink. And I never ate my dessert. I'm dying for a piece of that pumpkin spice cake."

He grinned at that. "She's back."

"Yes, she is." Riley smiled up at him. Then she let

him help her up. "And all things considered, I think today went well, don't you?"

He found her shoes and handed them to her. "Amazingly well. We're the talk of the town."

Riley was used to that, at least. So she stood, tested her equilibrium and gave him a wink and a smile. "Well, what else is new?"

Jackson grinned as they headed across the open landing to the stairs. And Riley realized that her ex-husband had changed.

Was he a new man after all? Only time would tell.

But he'd stayed with her. That and his kiss had certainly made her sit up and take notice.

CHAPTER SEVENTEEN

Riley checked her dress one more time.

The lightweight red wool sheath was A-line and sassy, with three-quarter-length sleeves and a nice round neckline that just begged for pearls. The dress hid her bulging tummy without being too tight. She'd decided to wear her tall brown boots and dark tights with it since the weather was turning nasty—rain with a chance of sleet—which only happened every few years around these parts. And why, oh why, today of all days? She'd worn her brown leather topper coat and brought a leaf-embossed scarf to throw on in case the magazine crew wanted to join her for lunch at the Hamhock.

Now all she had to do was wait for them to arrive. It should be a quick shoot since they'd saved two pages before they went to print next week. No margin for errors on such a tight timeline however.

Margie Sue twirled into the office, wearing a pretty green cashmere tunic-length sweater and black knit ankle pants. Her soft brown kid loafers made her outfit look effortless. And her serene smile calmed Riley's scrambled nerves.

"Almost time, honey," Margie Sue said, checking

her watch. "The shop looks great. Very Christmas-y. I hope we get lots of shoppers for the Black Friday open house."

Riley glanced around at her office, satisfied that she'd done the best she could with making it homey and holiday ready. Even little Killer looked festive with his big red bow. "The shoot today and then the open house in a couple of weeks. We're having a busy fall season."

"That's good, in this economy," Margie Sue replied. "How you feeling?"

"I feel great," Riley said. "The morning sickness has subsided a little and Jackson isn't pestering me as much since I've announced this pregnancy to the family."

Margie Sue played with a tassel on the hurricane lamp on Riley's desk. "But he still wants to be more involved?"

"Yes."

Riley thought of their kisses and how he'd asked her to let him in. Into her heart? Into her mind? He was already there. The man haunted her dreams and stayed front and center in her mind every day.

"You don't look so thrilled about this," Margie Sue pointed out. "Do you feel okay?"

"I feel fine," Riley said. She turned to an oval mirror centered over an antique hutch she used as a storage cabinet and patted her upswept hair. "It's been hard, you know, seeing Jackson again after so long. He says he's changed. He wants to prove that to me, but I'm so afraid. So afraid that if I give in, he'll just go back to the same old pattern of shutting me out."

"I'd like to see some of that change myself." Margie Sue frowned at Riley's reflection in the mirror. "Delton tells me Jackson is like a new man. He's making all kinds of improvements at the lodge, but he's staying within budget. And it's not like he can't manage the whole estate. He's certainly capable."

"But he never wanted all of that before." Riley turned and straightened the papers on her desk. "He loves Southern Hill. Nobody can doubt that, but he just seemed to give up on it and me." She wanted to tell Margie that she believed Jackson had been scared to be a father, thinking he wouldn't be any good at it. And she still wondered at the dynamics of his whole relationship with his own father. How could she have missed the undercurrents that had Jackson in such a state?

You were too busy planning your marriage and your pregnancy, she reminded herself. Maybe she'd been the one shutting others out. Especially her husband.

"Margie, does Delton ever talk about Mr. J.T.?"

"Jackson's father? No, why."

"I just…I guess I never really saw it. Jackson said his daddy had a mean side."

Margie crossed her arms and pursed her mouth, a sure sign that she knew something she wasn't saying.

"What?" Riley asked, hoping her sister-in-law could shed some light on this situation.

"It's just that—"

The bells on the front door jingled. Riley heard voices and glanced out the open office door. "They're here," she told Margie Sue. "But when we're done, I want to know what you've heard. I mean it. I need to understand Jackson. Okay?"

Margie Sue nodded. "Okay. Okay."

But Riley could tell she wasn't happy about being asked to share whatever it was she'd heard.

JACKSON SAT AT his desk, staring at the picture of his baby. The tiny little thumb-size fetus was his center of gravity these days. When things got to him, he'd stare at this picture and hope. And pray. Whenever he doubted himself, he'd stare at the baby and wish for things he had no right to have.

But even though he'd backed off a bit, he could tell Riley was warming up to the idea of having him around. Good. He might not get his wish of being her husband again, but he could be a father to their child.

Couldn't he?

Remembering his own daddy through the years, Jackson reminded himself it hadn't been all bad. He'd had a life of privilege for the most part. He'd always tried to please his parents, to do the right thing. Sports, good grades, a great social life that usually included Riley, and being an all-around good guy. But none of that had been enough.

"What did you want from me, old man?" Jackson asked, staring at the portrait of his deceased father.

"What was it I did to lose your respect, to make you become so critical of everything I ever tried to do?"

Jackson thought back on his father's last years. Had old age changed J. T. Sinclair? Or had his father always had that hard-to-reach core that demanded respect, no matter what?

"Would I treat my son that way?" he wondered, still mumbling.

He thought about how much Riley had wanted a child all those years ago, how they'd been devastated when they'd found out it would be hard for them to conceive. Then came the fertility tests and the expensive treatments and injections and the hours and days of waiting and wondering and trying to plan exactly the right time to conceive.

And in his mind, through all of that, Jackson remembered his father's words to him. "Too bad you can't produce an heir for Southern Hill. But then, that figures, huh?"

He'd asked his dad what that was supposed to mean. But J. T. Sinclair wasn't one to have his opinions questioned. His father had just walked out of the room.

He'd died in the car wreck about a month after that. And that left Jackson alone, with no answers and no way to explain his feelings to his wife. When Riley wouldn't give up about having a baby, they'd tried to make it work. But instead, they'd only drifted further apart.

Now it was up to him to put things back together.

Jackson stared up at the portrait of his father then he looked down at the ultrasound picture in his hand. He put a finger to the picture. "I didn't think I deserved to be a father," he whispered to the tiny baby. "I didn't think I could handle any of it."

So he'd treated everyone around him the same way his father had treated him—with distance and disdain.

"I messed up," he admitted. "But not again, never again."

He was stronger now. He'd gone away to find the pieces of himself that he'd somehow lost. But how could he ever make this up to Riley? He was too ashamed to tell her he'd felt inadequate and lost and that he'd panicked about being a good father.

He still didn't want to talk about it even though he'd let some of his angst slip when they'd had their picnic on the side of the road.

Now he was deliberately trying to stay away, except to be with her whenever it involved the baby.

"Just focus on the baby," he told himself.

He put the little picture back in his desk drawer in a safe spot, then glanced at the paperwork on his desk. The lodge was thriving thanks to Uncle Floyd and the people Riley had hired to help him. But Jackson had big plans to bring the place into this century, something he'd argued about with his father all the time.

He also wanted to get involved in the everyday happenings around the farm. Southern Hill was a treasure. He'd never take that for granted again.

So instead of hanging around waiting for Riley to notice him, he thought he'd try a new tactic. He'd work his tail off to show her that this time, he was in it to win it.

"OKAY, NOW TURN to your right, Mrs. Sinclair."

Riley did as she was asked, smiling into the camera. The morning had turned into afternoon and she was beginning to wilt. How many pictures did one magazine need anyway?

"That's great," the photographer said, his dreadlocks falling around his rugged face. "Thanks for your patience."

"No problem," Riley replied. She sent Margie a false smile. "Are we about done?"

The production assistant stepped forward, her notebook and cell phone cuddled to her chest. "I think we got some good shots and some great quotes from your staff and the customers. I'll go back over the interview with you and narrow that down and I'll make sure our editor has all the product information and your contact numbers, but I think, overall, we got what we wanted."

Riley took a sip of her water. "I do so appreciate this," she told the tall blonde, meaning it. "I especially appreciate how y'all were willing to get this into the Christmas issue. Most magazines have tight deadlines, so I'm impressed with all of you working to get us in at the last minute. Y'all take some of those red velvet cupcakes home with you."

"We will," the young lady said. "But we were hop-

ing to take you up on that offer for lunch at the Hamhock. We can do a sidebar about the restaurant, too."

"Of course," Riley replied, drained but not ready to
concede to fatigue yet. Dorothy Lyn would love the
publicity, so she couldn't say no. Besides, she'd offered
to buy their lunch. And she was hungry.

"Let me get my purse and freshen up a bit," she
said, giving Margie Sue a pleading look. "Want to
come, too?"

"Uh, sure," Margie Sue said. "I'll tell Jennifer we're
leaving. She's got extra help for the afternoon, so we
should be good."

In a few minutes, they were all trooping down the
street to the café. The wind was cold and wet with a
hint of winter in the air. Riley's stomach growled in
anticipation of a good, hot meal. Her appetite lately
had been beyond normal. But she was eating for two,
as Margie Sue liked to tell her. Well, the Hamhock
could satisfy any hunger. Dorothy Lyn was a great
cook and she hired other good cooks, too. Southern
comfort food always made things look better.

What doesn't look right in your life?

Riley almost stumbled as that question floated over
her head. But she knew the answer.

Jackson had retreated. That should be a good thing.
But she knew him well enough to know if he'd backed
off, it was only because he was fortifying his assault.
He'd come charging back with a new plan or a new
way to make her want him again.

It wouldn't take much, she reasoned. Which was

why she needed to use this time to plan her own mode of attack. Or rather, a withdrawal that could give her peace.

They were almost to the door of the restaurant when Fred Marshall called out, "Hey, Riley. Good to see you."

"Hello, Fred." She had to be polite. The man had called her several times and left messages. "How are you?"

"I'm fine," he said, grinning from ear to ear. "I was a bit concerned about you. Have you gotten any of my messages?"

"I did, yes." She pointed toward her companions. "Sorry I haven't had a chance to call back. I've been a bit busy." She introduced Fred to the three-member team from *Magnolia Magazine*. "We just wrapped up and decided we'd have a late lunch." Hoping he'd take the hint and keep walking, Riley gave him a sweet smile.

"Well, I'm headed in for lunch myself. Want to sit together?"

Margie Sue made a face behind his back, but Riley didn't want to appear mean. "I think we can find you a spot, that is, if my lunch guests don't mind."

"Not at all," perky Jennifer said. "We can get Mr. Marshall's take on Riley Sinclair."

"Oh, my, no," Riley said, wishing she'd thought better of allowing him to join them. "You don't need to know anything else about me."

They all laughed as they entered the restaurant.

Then Riley glanced around, looking for a big table, and saw Jackson sitting there with Allison and Curtis. Did the man just hang around with her family all the time?

Jennifer actually giggled. "There's that handsome man we met last time we came to town. Isn't he your—"

"Ex-husband," Fred offered up. "Very ex, right, Riley?"

"Uh, well now, Fred, we try to be civil."

Jackson glanced up and waved, his hopeful expression tightening to a glare when he spotted Fred Marshall with his hand on Riley's arm.

"So we can bring him in on lunch?" Jennifer said, already headed toward Jackson's table. "This will be great!"

"Yes, just great," Riley quipped, shaking her head at Margie Sue's surprised expression.

Curtis waved and motioned to Riley. "Hey, sis. C'mon and eat with us."

Dorothy Lyn didn't miss a beat. "Hey, Justin, pull up another table and some chairs by Jackson and Curtis and them. Looks like we got us a big friendly group of hungry people."

But Riley didn't miss the gleam of glee in Dorothy Sue's eyes. Her good friend was just shaking things up for the pure entertainment value.

No wonder people kept coming back to her diner. It was a virtual sinkhole for gossip and speculation.

And if Riley knew this town the way she thought

she did, she'd guess everyone was already placing bets on Jackson and her and who would survive.

And once they heard about the baby, things would really get rolling.

So she just went with it.

"Y'all find a seat and let's eat. I'm famished."

She sank down across from Jackson and gave him a sweet smile and chased it with a bit of daring.

After all, she wouldn't be impolite in front of her guests.

She just hoped he wouldn't try to pull something and embarrass her.

CHAPTER EIGHTEEN

"Place is hopping today," Curtis pointed out to anybody who happened to be listening. He leaned back and gave the group a once-over. "Riley, where'd you find these newcomers?"

The production assistant giggled. "We're from *Magnolia Magazine*."

Allison perked right up. "Oh, I love that magazine. I can't wait to see the Christmas issue. Y'all have the best recipes. And great decorating tips, too." She inhaled one quick breath then tossed her symmetrical brown bob. "So what on earth are y'all doing in Sinclair?"

Fred glanced at Riley. "Well, I never. What *are* they doing in Sinclair?"

Riley smiled and stared at Jackson. He smiled back then gave Fred a long, heated look as if to say "And what's he doing here?"

"They just finished up a shoot at the boutique," Margie Sue replied with her usual serene smile. "I'm surprised you hadn't heard already, Allison. The Life of Riley will be featured in a special two-page spread in the Christmas issue."

Allison's mouth dropped open and she sat there frozen, her gaze on Riley. "That's impossible. That issue is due out in about two weeks."

"We do have a short lead time," the cameraperson said. "Originally, we'd planned to do this in the spring, but we didn't want to wait."

The production assistant bobbed her head. "Yes, we were so impressed when we visited a few weeks ago, we talked our editor into holding a spot in the Christmas issue for the layout. We managed to get some great shots of all the cool items Mrs. Sinclair has to offer."

"Riley knows her stuff," Fred said as he looped his arm over the back of Riley's chair. His smug grin radiated across the table. "She is one savvy businesswoman. Why, in the past few years she's helped to put Sinclair back on the map."

She saw Jackson stiffen. She could have sworn his biceps thickened. It'd be just like him to cause a scene right here. She gave him what she hoped was an encouraging, pleading smile.

Be nice.

She didn't voice that, but she hoped he'd take the hint.

Jackson's cool appraisal moved from Fred to her. A lift of his dark eyebrows told her he wasn't happy. His scowl told her he'd like to do something about that. But he didn't comment.

Allison came out of her trance and bobbed her head, her eyes a dull, disapproving brown. "Well, that's so good of y'all. Riley, you must be beside yourself with glee."

Riley wanted to well, say, yes, she was beside herself right at this minute, but that would have been really uncalled-for and rude. She didn't know why she and Allison couldn't get along, but right now she didn't have time to figure it out. "I'm thrilled, of course," she said. "And very appreciative. That's why I'm buying the crew lunch."

"And we're going to mention the Hamhock in the spread," the production assistant's assistant replied. "We need to get a picture of your friend Dorothy Lyn."

"Somebody mention me?" Dorothy Lyn said from behind them, her arm full of menus, her ears full of diamond studs and dangling gold earrings she'd bought at Riley's shop.

Riley laughed at her friend's uncanny ability to be in the right place at the right time. "Yes, we did. I'll tell you all about it after you place our orders. I'm starving."

Dorothy Lyn passed out the menus. "Today's special is meat loaf and garlic mashed potatoes. You get dessert in the deal and today's dessert is chocolate pecan pie." She stood back, her hands on her hips. "And let me just say, I make the best chocolate pecan pie on God's green earth."

Riley's stomach actually danced. "Keep talking and you might get to share that recipe with *Magnolia Magazine*'s readers."

"That's the plan," Dorothy Lyn retorted, smacking

her gum and smiling. She sent Allison a wide-eyed stare. "Unlike some people, I know all about everything that goes on in Sinclair."

Everyone laughed and Riley almost felt sorry for Allison. Bless her heart, she really didn't deserve to be picked on so much. But she was an easy target.

Dorothy Lyn took everyone's orders and when she got to Allison, she put a hand on her shoulder and leaned in. "I'm just messing with you, honey, okay?"

Allison looked confused and finally smiled. "Okay. And I'll have a chef salad and sweet tea."

Riley grinned and waited her turn, her gaze flashing over to Jackson.

"How're you feeling?" he said underneath the buzz of conversation all around them.

"I'm great," she replied. *And please don't mention the baby right now.*

"When's your next—"

"I sure wish I could get a cup of decaf," Riley shouted to drown out his question. Then she held up two fingers in a quick flash. "Two weeks."

"We'll talk later," he mouthed.

She bobbed her head.

Then she looked over at Allison. Her sister-in-law had a smirk on her face. Uh-oh, payback time. Riley braced herself, but Allison's next words floored her.

"Riley, did you tell them your other news?"

Jackson cleared his throat and lowered his voice. "That's not public knowledge yet, Allison." He poked Curtis.

"Honey, you need to stop that now," Curtis said, his hand on his wife's arm. "We can talk about that later."

"What news?" Fred asked, his gaze swerving from Riley to Jackson and back.

"What other news?" the production assistant asked, her glass of water in midair. "Did we miss something important?"

"You sure did," Allison said, a gleam in her eyes. "Let me tell you—"

Riley let out a breath. "Well, yes. My sister-in-law is pregnant with her fourth child. Isn't that exciting?"

The three clueless people at the table all responded accordingly. "Oh, congratulations."

Riley kept her smile intact, but inside she was seething.

EVERYBODY COOED AND oohed while Riley kept her cold blue gaze on Allison. Jackson had to admit, Allison could dish it out with the best of them. But Riley could hold her own.

Jackson decided to kill the awkward silence. "Allison, what do you want this time, another boy or a girl?"

Riley gave him a thankful look, her eyes going soft again. She sipped her decaf and kept her head down, but he could see the agitation all over her face.

Allison played with her napkin. "Oh, I don't care as long as the baby is healthy."

Jackson figured she'd said that deliberately but not

even Allison could be that cruel or tactless. Maybe she was the other clueless person at the table.

"That is the important thing," Fred replied, his blush moving down his throat. "What a nice surprise, though."

Wait, make that five clueless people. Fred Marshall looked as lost as a puppy in a catfight. Poor sap. Jackson seriously wanted to toss the dandy out on his wingtip shoes.

Curtis let out a hiss of breath, his eyes on his sister, his hand on his wife's shoulder. "Let's get back to this story on Riley's place. When will this magazine be out?"

"December the first," someone said. "We'll have to hustle on this one."

"I want a copy," Curtis replied. "Allison, won't that be nice? This is good for the whole town. Mama and Daddy must be tickled, too."

"Yes, it sure is good for everybody," Allison said. She grabbed her water and downed half the glass.

Jackson sat back and watched.

Margie Sue managed to entertain the "newcomers" with stories about the good citizens of Sinclair.

Curtis managed to contain Allison by hovering and giving her pecks on the cheek and telling her how pretty she looked in her Christmas sweater. Okay, if you liked smiling reindeer, it wasn't a bad sweater.

Fred sat there twirling his straw in his diet soda, somehow managing to look broken and frustrated in a tailored suit.

And Riley, his Riley, kept her cool and kept her head held high, her pretty blue eyes still laced with a bit of ice. Each time she glanced his way, Jackson felt the warm parts of her stare. She gave him an appreciative look and a slight nod of her head.

He wished he could get closer but the big square table didn't allow for that. He wanted to tell her how gorgeous she looked in that lipstick-red dress and those killer high-heeled boots. He wanted to kiss all the red right off her pouty, pretty lips. Instead, he pulled out his cell and sent her a text message.

You look good.

When he heard her phone ding across from him, he watched as she hurried to check the message. Her eyes went wide then her gaze slammed into his across the table.

Thx.

Why don't you switch places with the camera guy so you can be closer to me?

That wouldn't be appropriate.

Nothing about this little get-together is appropriate.

I'm not going to respond to any more of your messages.

He grinned at that. Then he texted I want to kiss you.

She read that then snapped her phone shut and put it away.

Curtis nudged Jackson. "Quit working. Lunch is a sacred time, don't you know?"

Jackson tucked his phone in his pocket. "Yes, I sure do. I'm enjoying every minute of it, too."

He lifted his head and met Riley's bold look with one of his own.

While Allison sat there and watched his every move.

RILEY COULDN'T WAIT to get her clothes off and get herself into one of the soft velour lounge sets she carried in the boutique and wore herself. She had one in just about every color. Tonight, she didn't care which color she wore, she only wanted to get comfortable, have a bite to eat and go to bed early. Verde and Floyd were at a movie, so she had the run of the house but she didn't plan on staying up too late. She had too much on her mind to go to bed right now, though.

After the magazine entourage had left, she'd finally sat down with Margie Sue. "What do you know about Jackson's parents?"

Her sister-in-law shook her head. "Jackson used to confide in Delton. Not much. But he did tell Delton that when old man J.T. found out y'all were having problems conceiving, he kind of blamed Jackson. Told him that figured or something like that." She shrugged. "Delton said the old man was hard on Jackson in private, even while he bragged on him in public."

"That makes a lot of sense based on what Jackson told me the other day," Riley replied.

They'd talked about it a bit more, but at least now she knew Jackson had been chewing on this for a long time. And she'd never picked up on it at all.

"What kind of wife were you?" she asked herself, confusion and regret hitting her in a wave of sadness.

She needed to think about this and get things straight in her head, so her heart didn't trip over itself too soon.

So she grabbed a baby blue lounge set with wide soft pants and a longer, more tuniclike jacket. She put on a white T-shirt underneath then pulled on her tan fleece-lined boots. The cold, rainy weather made her shiver in spite of the heat kicking on.

For some reason, she was craving hot chocolate. The kind that Jackson had made for her the other night.

Drat his hide.

She'd made it to the bottom step of the stairs when she heard someone knocking on the back door. Wondering who was calling on a cold Friday night, she shuffled to the French doors and peeked outside.

Jackson.

Riley almost ran back upstairs. She didn't have enough energy to fight tonight, or to avoid temptation, either. Her mind was still on what Margie Sue had told her.

He waved to her and gave her one of those devastating smiles, so she felt obligated to let him in. Or so she told herself.

"Hello," she said, waving her hand at him.

"I hope you don't mind," he said, giving her a thoughtful look. "I was worried about you after lunch was over."

"Lunch," she said, squinting. "I think I remember something about meat loaf but by the time my lunch came, I'd sort of lost my appetite."

"Yeah, that was pretty awkward." He shook off his lightweight leather jacket. "I wish people would quit pushing us at each other."

Riley let out a snort of laughter. "Are you serious? You were the one doing the pushing. Flirt-texting me?"

He followed her into the kitchen. "I was bored and I wanted to sit next to you."

"So you could stir up even more rumors?"

"Might as well play it up for all it's worth."

"Yes, that would be nice," Riley said, a little jolt of disappointment surging through her system. "Let's make sure we have everyone gossiping and second-guessing us, too."

"Yep." He stood there with his hands in the pockets of his jeans. "Seriously, maybe they'll settle down once the word is out about the baby."

"Oh, I think that will definitely give them even more fodder. But nothing I can do about that."

His face went dark. "I guess not."

Riley wished there was something more to say. But the unspoken things hung in the air like a thick path of humidity.

"You look tired," he finally said. "Maybe I should just go."

Riley lifted her chin. Did she want him to go?

No.

"Or I could stay awhile. Make sure you're okay."

She pushed at her tumbling hair. "I'm all right, Jackson. I know you worry and I do, too. The odds of this baby being born too early like…like Jack Thomas… are strong. I've thought about that a lot, all the time. But things are different this time."

He shrugged, did a neck roll. "Because I'm not in the picture? Or rather, I wasn't in the picture. If me hanging around is gonna cause you any more stress, I'll—"

"Leave again?" she asked, her stomach going cold.

"I didn't mean that," he said, moving a step closer. "I meant I won't come around as much. I told you I'll only do what needs to be done for the baby. The birthing classes, the checkups, putting the crib together." He stopped, his expression softening, his words as soft as a caress. "Are you using the same crib?"

Riley let out a little gasp then searched for something to catch hold of.

And found herself in Jackson's arms.

Then she couldn't stop the tears. Or the jagged pain.

"I can't lose this baby, Jackson," she whispered. "Don't let me lose this baby."

He held his hand in her hair and tugged her close. "I won't, darlin'. I promise. We won't lose this one, Riley. We won't." Then he drew back, his eyes locking with hers, his finger tracing her tears. "And if that means I need to back off and leave you alone, that's what I'll do."

She bobbed her head and fell back into his arms, her heart begging him to stay even while she kept telling herself to let him go.

CHAPTER NINETEEN

SHE DIDN'T TELL him to leave.

Jackson kept thinking that each time Riley drew closer to him. He wasn't sure how long he held her there in the kitchen, but he didn't want to move for fear she'd realize she was in his arms and bolt.

Finally, she pulled away and touched a hand to his heart. "I'm craving hot cocoa," she said through a sniff. "The kind you made the other night."

Sensing she didn't want to discuss things anymore, he said, "I'll get right on that, ma'am."

He missed her already when he turned to find the milk and cocoa powder. "Don't go anywhere, okay?"

"I won't." She busied herself with pulling out bread and sandwich meat. "I'll make us a grilled ham and cheese. Is that all right?"

"Sounds great to me."

Jackson didn't care if she burned the house down, so long as he had her in his sights. Even though he'd upset her by mentioning the crib they'd picked out for Jack Thomas, Jackson felt as if he'd somehow broken down a cement wall of resistance.

Yes, he'd kissed her once or twice and declared he'd have her back before the baby was born, but he hadn't actually believed that might happen until now. Until tonight.

Riley hid her vulnerability and her fears behind that mask of serenity and sophistication. She'd never let anyone in before, not even him. But tonight, with her here in his arms, he saw and felt all that pain and anguish that he'd also felt and it tore through him like barbed wire, sharp and piercing, his guilt cutting hard right along with the knowledge that he'd left her when she needed him the most.

He should have fought harder to stay.

He would this time. He would. For both Riley and their unborn child. And for his own salvation.

"Sandwiches are ready," she said from her side of the big stove. Glancing at the still-cold milk in the pot he was supposed to be stirring, she asked, "How's that cocoa coming?"

Jackson snapped back to attention. "It's getting there, darlin'. All in good time." *All in good time.*

He made their cocoa and together, they sat at the old kitchen table and laughed and talked until late into the night. They caught up on a lot of things. And he told her about his travels and how his trip had gone from running away to finding something he thought he'd lost. It felt right to Jackson to be able to enjoy a normal conversation instead of going through a sparring match. So right, so nice, he could do this the rest of his life. He wanted this for the rest of his life.

But right now, Riley needed her rest. She was yawning into the dregs of her marshmallows.

"What are you doing for Thanksgiving?" she asked when he got up to leave.

He shrugged. He wanted to be with her. But he pretended otherwise. "I haven't given it much thought. I guess I'll hang out at the lodge."

"No, you will not," she said, back to being bossy, firm Riley. "We'll all be at Mama and Daddy's and we'll have more food than we should be allowed. Plenty of room for one more."

"Are you inviting me, Riley?"

"Yes," she said, her hands on her hips. "Unless you want to spend the day alone. Take it or leave it."

He laughed to hide his surprise. Did she pity him? Well, he didn't want to be alone. "I'll take it." He wanted to ask if that meant she was removing all remaining walls between them, but he didn't. He'd promised to back off. But it sort of rubbed him the wrong way that she might be doing this out of kindness and nothing else.

He should have said no, thanks, to the invitation. But how could he do that? It had hit him hard the day of the barbecue—he craved being around family. And since most of his family was long gone, he craved being with Riley and her family even more. He now understood the importance of family. He now understood why he'd been so afraid to embrace that concept.

Only now his ex-wife felt sorry for him. How low could a man sink? He didn't want to be a failure. He didn't want to disappoint. But the alternative would mean never having Riley or their child in his life. So he'd suffer anything to make that happen. And he'd work hard on his inadequacies in the meantime. After all, he had close to seven months before the baby came to make Riley his wife again.

THE PHONE ON Riley's desk jingled impatiently.

"Hello," she said, out of breath from hurrying across the room. Even though she had a tiny baby bump, her body was constantly changing. She was close to making it through the first trimester.

"Guess who's back in town, suga'!"

Riley grinned big and sank down on her chair. "Let me see, could it be that globe-trotting, gorgeous Mary Ann Winebarger?"

"The one and only," her friend Mary Ann replied. "And from what I hear, there's been a lot going on since I left."

"You can say that again," Riley retorted. "But I want to hear all about your trip to Europe. Did you find any fascinating Italian men?"

"Lots of 'em," Mary Ann replied. "And let me just say, they are yummy."

"I can't wait to hear all about it." Riley had missed her dazzling red-haired best friend. They'd been friends since grammar school. Along with Dorothy Lyn, they'd cut quite a flashy path through school and bad boyfriends and angry parents.

"Come to the country club for lunch—my treat," Mary Ann said. "I insist."

"You don't have to insist," Riley said. "I'm always hungry these days. And if you're buying, I'm eating."

"Uh-huh. Meet me at noon. We have a lot to catch up on." Mary Ann said a breezy goodbye.

"Yes, we sure do," Riley said to herself.

She checked the clock, checked her lipstick and headed out a few minutes later, her thoughts on Jackson.

He was behaving.

He'd been a perfect gentleman during the Thanksgiving meal last week. He'd chatted and hooted with the boys, cheered on their favorite team during afternoon football and helped with the dishes after dessert and coffee. He'd smiled at her, laughed with her and stayed a safe distance from her. In fact, he'd been kind of subdued around her.

While everyone else wondered what was going on.

She didn't know, couldn't tell them. Wasn't sure herself.

Even Allison seemed happy about having Jackson back.

"He keeps Delton occupied," Allison had exclaimed when they were serving up the pumpkin pie. "Not that I don't love my husband, but he likes to hover, you know. Especially with this being our fourth."

"Is everything okay?" Riley asked, her concern real. No woman should have to go through the loss of a child.

Allison looked down at the pie plate. "It's just I'm older now, and well, I've had three big boys. But I'm fine, really. I get tired so easily, that's all. This one seems to want to fight me at every turn."

Riley could understand that. For the first time in a long time, she and Allison had something in common. They'd bonded right there over the pie and whipped cream.

Riley chalked that up to her maternal instincts kicking in.

Maybe that was why she was able to tolerate being around Jackson. *Tolerate* being the operative word there. She thought about the man day and night. And he'd looked great on Thanksgiving in his standard jeans and button-up shirt, his leather jacket smelling like the outdoors. Of course, he'd settled right in with her family, almost as if they'd never gotten a divorce. But with so many others around, Riley was able to relax and enjoy the day even if she did go home tired.

But she wasn't ready to go into forever with him again.

So she put him out of her mind today and headed out to the Sinclair Country Club, located at the edge of town, to see her long-gone friend, Mary Ann. Riley had missed Mary Ann's sage advice and feisty attitude, even if she'd kept this whole pregnancy thing a secret. Mary Ann, widow of a pro golfer, was now manager of the Sinclair Country Club. When she wasn't traveling, that is. Riley loved hearing about her friend's grand adventures.

But when she got out of her car and handed the keys

to the valet, Mary Ann came screaming out of her office, her hands waving in the air. "You're pregnant?"

Riley cringed while all the valet boys turned to stare.

Grabbing Mary Ann by her sequined green sweater, she nodded. "Yes, but do you have to announce it into the next county?"

"I thought everyone but me knew it already," Mary Ann said with a mock frown. "And why didn't *I* know it already?"

"I didn't tell *anyone* at first." Riley hugged her friend close. "And not everyone knows already. The word is slowly getting out, though."

"I'll say more like fastly getting out—as in wildfire rapid." Mary Ann looped her arm in Riley's and marched them back into her swank office, where one entire wall looked out over the manicured hills and holes of the country club. "I need details. And the truth. I've heard everything from aliens invading and impregnating you to Jackson swooping you up like Rhett did Scarlett and letting you have it good and proper."

"None of the above is true," Riley said. Although that Jackson swooping her up part was kind of nice to think about.

"But you are pregnant?"

"Yes."

"And it's Jackson's child?"

"Yes."

Mary Ann sat her down at a round table in the office

and opened the lid on their lunch. Lemon chicken and fluffy rice, green beans and a roll. And bread pudding.

Riley almost cried with joy. She went for her soft, hot roll with gusto. But Mary Ann ignored the food and went right on talking. "How did this happen without me knowing?"

"You knew I was thinking about it."

"Yes, but…but I've only been gone a couple of months."

"You left before I knew for sure."

Mary Ann grabbed a roll and buttered it. "But, Riley, you never once told me you were gonna…get yourself pregnant. You must have been preparing your womb even before I left."

"I didn't tell anyone," Riley admitted. "In case."

Mary Ann dropped the roll and took Riley's hand. "Honey, you shouldn't have gone through that alone."

"I had to," Riley said between bites. "I couldn't stand it if anything bad happened. And I didn't want to tell anyone until I was one hundred percent certain I was really going to have a baby."

"Oh, I see." Mary Ann cut her chicken in tiny bites, her green eyes flashing. "So Miss Independent did all this on her own? Literally. How'd that go over with Jackson?"

"Not too well at first. But…he's getting used to the idea."

"And how about you and him? Are you getting used to him?"

Riley chewed her roll very carefully on that one.

"He's growing on me, but we've reached a truce of sorts. He's only allowed to help with baby stuff. Nothing else."

She didn't tell her friend about how he'd spent Thanksgiving with her family. Mary Ann would jump to the wrong conclusion.

"Really now," Mary Ann replied. "That's odd, since the man called me this very morning and reserved two tickets for our annual Christmas party, which is in two weeks, by the way. Said he was bringing you as his date."

JACKSON LOOKED AT the date on the calendar. Two weeks until his big date with Riley. They'd always enjoyed the country club Christmas party before. Or at least they had until things started deteriorating in their marriage. That last few months after she'd lost the baby had been rough.

She'd cried a lot.

He'd drunk a lot.

They'd fought a lot.

He wanted to make all of that up to her. Riley was trying to have a second chance. A do-over. He needed the same. But he needed a fresh start, not a do-over.

Because if he had it to do over again, he'd do it right.

His phone rang so he turned from the big window of the lodge office to answer it. "Jackson Sinclair."

"Since when do you make reservations without asking me if I want to actually go? And, this does not qualify as baby time."

Riley. The fighting-mad Riley. "I knew Mary Ann would call you right away."

"Yes, we had lunch together. Jackson, what if I don't want to go to the party with you?"

"Don't you, though?"

"What if I've made other arrangements?"

"With Fred Marshall? Tell him you're sick."

"And show up there with you. Yes, that'll go over well."

"He's your accountant in regards to your finances, not your personal life. You don't owe that man any explanations."

"And I don't owe you a date. We're supposed to keep this about the baby. Just about the baby."

"Look, I made the reservation, and yes, I want you to go with me. Think about it and get back to me, okay?"

He hung up before she could say no. He'd let her stew but he was pretty sure she'd come around. Riley never missed a good party. And if she refused to actually go with him, well, he'd certainly see her there. And he'd make sure Fred Marshall was tied up all night. Literally. Jackson knew where all the broom closets at the country club were located.

Uncle Floyd came in, his hands in the pockets of his overalls.

"What's up, Floyd?" Jackson asked, his good mood making him smile.

"I think we've had some trespassers up near the

highway. Fence is cut and I found lots of footprints in the mud."

Jackson got up and checked his watch. "Wanna ride out there and check it out? We might need to reinforce that fence. That's always been a prime spot for people to sneak in."

Floyd nodded. "Poachers almost year-round. I guess they like that spot because it's so isolated."

"And when it's open season, they think they should be entitled to traipse all over Sinclair land and hunt whatever they want."

Floyd scratched his head. "Well, most of this county is Sinclair land."

Jackson couldn't argue with that. "True. Let's go give it a look and see what we can find."

He grabbed his keys and headed out with Floyd, but Jackson's thoughts were on Riley and the baby. She had one more appointment before Christmas. He would be there with her.

And then, he'd take her to the country club Christmas party. Officially. He hoped that would be the official beginning of him winning her back, too.

CHAPTER TWENTY

SHE WAS BEGINNING to show.

Riley touched the bump of her belly and wondered if she'd ever be the same size again. Did she care? She'd always taken care of herself and she'd been active all of her life. Cheerleading, dance lessons, horseback riding and running around on a big farm had given her an athletic body and a sense of adventure.

But having a baby in her mid-thirties might change all of that. She'd been careful so far. She'd tried to eat the right things and exercise, but she craved sweets a lot. She'd been getting up early to take long walks around the property at Southern Hill. So far, Jackson hadn't made good on his offer to walk with her, which was okay by her. Besides, it was getting too cold for that now that winter was setting in. She'd started exercising after work in the comfort of her bedroom, too. She didn't mind that, since she loved the stretches and walking in place. But Riley knew she'd bundle up and go for some more long walks before winter was over. She liked the solitary walks. They gave her time to think.

Now she sat down at the dressing table and wondered why she was going to this Christmas party with

Jackson. She'd tried to get out of it, had told him she might not even go to the party at all. But he'd insisted. And two days ago, he'd had an hour to and from Atlanta to convince her.

A minute into the drive for her next checkup, he said, "I heard ole Fred will be out of town the weekend of the country club party. That's too bad."

"You probably planned that," Riley retorted to Jackson's smug information. She'd show him. She'd stay home and wear her favorite flannel pajamas. But knowing Jackson, he'd bring the party to her if she didn't attend.

He lifted his hands off the steering wheel for a brief second. "I didn't have anything to do with that, darlin'. Call it divine intervention or dumb luck, but I'm happy Fred won't be there with his paws all over you."

"Fred doesn't put his paws all over me," she replied. "We have an occasional dinner or lunch together, mostly to discuss business. Besides, it's really none of your concern."

"No, it's not," he agreed, his fingers tapping the leather on the steering wheel. "But he's not your type, Riley. And I'm not so sure I want him around any kid of mine."

That comment really riled her. "What? Are you telling me that I can't make that decision on my own? That I can't pick good friends to influence my baby? I know how to protect my child and I think Fred Marshall would be a good role model for any youngster.

I'm also fully capable of being a good parent, without your input."

"Are you sure about that? I mean, you work day and night. You were so tired a few weeks back when that magazine followed you around all day, I was afraid you'd fall over on your feet."

Riley couldn't believe this. Thinking Jackson was just trying to irritate her, she breathed deep and let it go. For now.

"I loved doing that shoot," she said. Then she smiled big. "And the issue turned out great. It was a good business move for us. We've had people waiting at the door just about every morning this week. Instead of being tired, I feel exhilarated."

That wasn't exactly the truth but she had been enjoying seeing so many extra Christmas shoppers. She'd been shocked, however, to find a picture in the magazine spread of her and Jackson together, his grin full of male persuasion while her expression bordered on panic. The caption read, "While divorced, Mrs. Sinclair still manages to have a good laugh with her ex-husband Jackson Thomas Sinclair, the lone heir to Southern Hill Plantation and one of the last remaining members of the family for which the town of Sinclair was named."

She'd gotten more attention from that one picture than from the whole darn spread. Well, if Jackson's good looks would bring in customers for Christmas, so be it. She had to admit, the man sure photographed like a pro.

Jackson aside, this could turn out to be her best year since opening the shop. Her best year, personally, too, she thought. She would have a little person to love in the early summer of next year.

But…she still had to somehow come to terms with the man beside her, too. "I'm taking care of business, Jackson."

"Well, good for you then." He navigated the heavy traffic into the city. "But don't let this Christmas season get you all run-down and tired. I've seen you running around that shop in high heels. You can't keep up this pace."

Angry that he was hovering too close and telling her what to do, Riley glared at him. What did he know about high heels, anyway? "I think I can be the judge of that, thank you very much."

"I get it," he said. "Stay out of your life, right?"

"Right."

But the silence that followed only made her wonder if he was remembering her first pregnancy. She'd been busy back then, too. While she hadn't had a shop to run, she'd kept herself busy with the household and all of the bookkeeping for the lodge and the farm. She'd somehow gotten it in her mind that she had to take over where Jackson's sweet mom had left off. But Riley was no Susie Homemaker, even though she admired women who chose that path. She'd done too much, tried too hard. But the doctors had told her repeatedly that she hadn't done anything wrong. The baby was born too early. They told her no one could have predicted it would happen that way. And while Riley wanted to make sure that didn't happen again, her doctors had urged her to go about her business and to be careful.

Maybe Jackson was right in fussing at her. The last thing she wanted to do was give him a reason to accuse her or judge her.

But hadn't she done that with him?

"Do you blame me for...losing Jack Thomas?" she asked Jackson while they waited in the reception area.

"Of course not," he replied, shock and resolve clear in his expression. Then the nurse had called her in and the conversation had ended. Neither one of them brought it up on the way home.

But she had to wonder what Jackson thought. She'd been so caught up in her own grief back then, she hadn't considered his feelings. Maybe because she didn't believe he cared as much as she had. Should she tell him she'd been wrong about that?

JACKSON TUGGED ON his bow tie again and checked his distorted reflection in the glass-paneled French doors of the sunporch. He hadn't gotten all dressed up in a tux in a long time. But it would be worth it to enjoy Christmas with Riley.

He heard her high heels clicking on the wooden floor.

She rounded the corner by the stairs, one hand touching on her pearls. She wore red. Sparkling red. A sleeveless, clingy bright red with sequins across the rounded neckline. The dress flared out around her and floated against her in pleated elegance. Her hair was held up on her head with a sparkling clip, but she'd left a few silk strands around her face to tease him.

So far, so great.

Then he looked down her legs to her shoes. Sparkling black, dainty and flashy and strappy. Not practical in this cold weather, but then sometimes being practical was overrated.

Jackson looked back up to her face. She was beautiful. Red lips and diamond earrings beautiful. This was gonna be a tough night. She'd only agreed to go with him as a...friend.

Yeah, right.

Since when had they ever been just friends?

It was always all or nothing with them.

And tonight would be no exception.

"People are talking," Jackson told Riley an hour later. They were well into the evening. The dinner of steak and all the trimmings had been served and now a jazz ensemble played Christmas tunes while dessert was being served.

"Did you think they'd ignore us?" Riley quipped, grinning at him.

"No," he said. "I knew they'd notice you. You look great."

She eyed him with appreciation. "And you still fill out a tux nicely."

"Do you care that we're being talked about?"

"Why should I? Everyone called me a gold digger after our divorce. I'm used to being the subject of gossip around here."

"You did what you had to do," he said, nodding toward her. "I was a mess back then. You saved Southern Hill."

Riley stared across the room then glanced back at him. "I'm glad you get that. I worried after you left. I didn't want you to think the worst." She lowered her head, her lashes hiding her eyes.

"I was the worst," he said. "I was bitter for a while, but when I finally sobered up I saw the logic of your actions. Didn't like it, but the truth of it hit me square in the head."

She fluffed her hair. "How are things at the lodge?"

He lifted his eyebrows, worried about her. "You never ask about the lodge."

"I try not to think about it, but it's there. Kind of hard to ignore. As long as it's bringing in a profit I can live with that."

"Then you'll be happy to know we're holding our own."

"Good."

The waiters brought out their dessert.

"Italian cream cake," Jackson said. He pushed Riley's share toward her. "Want some decaf with that?"

"Uh, maybe." She sat up straight in her chair. "Have you seen Allison? She went to the ladies' room a while ago."

Jackson searched the crowd. "No. I see Curtis over by the bar. Maybe she's with him."

"I'm gonna check on her," Riley said. "She's been quiet all evening."

Jackson grabbed her hand. "Hey, are things okay with you two? I was surprised when you asked them to sit with us."

"We're good," Riley said. "I think both of us being pregnant at the same time has…mellowed things between us." She gave him a quick smile. "I'll be right back."

Jackson watched her sashay toward the open doors to the lobby, his heart doing that funny little flip-flop. Curtis sat down and tapped him on the shoulder. "Have you seen my wife?"

Jackson shook his head. "No, and Riley just asked me the same thing. She went to the ladies' room to check on Allison."

Curtis frowned and chewed his lip. "Allison was in a mood earlier. This pregnancy is taking its toll on her."

Jackson could sympathize. "It's amazing what a woman goes through, huh?"

"Yep." Curtis lifted his drink. "Which is why I try to say the right things at the right time."

"You're one smart man," Jackson replied. "Maybe I need to try that myself."

He glanced toward the lobby doors but didn't see either Riley or Allison.

RILEY WALKED INTO the women's lounge and checked the bathroom stalls. "Allison?"

"Riley?"

Going to the last stall, Riley touched the door. "It's me. Are you all right?"

Allison didn't speak but Riley heard a low sob.

"Allison?"

"I'm spotting. I don't know what to do."

Riley glanced around to make sure they were alone. "Are you cramping? Do you hurt?"

"Yes," Allison said on a soft wail. "Both."

"Okay, we need to get you to the doctor," Riley replied, pulling her phone from her purse. "Honey, can you come out? I'll text Jackson and Curtis to get the cars. We'll take you to the emergency room right now."

Allison finally opened the door. She looked pale, her dark eyes full of fear. "I've never had this happen. Do you think—"

Riley's phone dinged. She touched a hand to her arm then read Jackson's reply.

We're on it, his text stated.

Riley tugged her black shawl around Allison's shoulders. "The boys are getting the cars. Don't worry. It could be anything and it might be nothing at all. But we need to get you checked."

Allison held to Riley like a lifeline. "I'm scared. I've never felt like this. You know I breezed through all my pregnancies. But I hurt, Riley."

Riley guided her out the side door, making sure no one was lurking about. "It's okay. You'll be okay. I'm sure it's nothing to worry about."

"But you know what this is like? I can't deal with that," Allison said, her face marred with fear. "I can't. I promised Curtis a little girl this time."

Normally, Riley would have been hurt by Allison's clueless reminders and her need to keep producing to please her husband, but not tonight. She steeled herself and took Allison's arm. "We're not gonna think about that right now. We'll let the doctors decide, okay? You hang in there, you hear?"

"I hear," Allison said. "I've felt funny all day. Kind of sick. I almost didn't come tonight."

Riley let her talk while she nodded and guided her out the doors.

Curtis met them underneath the catwalk. "What's wrong?"

"She's having some cramps and spotting," Riley explained, her gaze landing on Jackson. "Take her to the E.R. We'll be right behind you."

"Okay," Curtis said, his eyes wide with worry. "Mama and Daddy didn't see us leave. Will you call them?"

"Yes. Now go." Riley watched as he helped Allison into the car. "We'll be right there."

Then she turned to Jackson. "I—"

"Let's go," he said, tugging her close. "She'll be fine, Riley. She'll be okay."

Riley prayed Jackson was right. Allison wasn't cut out for this kind of hurt.

But then, what woman was?

CHAPTER TWENTY-ONE

BUCKINGHAM RELATIVES WERE coming out of the woodwork. Jackson stood at the end of the emergency room hallway, marveling at how many aunts, uncles, cousins and even distant relatives Riley and her big family seemed to have. Add to that mass of humanity, Allison's hyper mother and stoic father and well, the head floor nurse was about to send half of them packing.

"This isn't a party, people," the stocky spiked-hair nurse said, her green eyes as bright as the fake Christmas tree in the corner. "Either settle down or go out in the parking lot. We got sick people here, understand?"

Curtis tapped the woman on her arm. "What about my wife? Allison Buckingham? When can I see her?"

The nurse gave him a sympathetic stare. "The doctor will be out in a little while. Just keep your entourage quiet until then, okay?"

Curtis looked lost. Jackson glanced toward where Riley was sitting with her mother and Margie Sue. Their eyes met in a long-held gaze that said everything without saying a word.

They'd been here before.

Riley had been here before.

Now Jackson wondered if this was how it had been

that night years ago when he'd been out in the woods, camping with his buddies. No cell reception and not a care in the world.

While his wife lay there crying as she held her tiny baby.

Jack Thomas.

His son. He'd been away and out of reach when his tiny son had breathed his first and then later, his last breath.

How did a woman forgive a man for something like that? It didn't matter that the baby had come way too early. Or that Riley had seemed fine when he left the house. No, there was no excuse, no words, for him being a no-show at one of the most important events in his life.

He got up, ready to bolt toward the door, when he felt a hand on his arm. Jackson looked up to see Riley's father giving him a strong appraisal. "Going somewhere, son?"

"I thought I'd get some air," Jackson lied, sweat popping out along his backbone. The waiting room tried to close in on him.

"Stay where you are," Charles said, his grip like steel. "I don't like hospitals, either, but you need to stay, you hear me?"

Jackson nodded. "Yes, sir." He glanced at the cool open world outside the sliding doors. "I just—"

"You just wish you could go back and change things, right? Son, we all want that chance but you can't go back. What you can do, though, is go forward. But if you walk out that door, you're gonna wind up in the wrong dang direction. Or worse, lost forever."

Jackson scrubbed a hand down his face, his gaze hitting on Riley. She glanced up and caught his eye. "I messed up. I don't know how to fix that."

Charles leaned close. "You fix that by never making the same mistake again. You do what makes you uncomfortable and you get through it. It's called showing up. You've got to learn to show up and then you've got to learn staying power, Jackson."

Jackson let out a sigh. He felt sixteen again. "I'm here, Mr. Charles."

"Good," Charles said, winking at Jackson. "Stay here. We need you."

Jackson swallowed and leaned against the wall, the swish of cool outside air hitting him every time someone came in or went out the emergency room entrance doors. Did anyone really need him, he wondered. But hearing it declared by Charles Buckingham, a man he admired, helped a lot. Jackson still wondered if Riley would ever need him again. Or if she'd ever really needed him at all?

Finally, an hour later, a lone doctor walked out to where the crowd had settled into a hushed vigil. The tall, tired doctor looked around until he saw Curtis.

Curtis jumped up and met the doctor halfway up the hall. The doctor leaned close and said something into Curtis's ear.

Jackson watched as Curtis slumped into himself, the tall, proud man now crumbled, a hand over his mouth. When Curtis started shaking his head, Bettye Buckingham gasped and hurried toward her son. Curtis grabbed his mama close and spoke in a whisper. Bettye hugged him and over his shoulder, she looked out at the waiting family and shook her head, tears falling down her face.

Jackson searched for Riley.

She stood away from all the others, her body shoved into a corner, her hand on her stomach. The look on her face spoke of memories and regret. And fear. He walked over to her and tugged her into his arms.

"She lost the baby," Riley whispered over and over. "Allison lost the baby. She's not supposed to do that. She's the strong, healthy one."

Her voice rose with each word. Her eyes misted over. "Jackson, I…I don't think I can do this again," she said. Then she pulled away from him and hurried to her brother.

AN HOUR LATER, Riley knocked on the door to Allison's room.

"Come in," a small voice called.

Riley wiped her eyes and held her head up then planted a smile on her face. But when she entered the hospital room and saw her sister-in-law lying there with tears rolling down her face, Riley couldn't stop her own tears.

Hurrying to the bed, she pulled Allison into her arms. "I'm so sorry. So sorry."

Allison patted Riley on her back then fell against

the pillows. "Me, too," she said, shaking her head. "I would have never dreamed—" Allison held Riley's hand tight to hers. "I never understood what you went through. I should have done more for you back then."

Riley patted Allison on the arm. "It's okay. It's hard to explain to someone. And, I pushed everybody away after…after I lost Jack Thomas." *Even my husband.* She didn't know what else to say, so she just sat there holding Allison's hand.

Allison stared at the ceiling. "My doctor said this was a blessing. That something was wrong."

Riley had heard that one, too. She could never see the blessing in losing a child, but people meant well, telling her that. At least her mama had kept telling her everyone meant well, talking in platitudes and clichés. But Allison was right. No one could ever understand the pain. "Did he say if you could try again?"

Allison nodded. "He thinks I'll be okay, but he wants me to wait a few months." She started crying again. "You know, I'd envisioned our babies growing up together."

Riley had thought about that, too. It had been a driving reason behind her trying to reach out to Allison at Thanksgiving. "Well, maybe we can still have our babies doing that. You'll have another chance."

Allison gave her a watery stare. "I don't know. I didn't realize how tired I am." She put a hand to her mouth. "Riley, if I tell you something, promise you won't say anything to anyone. I'd be so humiliated."

Worried, Riley leaned close. "What is it?" When

Allison held back, she said, "You can tell me anything. I won't repeat it."

Allison grabbed some tissue and wiped her eyes. "I didn't want another baby." She paused, her gaze holding Riley's, her eyes watching for censure. "Is that horrible or what?"

Riley, never having had the opportunity to raise a child, wondered why Allison felt that way, but she didn't rush to judgment. "I don't think that's so horrible. It's a full-time job, after all." Now she was using clichéd language.

Allison bobbed her head. "Yes, and my three boys are so…active. But I did want a little girl. And Curtis said he did, too. So we decided to try again. I couldn't wait to buy frilly little dresses from your shop." She wiped at her eyes. "I even bought a few ahead of time."

Riley had sold her a dainty little dress a few days ago. "You can return those, honey."

"I know," Allison replied, her hand hitting on the sheets. "But I resented this pregnancy. Secretly. Even when I was full of joy and anticipation, I still had these thoughts about having to go through this all over. When I heard you were expecting, I felt so much better about things. Now, I feel as if—"

"You can't think that way," Riley said. "You can't. The doctor told you something wasn't right. You have to know your thoughts didn't cause this."

Allison looked down at her hands. "I feel so guilty, though. If Curtis knew—"

"He'd tell you the same thing I just told you," Riley said. "Don't blame yourself." She stopped, shook her head. "I know I sure did that. I blamed myself and…I especially blamed Jackson."

Allison pushed at her dark curls. "We didn't talk much back then, did we?"

Riley laughed. "No. I was mad at the whole world. Talk about resentment. I hated hearing my own nephews laughing and having fun. I wanted my little boy to be right there with them."

Allison took Riley's hand again. "I guess if any good has come of this, at least we've gotten closer. I'm glad."

"Me, too," Riley said, meaning it. "Me, too. Now you need to rest. I'll come by tomorrow."

Allison pushed down against the covers. "Will you tell Curtis I'd like to kiss him good-night?"

"Of course," Riley said. "Anything else?"

"He's gonna need some help explaining this to the boys."

Riley nodded. "Maybe Mama and I can help with that."

"They'll need their grandmother…and their favorite aunt."

Riley smiled at that. "Okay. Good night."

Allison bobbed her head, tears falling down her face again.

Riley wanted to go back and hug her, but then she'd burst into tears herself. She'd held it together as much as she could, except for when she'd first heard the news and fallen into Jackson's arms.

But right now, she wanted to go home and let this soak in and then thank her lucky stars her baby was safe.

But what if this happened to her again?

Riley knew she'd never recover from that.

And after tonight, she knew she'd never recover if she let Jackson back into her heart and he left her again, too.

CHRISTMAS EVE.

Jackson took his cup of coffee and walked onto the long front porch of the lodge. The place was quiet today. All the day hunters had gone home to their families and the lodge didn't have another group hunt booked until the end of the week. He'd sent Floyd home early this morning.

"Go spend Christmas Eve with Aunt Verde," he ordered after they shut the main gate and checked the new security system.

"Why don't you come with me?" Floyd asked, his baseball cap slung low over his eyes.

"No, not today. I might try to get by tomorrow."

"Whole family's coming to Southern Hill tonight, but Bettye insisted on doing most of the cooking."

"Wise woman," Jackson retorted, remembering Riley's burned roast. "Maybe she'll save me a plate."

"If I know Bettye, she'll sure do that."

Now in the still of a bright, sunny winter sunset, Jackson sipped his coffee while the lodge's two hunting dogs got some exercise and wondered when he'd become comfortable being alone. As long as he could remember, he liked hanging with other people. Growing up, he'd beg his mom to let him go visit a friend, any friend. Just so he had someone to talk to and goof off with. Being an only child had its advantages, but for the most part it was a lonely life. His friends always told him how lucky he was, to be spoiled and pampered. He let them believe that and never told them he had to work hard for any praise from his somber father. So Jackson had also worked hard at being the life of the party. That way he'd always have someone around. His friends came to Jackson when they wanted a good time. Swimming, hunting, fishing, riding around, drinking, chasing girls. He knew all the tricks and he had all the lures. He'd throw a party and half the town would show up. He was a part of something. And he convinced himself he had lots of good friends.

"Lots of fair-weather friends," he said to himself now, the quiet enveloping him like a welcome blanket while the dogs ran around searching for some action. Where had all his good-time buddies gone? Those who expected him to give them a fun agenda had come around after the divorce, but Jackson hadn't been in a partying mood then. Some of them had even suggested he let them go with him on his around-the-world adventure. But he'd politely declined, wondering how they'd planned on explaining that to their wives waiting back at the house.

Probably in the same way he'd tried to explain to Riley why he couldn't be reached the night she'd gone into labor.

There was no excuse for that.

The life of the party had become a broken, silent man. And he'd realized he'd never really seen the world. Jackson had been so caught up in his own little world, he'd overlooked the importance of having compassion and understanding for strangers and the importance of understanding someone you loved.

But…out there…he'd seen what family was all about. He'd helped people who had lost everything and yet still smiled at him each time he passed them. He'd lost everything, too, so that he could understand. But how did they keep going?

He thought about the woman in Mexico who'd lost her baby after giving her life to have that baby, then he thought about Allison, so prim and smug, so sure of herself and her station in life, and he hung his head, knowing that it didn't matter. All the money and status in the world didn't matter when your heart was broken.

Then he thought about Riley and how much she must have hurt, and what had he done? He'd shut her out, gone on about his business, tried to smooth over the rough patches. But she'd done the same, shutting him out, too. They passed each other like two strangers, hurting and broken.

Some things couldn't be smoothed over.

Jackson finished his coffee. Then he looked out across the big, deep pond and watched as the wood ducks started their morning glide. He went inside and found some bread and then he strolled out to the water's edge and tossed some crumbs. Even though the dogs huffed and barked, the ducks quacked their thanks as they waddled out of the cold water and enjoyed this Christmas treat.

Jackson sat down on a bench and stared across the way to the big Victorian house he'd always called home.

And even though his heart ached to be there in the middle of all that love and chaos, he realized something about himself.

A man didn't know himself until he felt comfortable in solitude. Jackson felt comfortable now. He wasn't as frantic, as needy as he'd been when he'd left here.

But he was stronger now, too. Strong enough to back off and wait this thing out. He loved Riley with each breath he took but he wanted her to love him in the same way. He wanted her to forgive him and give him another chance.

Mostly, he wanted to be a good father to their baby.

That was his Christmas wish.

He hoped and prayed that wish would come true, but last week at the hospital, he'd felt her slip away, felt her slip right out of his arms and back into her despair and misery.

And he hadn't heard a word from her since that night.

"I'm not going anywhere this time, Riley," he said, his quiet words echoing out over the water. "I've stopped running."

One of the mama ducks quacked at him then slipped back into the water and glided away.

CHAPTER TWENTY-TWO

"Where's Jackson?"

Riley glared at her brother Bobby and turned to head back into the kitchen. She grabbed some pot holders and started helping Margie Sue put the food on the buffet table. "If one more person asks me where Jackson is, I'm going to scream."

"Well, where is he?" Margie Sue asked, grinning.

"Not you, too." Riley placed the sweet potato casserole next to the baked ham and fried turkey.

"He kinda grows on you," Margie Sue said without apology. "And he was part of the family for so long and well, this is…was…his home."

"Was," Riley retorted, her gaze moving over the pan of corn bread dressing and on to the ambrosia salad, pecan pie and buttermilk pound cake. Food seemed to be her only friend these days. "This *was* his home. We're not together anymore." Frowning toward the crowded den, she added, "And we all need to remember that."

Margie Sue stopped grinning. "Did something happen between you two?"

"You mean, besides the obvious?"

Riley glanced toward the den once more. The scene

moved her heart even while that heart twisted in grief and longing. Her family all gathered by the fire, the big Christmas tree decorated in bright red and lime greens, the many gifts wrapped with fancy bows she'd made herself. It was a beautiful scene.

But Jackson wasn't in it. And he wasn't supposed to be in it. So why did she miss him so much?

Throwing the pot holders down, she put one hand on her hip and leaned against the kitchen sink. "It just hit me the night Allison lost her baby—I was reliving it all over again. And I remembered the pain...and how my husband wasn't anywhere nearby to help me through that pain."

Margie Sue's expression filled with sympathy. "Honey, I know that was tough. It was tough on all of us. But what happened with Allison isn't anyone's fault."

"Yes, it was tough for everybody," Riley said on a low whisper. "And I'm not blaming anyone. But it reminded me of why I'm a divorced woman and why I decided to have this child without any help from... Jackson."

"So you're punishing him because of what happened to Allison?"

Riley checked the kitchen to make sure they were alone. But the whole family was watching a sappy Christmas movie. Allison sat with Curtis, her hand over his. Even though it'd been a couple of weeks since she'd lost the baby, Allison looked gaunt and fatigued. "No, I'm not punishing him at all. I'm just remembering the pledge I made to myself when I decided to go this route. I can't count on Jackson to help me through this pregnancy. I can't count on him for anything. And I was wrong to give anyone the impression that we'd taken back up where we left off. We left things in a bad way when we parted. I can't forget that."

Her sister-in-law started back with the busywork, folding napkins into tidy little triangles, but Riley could see Margie Sue's concern in the frown etched on her face. "I guess we all thought y'all were getting along better."

"I did try, but what else can I do?" Riley asked, wishing everyone would leave her alone.

"You can forgive him," Margie Sue said. Then she shrugged. "I'm not in your shoes, so I don't have any right to butt in but it seems to me you were happier a couple weeks ago than you are right now. So maybe you could tolerate him for the baby's sake? It's something to think about."

"I have thought about it," Riley said, shocked at Margie Sue's bluntness. "More than anyone can ever know or understand. Yes, I can allow him to be a part of the baby's life, but that also means I'd have to allow him back into *my* life, too. I'm not ready for that."

"But, Riley, a lot of parents are divorced and they manage to work things out between them. Just think about it."

Riley nodded. "I will. Later. I need to let this soak in, get used to the idea of Jackson being here. He wants to be involved right now and I thought I could handle that, but I can't."

Margie Sue put the rolls into a basket. "Okay. It's your call. I'll stay out of it."

"Thank you," Riley said. "For being there, for being the voice of reason and for understanding my concerns."

Margie Sue's smile wasn't all the way happy. "Ready to eat dinner?"

Riley nodded. "I think so. Everything's out on the table."

She checked the dining room, where a white cloth graced the long table. She'd put a red satin runner across that and placed two poinsettias surrounded by golden candles in the middle. The sideboard held a small potted tree decorated with shiny white lights. The whole room sparkled with Christmas flair.

But Margie Sue was right. Jackson was missing.

Riley wondered what he was doing this Christmas Eve.

HE ATE A TURKEY SANDWICH and decided to take the dogs for a long walk. The two chocolate Labs—Sport and Gertrude—had a nice dog run behind the lodge kitchen, but Jackson loved taking them out to stretch their legs. It kept him and the dogs in shape. And tonight, with the sun setting to the west and Riley and her family celebrating Christmas to the east, he needed to stretch his own legs.

Besides, while the dogs ran on ahead, he could at

least cherish the memories of the few weeks Riley had been nice to him. But the more Jackson thought about it, the madder he got. She had been nice. She'd begun letting him in, calling him to come and eat, laughing and talking to him when they went to the doctor. What was her game, anyway?

He did have a right to that child, same as Riley.

He did have a right to…

What? Demand that Riley let him follow her around like a puppy dog, begging for scraps?

The woman still had control over him. Well, that had been just fine, even while she held him at arm's length. But she'd changed the night Allison had the miscarriage. Or maybe she'd just woken up and remembered why she still hated him so much.

The cold seemed to penetrate to his bones, but Jackson kept walking. He wouldn't sleep tonight. He knew that. He might not ever have a good night's sleep again. Maybe he should have stayed out there on the water, or down there in South America somewhere. Too much water under the bridge here. Too many memories and sad things to consider.

And yet, tonight, he didn't want to be anywhere else in the world. Even if he couldn't be with the one person he needed.

By the time he'd walked the dogs around the whole farm and back, he was pretty tired. But glad he was home. In spite of being alone, he wanted to be home.

When he looked up and saw the old Sinclair family graveyard, Jackson took the dogs inside. No one had been buried here for years and from the look of the place, no one had bothered to maintain the grounds, either. But this site held a lot of his ancestors' bones. Jackson had always been aware of the old cemetery, but growing up, he tended to bypass it for more exciting things.

His parents were buried in the main cemetery in town. And so was little Jack Thomas. Thinking it might be an interesting distraction to look at the tumbled and crooked gravestones, Jackson let the dogs run loose while he opened the creaky gate and strolled through the dry weeds to the grave markers. Squinting toward the names, he got out his cell phone and used his flashlight app.

After about twenty minutes of reading the names and deaths of his grandparents and great-grandparents, a few cousins and aunts and uncle, he stood to leave.

And that's when he stumbled on another tiny grave that reminded him of Jack Thomas's.

Had another Sinclair baby died after birth? Curious to see the name, and wondering if his family history could have contributed to the cause of his son's death, he bent down and scrubbed a hand over the rough stone.

J. T. (Judson Terrell) Sinclair, Infant, born June 10, 1973, died June 12, 1973.

1973. A two-day-old baby.
Three years before Jackson had been born.

He'd had an older brother that died as an infant?

Jackson blinked and looked again. But it was all still there. He sank down on the cold ground and stared into the dark.

His parents had never told Jackson about this.

Maybe they'd never told anyone.

Because he was pretty sure he'd never heard any mention around town of his long-deceased infant brother.

RILEY PUT AWAY the rest of the pies and cakes then went into the den. Margie Sue and Delton and their adult kids had already gone home. Bobby was out with his latest girlfriend. Her parents had said good-night after the kitchen was cleaned. Bettye didn't want to leave Riley and Aunt Verde with all the dishes. That left Uncle Floyd dozing in his recliner and Aunt Verde visiting with Curtis and Allison's three boys.

Allison had gone to the bathroom, but Curtis stood when Riley entered the room. "Could we talk a minute?" he asked, timid and quiet.

"Of course. Want some more chocolate cake?"

"No, I'm stuffed." He cut his gaze down the hall toward the powder room. "I'm worried about Allison."

Alarm rushed through Riley. "Is she having problems?"

"Not physically, but honestly I've never seen her like this. You know how she goes all out for Christmas? She'd already done most of her Christmas stuff before…before we lost the baby, but she just seems so sad now. It's like none of all that shiny, glittering stuff she loves means anything anymore. She barely talks to me or the boys. What should I do, Riley?"

Riley hurt for her brother. And remembered how Jackson would stare at her with a kind of dread in his eyes each time she entered a room. What could she tell her brother? There were no easy answers.

"Let's sit," she said, tugging him back into the kitchen. Pointing to the stools tucked under the big island counter, she pulled one out and sat down. Curtis did the same, but he seemed so stiff and uncomfortable, she wondered if they should go somewhere more private.

"How are *you* doing?" she asked, her heart hurting.

"I don't know." He cupped his hands together and stared down at them. "I've never had to deal with this. I mean, I remember what you went through and it was awful, knowing how much you wanted that baby. Now it's my wife. And it's Christmas and…I hate seeing her this way."

Riley leaned against her chair. "It's only been a couple of weeks," she whispered. "You might have to give her more time to grieve. The holidays make it hard, so just be patient."

"She won't talk about it," Curtis replied. "And you know me. I'm not good at talking, either. I hate the silence, but I don't know what to say."

Riley remembered that same silence. It was a cold, unyielding blackness that screamed with angst and grief. And guilt.

How did a person fill such a silence?

"I don't know what to tell you, Curtis. But I do know that Jackson and I both kind of shut down after we lost our baby. That was a mistake. We should have turned to each other for comfort, but I blamed him for not being there when I went into labor. And maybe he resented me because I was so caught up in having a baby and then losing that baby, I pushed Jackson aside."

Curtis lifted his head. "But I'm trying to show her I care. I'm trying to encourage her to try again. I don't think she wants to do that."

"Give her some time," Riley said, remembering her conversation with Allison at the hospital. "She might not be ready to try again so soon." She stood and hugged her brother close. "Keep loving her, Curtis. Hold tight. You have three beautiful boys and…you have another chance. Be kind to each other and hold tight to here and now, instead of forcing another pregnancy. Maybe go and talk to a counselor or a minister. That might help."

Her brother held her then leaned back. "You're so smart. I appreciate you helping Allison through this. I always wondered why you two seemed to butt heads, but now you're the only person she can trust to understand how bad this is."

"Allison and I are fine," Riley said. "We'll always be two different people, but yes, we have a bond now. I won't take that lightly, I promise."

"What are y'all doing all huddled up?"

Riley whirled to find Allison staring at them.

"I was just giving my brother a pep talk," Riley replied. "And wishing both of you a good Christmas."

Allison didn't force a smile. She nodded, her lips a tight line across her pale face. "Yep. We'll have a good Christmas. The boys are getting a lot of gifts from Santa. It'll be okay."

She didn't sound convincing, Riley decided. "Allison—"

"I'm tired," Allison said. "Curtis, let's get the boys home. You know how wound up they get waiting on Santa. And we still have a lot to get done before sunup."

Curtis shot Riley a futile glance then called out to the boys. "Get your coats. Time to get to bed. Santa won't come until you're asleep."

Allison watched as the boys squealed and started gathering their things. "I've always loved this time of year," she said to Riley. "I have to be strong for my boys, don't I?"

Riley put her hands on her sister-in-law's shoulders. "You don't have to be too strong. Rest and enjoy your family. Curtis loves you so much."

Allison smiled at that. "I know and…he's hurting, too."

"Yes, he is. Both of you need to not try so hard. Don't force things you can't feel. Just remember your boys and what a gift they are."

Allison's eyes misted over. She gave Riley a silent nod. "Thank you—for understanding."

Riley thought of Jackson. He'd had no one to turn to after their tragedy. No parents, no brothers or sisters, no one. Since they'd met in grade school, he'd had her. And what had she done? She'd blamed him and pushed him away and then taken his home right out from under him. No wonder the man left town.

After she'd waved goodbye to the last of her relatives and kissed her aunt and uncle good-night, Riley went up to her bedroom and stood staring out into the night.

She'd never felt so all alone.

She stared at the phone, wondering if she should call Jackson.

JACKSON STARED AT his cell phone.

He needed to talk to someone.

But he had no one.

He couldn't wake any of his buddies. They all had families to deal with, Santa stuff to sort through.

He thought of Riley. His Riley. She'd always been his best friend, his go-to girl, his heart. Used to, he could talk to Riley about anything. And yet, he'd kept so much held inside.

Did he dare call her now?

It was nearly midnight. He'd walked and walked after discovering the little grave.

How could his parents have had another child and never mentioned it to him? Did anyone else know about this?

His parents had met and married late in life. They'd

both been well into their thirties. His mother always told the story of how J. T. Sinclair had come to Atlanta to visit a relative and handle some business and had come back to Sinclair with a wife.

In 1973. They'd married in 1973. The same year their first child had been born and then died.

The truth hit Jackson like a two-ton truck.

His parents hadn't just wed out of love.

They'd gotten married so quickly because they were going to have a baby. And they'd lost that baby before anyone had ever discovered the truth.

CHAPTER TWENTY-THREE

RILEY HAD JUST turned off the lamp when her cell began buzzing. Grabbing it from the nightstand, she held it while she turned the light back on.

Jackson.

"Hello," she said, breathless for way too many reasons.

"They lied to me," he said, his voice sounding distant and dangerous.

"What? Who are you talking about? Jackson, what's wrong?"

He let out a ragged sigh. "My parents. They—" He stopped and went silent again. "Never mind. How are you?"

Worried that he'd been drinking, Riley asked, "You called me at midnight to see how I'm doing?"

He didn't speak for a couple of seconds. Then he said, "I need you, Riley. I really need you. I just wanted to tell you that."

Riley's heart skidded and sputtered. "Jackson, are you all right?"

"No. I'm not. I…it's Christmas. I came home for you, for Christmas, for all the holidays I'd missed. No,

I'm not all right. I don't think I can make this right. And now I'm beginning to understand why."

Riley sat up. "Where are you?"

"I'm…at…the lodge, of course. My new home. My big ole rambling, lonely home."

"I'm coming over there."

"No, no. I'm fine. Really. Just needed to hear your voice."

She stood and began searching for clothes. "I said I'm coming over there."

"You have to take care. You have to avoid me."

"A long walk won't hurt me. And I'm not trying to avoid you." At least, she'd tried and it apparently wasn't working.

"It's cold."

"I'll put on a coat and a scarf."

"I could come there."

"No. My aunt and uncle are asleep. We don't need to disturb them. I'll take the shortcut along the lane."

"Bring a flashlight. I don't want you to stumble."

"Okay. Give me about fifteen minutes."

"Riley, you don't have to—"

"I'll be there, Jackson."

She put down the phone and scrambled for her fleece sweatpants and a warm sweater. Then she grabbed a down jacket and wrapped a wool scarf around her neck. Throwing on some suede, low-heeled boots, she hurried down the stairs and out the back door, her phone in her pocket in case her aunt or uncle realized she'd gone missing. She found a big flashlight in the utility room and started along the back of the yard, following the fence line and the moon the half mile or so to the big lodge.

Luckily, she'd installed several security lights along this particular dirt lane since visitors at the lodge and at Southern Hill liked to walk the pretty trail. And she often rode her horse along this same trail. Riley knew the way by heart, but the lights gave her a certain amount of security now.

Her mind whirled with fear and concern. Had Jackson taken a drink and called her maybe to talk? Or had something happened to upset him? He said his parents had lied to him. But what did that mean?

Was she crazy to do this? To run to him in the middle of the night after she'd decided to stay away?

No. It was Christmas. She couldn't let him sit there all alone, no matter how much he got under her skin. She wasn't as unkind as people might think. Her thoughts propelled her, causing her to walk as fast as she could. By the time she'd reached the grounds of the lodge, she was panting for breath.

But she'd made it.

Jackson must have been watching from the porch. She saw him in the hazy security lights. He hurled himself down the steps and hurried toward her.

And pulled her into his arms.

Riley tried to speak but he hushed her.

"Just...don't say anything, okay?"

"Okay." She let him hold her, let herself respond by wrapping her arms around him and closing her eyes to whatever pain had brought him to this state. She must have contributed to that pain but she'd been too self-centered to see that. It had taken five years of him being gone and then returning to show her how cruel she had been to him.

After a few minutes, the warmth of his body penetrated her soul and Riley decided she could probably stay in his arms for close to forever.

But he pulled away and stared down at her. "You shouldn't be here."

"I know," she admitted. "I know."

He touched her face, his hand holding her chin and then he leaned in and kissed her. His lips were warm in spite of the biting cold. His hand felt rough against her skin and made her whole body tingle with awareness.

"Let me get you in by the fire," he said against her earlobe.

Riley could only nod.

He put an arm around her waist and guided her toward the looming lodge. "It's warm inside."

Riley almost bolted. If she went in there with him, she might not ever leave.

But…he'd said he needed her.

And that was something new and special and… touching.

And it was Christmas after all.

JACKSON STARED AT the woman sitting across from him in front of the big fireplace. He'd built up the fire to a roaring blaze. The golden hues reflected off Riley's hair, giving it a shimmering quality. It felt a bit strange, having her here. Riley rarely came to the lodge.

"Want another cup of decaf?"

She shook her head. "No. But thanks."

"Are you warm enough?" he asked, his hands reaching toward the fire.

"Yes. It's very cozy." She glanced around. "I haven't been in here in years. You must have done some updating."

"A little. We have a fairly large maintenance budget, thanks to you. But then, you'd already renovated it quite a bit."

Riley looked back into the fire. "I didn't do much. Just told Aunt Verde and Uncle Floyd to hire someone to make sure the place was up-to-date. I found pictures in magazines and used those as suggestions. But I didn't bother seeing the final results. Verde vouched for the improvements. Said they worked out great. I have to agree."

"Why do you hate this place?" he asked, hoping to stall her on why he'd panicked and called her. While he loved having her here, now he felt silly and embarrassed about dragging her out on a cold night. Even sillier about his reasons. What did any of this matter? But then, this could be at the crux of why he'd been such a loser, marriagewise. Fatherwise.

"I don't hate it," she replied a little too quickly. She shrugged, stared at the fire. "I guess I resent it. I'm envious of the power this place holds over you."

"Not just me, sweetheart," he retorted, trying to

lighten things. "It's a hunting lodge, the ultimate man cave."

"Yes, and it kept you away for most of our marriage. I wonder how the other wives and significant others feel about this place."

Jackson got up and stood facing her, the fire behind him. "I can admit that it did indeed keep me away. I didn't see the damage or understand it before. I grew up thinking it was perfectly acceptable to spend time with my buddies. That's what my daddy did. He went about his business and his pleasure, without consulting anyone, including my mother. But she never complained. She waited on him hand and foot and then waited for him to come home. I took for granted that you'd always be waiting for me, that we'd always be together."

"Yes, you did, because your mom was always there for your daddy. Which made me worry so I fretted that I'd somehow lose you if I didn't behave, or if I fussed at you too much. And I lost you anyway." She shot a glance at the fire. "And somewhere in there, I lost myself, too."

"But you found yourself again," he said, the statement bittersweet. "When I came back and saw you, I thought 'There's my Riley.' You looked so…confident, standing there in all your glory."

"I thought I was confident."

She leaned back in the oversize leather chair. It made her look like a little girl, sitting there. And made

Jackson hate the way he had taken their marriage and her love for granted.

Riley sat silent for a minute, then said, "One of the reasons I wanted a child so much was so you'd stay home more. Or at least, that's what I told myself. What father would neglect a newborn baby, after all?"

"My father," he said, blurting the words out in a burst of pain.

"What?" She looked up at him then, her eyes bright against the blinding fire. "What are you talking about, Jackson? What happened with you earlier?"

He sat back down then gazed over at her. "I found out something tonight that helped me understand my entire childhood."

Riley sat up again, her hands folded across her legs. "What on earth?"

He hadn't planned on telling her or anyone else, but he needed to get this off his chest. "My parents had another son, Riley. He would have been about three years older than me."

"Another child? A boy? You're joking, right?"

"Why would I joke?" He came and sat down in the matching chair across from hers. "I saw his name."

"Where?"

"On a grave marker in the old Sinclair cemetery."

She put a hand to her heart, her expression full of shock. "You had a brother but…he died?"

Jackson bobbed his head. Hearing the words out loud made him even madder. It was like living Jack Thomas's death all over again. "Yep. He was born in

1973 and died two days later. Riley, my parents got married in 1973."

"Yes, I know that but—"

She stopped, gasped, her gaze hinging on him. "Are you saying they had to get married? That your mother was pregnant?"

"I believe so," Jackson replied. He closed his eyes for a minute. "They obviously didn't tell anyone or we would have known about the baby. I've sat here all night trying to piece things together. I believe they got married while my dad was up in Atlanta. They always told the story of how he went up there for a few months on business, some big project with her father. They fell in love and…when he came home, he brought her with him as his bride."

"I remember the story," Riley said. "Your grandparents weren't happy that they'd eloped but they welcomed your mother into Southern Hill."

"Yes, and threw a big party as a kind of reception."

"We have pictures of that. Your mother didn't look pregnant in those pictures."

"That's because she probably wasn't as far along as you are now. She wasn't showing."

"Or she hid it very well." Riley sat there staring at him. "I don't know what to say." She folded her arms against her stomach. "Are you sure, Jackson?"

"I'm sure of what I saw on that grave marker. It was almost buried underneath an azalea bush, but I found it."

"I can't believe this," Riley said. "That's quite a discovery."

"Now you can understand why I…I was so upset."

She gave him a long hard stare. "Why would they keep this from you? Or anybody else for that matter?"

"Pride," he said. "Think of the scandal. My father was the same as me, the lone heir to a vast fortune of land and holdings. They probably planned to announce it after they'd settled in and who knows what excuse they would have used when the baby actually came. I don't know. But I do know my mother suffered a miscarriage and they quietly buried that baby in the old cemetery. And this is the weird part. He has my initials—JTS, but they named him Judson Terrell."

"That is odd," Riley said. "Why didn't they go ahead and name him J. T. Sinclair III?"

Jackson stared at the fire. "I think they talked it over and decided to try again and save that name for another boy."

"You," she replied. "They did try again and they had you."

"Yep." He got up and paced back and forth. "I was second best. I've always felt that way, you know. I didn't measure up to my daddy's expectations. I didn't do anything right. So I followed him around, trying to learn, trying to figure out what he expected of me. And even as an adult, I still followed him around and neglected you. After he died, I couldn't break that habit. I've been following a ghost. Make that two ghosts—my brother and my father."

"Jackson, your daddy loved you. You know that."

"No I don't. He never told me. Never. I'd walk in a room and feel his eyes on me and think I'd done something he didn't like. But it wasn't that, Riley." He turned to stare down at her. "It was just that he was always thinking of his real firstborn son. The one he buried away in a hidden grave. All of my life, my daddy compared me to my dead brother. And I guess he always wondered why Judson Terrell had to die. The same way I wonder why Jack Thomas had to die."

She put a hand over her stomach. "Are you going to resent this baby then?"

He walked over to her and pulled her up and into his arms. "No, and that's why I had to talk to you. You're the only one who ever understood me, Riley. You've been right there beside me all the way…until I messed up everything and drove you away."

"Jackson, I'm partly to blame, too. I treated you horribly and told you to leave."

"But you didn't know, could never understand why I acted that way. I was afraid to be a father. So afraid I'd be a disappointment to my kid in the same way I'd been a disappointment to my daddy." He touched a hand to her cheek. "That's why I ran, Riley. And I ran because I'd always felt less-than growing up and no matter what I did or said, my daddy never tried to convince me otherwise. I can see it all in my mind now—my sweet mama, so passive, so accommodating. She was trying to make it up to the man she loved. She lost their child and I think the guilt of that ate away at her all of her life."

"And she never said a word," Riley whispered. "Nothing. No wonder she was always so quiet."

"Yes. She was trapped in a horrible nightmare and she didn't really have anyone to talk to." He shook his head then touched his chin to Riley's hair. "And me—I often wondered what I'd done to displease my father. And now I know why I felt that way. I was competing with a tiny little baby that never got a chance to prove how perfect he could have been." He backed up and pulled away from Riley. "And that's hard, trying to live up to someone you didn't even know existed. Too hard. That's why I failed at marriage and trying to be a father. What if I fail again, Riley? What then?"

CHAPTER TWENTY-FOUR

RILEY WAS SO astonished, she didn't know what to say or how to respond. She'd never seen Jackson like this, even when they'd gone through the worst and the fighting had increased.

Even during the horrible silence of a marriage dying a slow death.

"Do you really believe you can't be a good father?"

He backed away and dropped his hands to his side. "I want to be. I thought I was ready. I thought I'd gotten past all the doubts my father somehow drilled into my subconscious. But now that the proof is right there and my own parents didn't bother to tell me, I feel a kind of relief, yes. This explains a lot of things that didn't make sense before. But I also feel sick to my stomach and wondering if maybe my daddy was right."

Anger coursed through Riley's system. "Jackson, stop this, right now. You would…you will…be a good father. You were a good husband in so many ways." She hugged her hands to herself and let the fire warm her. "We had everything, Jackson. We had it all. We were made for each other. Everybody said that. But maybe it was all an act, a charade that we had to play out." She hated to say what she was thinking. "Maybe we were just convenient for each other and as long as things were going great, we could keep up the facade. When things got rough, though, we gave up. We caved in."

He rushed to her, dragged her hands into his. "Riley, we were real. We did belong together. I don't doubt that. But I blew it. I messed up. I sabotaged the thing I wanted the most in the world—you and our child—a real family. Now I think I can at least understand why I was so self-destructive."

"And you think you did that because of the way your daddy treated you?"

"Yes, but I'm not using that as an excuse. I was a lousy husband at times. I don't have any excuses. But in spite of all of that I'm a different man now."

"And yet, you're still making excuses." She started gathering her things, unable to look at him. "You know the truth now, or you think you know the truth. You think you're just second-best but I believe your parents loved you and did the best they could with you. Maybe they never mentioned your brother because they *didn't* want you to feel inferior. And I'm sure the subject of losing their first child was painful for them in the same way it is for us. Maybe that's how you need to look at this."

He kept his gaze on the fire. "Even if they kept my brother's existence from me for my sake, it's a lot to take in, don't you think?"

"Yes, it is," she agreed. "A big shock. But it doesn't change anything between us. We're here now, Jackson. In the same spot we were in before. I'm pregnant and you're in a panic over being a father. That doesn't change anything. If you're already having doubts about helping me raise this baby, then you haven't really changed at all, and that brings us back to square one."

She turned to leave, disappointment and frustration making her blunt and bold. "You called me and told me you needed me, and yet you tell me you're worried you might mess up again. Maybe you don't need anyone."

"I do need you," he said, following her to the door. "I thought you'd understand. You were the one I called, Riley. The one I knew I could trust."

She turned and started wrapping her scarf around her neck. "I do understand this—you've been through an awful shock. Your parents withheld vital information from you. That's hard to deal with, but, Jackson, you can get past that. You did get past whatever you went through with your daddy. Trust your own instincts on this. Don't give up on yourself or our baby, please?"

"Are you willing to let me in?" he asked, his own anger bubbling just beyond the question. "Are you willing to meet me halfway and let me show you I've changed?"

"That's exactly what I've been trying to do," she reminded him. "I made some mistakes back then, too. I see that now. I was so wrapped up in my own pain, I didn't see how much you were grieving, too. I wanted things to be better for you this time. I wanted things to change between us so I tried to let you in to my life again. To make up for the past and for the baby's sake, at least."

He pushed a hand down his face. "But you shut me out for the same reasons I'm afraid to let go, Riley. After Allison lost her baby, you went right back to your old ways, too. You pushed me away, ignored me, left me hanging. Again. You told me right there in the hospital that you didn't think you could do this again. And as you pointed out, here we are right back where we left off."

His words cut Riley to the core, but he spoke the truth.

And that truth was glaring at them almost as brightly as the fire burning in the fireplace.

"We're not gonna make it, are we, sweetheart?" he said, his hands in his jean pockets, his tone full of acceptance and regret.

Riley hated hearing those words, hated defeat. "No, I don't think so."

She turned to leave, her hands shaking, her world tumbling down around her. Then she whirled, her hand on the doorknob. "I would have been fine, Jackson. Fine with this baby, happy on my own. I'd finally learned to live without you. But you had to come home and…make me hope again. That was cruel."

"Don't talk to me about cruel," he replied, his words hitting her in a controlled rage. "I just found out my brother died in pretty much the same way as my son. Before he'd ever really lived. So don't talk to me about hurt and pain and cruelty, Riley. I think

I've pretty much cornered the market on all of that. I thought I'd learned it from my daddy, but I think I've seen it one too many times in you, too." He stepped close then leaned in. "You were so bent on keeping me away that you went and got yourself pregnant without me. Without me, Riley. No one can be any crueler than that."

The look of disgust and regret in his eyes burned her. Riley couldn't breathe, couldn't find the words to defend herself. So she opened the door and started back on the long way toward her home. But this time, the trip seemed to take a lifetime. And this time, she knew, there would be no turning back.

He'd lost her.

Jackson watched as the last of the fire's embers died down to a smoking pile of ashes. His life seemed to be following suit. He'd come home on a triumphant wave of hope, determined to prove to everyone that he was a changed man. And now, weeks later he was dying a slow death, alone and angry. But this time the hurt was doubly blinding.

The pain of losing Jack Thomas hit him full force, coupled with the pain of the deliberate deceit his parents had used to shield him and mold him. If they'd just been honest with him, his life might have taken a different turn. He would have looked at his brooding father in a different way, maybe would have felt a little sympathy for the man. He would have understood why his sweet, quiet mother tried so hard to please her husband over and over again.

But it was too late now.

He'd come home, determined to win his wife back.

Now on this night of revelations, he'd lost Riley and their second baby, too. So much for Christmas and reconciling during the peace and beauty of the season.

Jackson stared into the still remnants of the fire and then finally got up to go to bed. He lay there in the dark and thought about packing up and leaving. But he didn't want to go back out into the world. He'd conquered his wanderlust and while that journey had forced him to see behind his happy-go-lucky facade, he didn't need to run away to find the truth.

He'd found it right here.

He loved Riley, but they couldn't work things out.

He wanted to be a father to their baby, but Riley would keep him from doing that full-time.

And he had a brother he never knew about, but there was nothing he could do about that now.

So Jackson resigned himself to growing old alone and lonely. Maybe if he stayed around, he could at least have some part in this baby's life. Maybe. It was his only hope.

"I won't lie to my son or daughter," he said into the night. "And I won't hide, either. I'll be right here. I'll show all of them that I'm here to stay this time. Whether they like it or not. I'll stay in spite of everything."

Having made that decision, Jackson turned on his side and tried to go to sleep.

As he dozed, he realized it was Christmas. A lonely Christmas for him.

"Do you want me to invite Jackson over?" Margie Sue asked Riley the next day at noon.

"No." Riley turned to help her obviously concerned mother put out the dishes for their Christmas brunch. "No, I don't think that's a good idea."

Bettye shot a questioning gaze to Margie Sue before she focused on Riley. "You two fighting again?"

Tired and frustrated, Riley retorted, "When were we not fighting?"

Margie Sue gave the mashed potatoes another heavy stir. "I thought y'all had called a truce for the baby's sake."

"I thought that, too," Riley admitted. "But you know how it is with Jackson and me. We always managed to destroy each other."

"It wasn't always that way," Bettye pointed out. "Y'all need to get back to what's important, honey. If you love each other, you need to learn to be with each other."

Margie Sue nodded in agreement. "She's right, Riley."

Riley stared at her well-meaning mother and sister-in-law. "What if we love each other, but we just can't live with each other?"

Margie Sue must have sensed the defeat in her

words. "I don't know. We just hate to see you this way."

Bettye pursed her lips and remained silent. But Riley saw the disappointment in her mother's eyes.

"I don't like being this way," Riley said. "But I have to concentrate on the baby now. That has always been my plan and in spite of Jackson being back here, I have to stick to that plan."

"Uh-huh."

Riley couldn't talk about it, not even with Margie Sue and her mother, not today. "The coffee and other drinks are ready. I think we can tell everyone it's time to eat."

"Uh-huh." Margie Sue whirled to announce the meal.

Bettye walked over to stand beside Riley. Her mother grabbed her hand and squeezed it. "Whatever you decide, we'll be here for you and the baby, honey."

"Thanks, Mama."

Riley thought about all the meals she'd had here at her parent's house and at Southern Hill, too. Over the past five years, she'd gotten used to her cushy, comfortable life. She'd thought of Jackson a lot during that time, usually late at night when she couldn't sleep. She'd always wondered where he was, if he was safe. And she'd wondered how he could leave everything he loved to go off on some grand adventure. What had been missing here with her? What had she done to cause him to leave and stay gone?

Now she had to accept that it hadn't all been about

her or their doomed marriage. It had been about something inside Jackson that hadn't allowed him to feel fulfilled or nurtured. He'd gone off on his own to heal himself and maybe he'd accomplished that. Or maybe he still needed to work on things a bit more.

But finding that little grave. That must have been such a shock. And what had she gone and done when he'd reached out to her? She'd turned away, angry that he couldn't commit to her and their baby. Would he ever be able to make a permanent commitment? And would she ever be able to forgive him and trust him? Either way, they couldn't go on hurting each other.

Those questions haunted Riley through opening gifts and eating a lazy Christmas Day dinner. She nibbled at her food and got up to leave early, giving the excuse of being tired.

But Allison caught her in the guest room where they'd put all the coats and hats. "Are you all right, Riley?"

Riley turned to her other sister-in-law. "I'm okay. How about you?"

"Better," Allison said, her usually bright eyes still a bit dull. "I'm still blue but I'm trying for the boys' sake. And for Curtis. He worries so much."

"He loves you," Riley replied. "You're blessed. You have three little boys who are adorable and so full of life."

"Yes, I keep telling myself that," Allison replied. "Riley, I hope you make it all the way with this pregnancy. I truly mean that."

"Thank you." Riley turned away, afraid she'd burst into tears if she looked at Allison again. "I appreciate that."

Allison touched Riley's arm. "I also hope you and Jackson can work things out."

"I wouldn't count on that," Riley said. "We can't seem to agree on anything these days."

"Keep trying," Allison said. "Some things are worth fighting for, you know."

Riley gave Allison a quick hug. "Everyone seems to think Jackson is worth it, but I'm not so sure I am."

Then she turned and left without another word to her big, loud, loving family. She did love them and she cherished these times together. But right now, she needed to be alone with her thoughts. And she needed to figure out what to do about loving Jackson.

CHAPTER TWENTY-FIVE

Riley heard fireworks.

Nothing like spending New Year's Eve alone, wearing sweats decorated with sequins instead of a cocktail dress and sparkling shoes.

She'd sent Uncle Floyd and Aunt Verde out the door earlier. "Don't worry about me. Just have fun with your church group."

They planned to have dinner at a local steak house then watch the fireworks out at the country club.

"I thought you'd at least go to the party with Fred," her aunt had said before leaving.

"No. Fred and I...aren't dating anymore."

She'd finally told Fred Marshall that she *couldn't* date him anymore.

"Is it because Jackson's back?" he'd asked with that hang-dog look he liked to give her.

"No, it's because I'm expecting a baby. Jackson's baby."

That had taken some time to explain.

"I'd heard rumors," Fred admitted. "I was hoping you'd tell me the truth."

She did tell him the truth. And that truth was her only company on this cold winter night. "Yes, Jackson is the father, but no, we're not getting back together."

End of discussion.

But because of that truth, everyone had been coddling her and watching over her. Which meant her phone rang all day long.

Margie Sue called around seven. "So you're staying home tonight?"

"Yes. Just me and my tummy. I plan to eat low-fat ice cream and fruit in celebration of the New Year."

At seven-thirty, Mary Ann called. "Riley, you're the life of the party. We can't enjoy our annual New Year's Eve bash without you here. Throw on one of those fabulous dresses from your closet and get on out here."

"Sorry, but I'm already in my lounge clothes," Riley replied. "You know you'll have a sold-out crowd and no one will miss me at all."

"Oh, I don't know about that," Mary Ann said. "I think the handsome man sitting alone in the bar sure will miss you."

"Fred?"

"Heck, no. He's dancing with Barbara Dixon. Guess again."

"Jackson?" Riley's heart betrayed her determination to stay calm.

"The one and only. And from the way he keeps calling to the bartender, I think he might be backsliding just a tad."

Riley willed her heart to stop racing. "Don't let him drive home, okay? Call him a cab or get Delton to drive him."

"We'll take care of him," Mary Ann promised.

Dorothy Lyn called at eight. "We miss you, suga'. I know you can't drink, but you still have to eat. Mary Ann's got a spread to die for. Just come on out and have a bite."

"No. And don't tell me Jackson is sitting there, pining away for me. I can't deal with that guilt on top of everything else."

"Okay, I won't tell you that. But I will say he's not exactly pining away. He's dancing with every woman in the place, including Miss Maxine."

"The librarian?"

"The long-retired librarian who just celebrated her eighty-second birthday. That sister can cut the rug even wearing orthopedic shoes, let me tell you."

Riley smiled in spite of worrying. "Don't let Jackson drive, okay?"

"No, ma'am. We've got cabs standing by for all of the guests. You know how Mary Ann feels about being responsible."

"Good. Now go back to having fun. I'm fine."

"Yeah, you sure do sound just fine."

Riley wondered why she'd bothered staying at home since the phone didn't stop ringing all night. Her mom called. Then Allison called.

"I'm at home with Curtis and the boys," Allison told her. "Want to come over and watch the ball drop in Times Square?"

"No, thanks. I think I'll watch an old movie and ring in the New Year all tucked in."

She was on her way to doing just that when she

heard the fireworks. Riley went to the big bay window in her bedroom and stared out at the sparkling lights shooting over the tree line.

Beautiful.

She remembered other New Year's celebrations, standing here with Jackson. Then turning to go to bed. Wonderful memories.

Now she was alone. That used to scare her, but now she was content with her solitary confinement. She was happy that her baby gained more strength every day.

But she couldn't stop thinking about Jackson.

Finally, the fireworks show ended and she turned to go back to bed. The old grandfather clock downstairs chimed the midnight hour. *Happy New Year to me,* she thought.

Riley settled underneath the covers, her soft sweatpants and long-sleeved jersey tunic keeping her warm while she tried to put Jackson out of her mind. Had she been wrong to walk away after hearing his devastating news?

Her thoughts whirled in a mist of regret as she drifted into a restless sleep.

But she woke with a start after hearing something ping against the side of the house.

Her heart racing, Riley stepped back to the bay window and squinted into the muted darkness. Pranksters always came out on New Year's Eve.

Ping!

There it went again. Something hitting the side of

the house. Then another ping, this time on one of the big windows right in front of her.

She looked down and saw him standing there. Or rather, barely standing there.

Jackson. Weaving and bobbing and waving his hands.

How on earth did he get here? She hadn't heard a car. She didn't see his car in the driveway.

Another pebble hit the window.

She opened one of the panels and leaned out. "Jackson, stop that!"

The man standing in her yard did a deep bow. "Ah, the fair lady of the manor is in her ivory tower."

Riley recoiled from the slur of that statement. "Jackson, let me call you a cab?"

"Nope. No cab. No car. I walked."

"From the country club? That's almost three miles."

"Yep. And pretty cold out here, too. Got any coffee?"

She shouldn't. She wouldn't. But she couldn't let him freeze to death. That would leave a messy situation to explain in the morning.

Okay, so it wasn't that cold but it was chilly. Maybe if she brought him in long enough for Uncle Floyd to get home and give him a ride.

But she and Jackson weren't supposed to be talking. They had ignored each other for the better part of a week now.

"Riley, dear beautiful Riley, won't you please come to my rescue?" Before she could answer that shouted plea, he went on with, "Rapunzel, Rapunzel, let down your hair. I mean, your guard, let down your guard. Or maybe, just let me in out of the cold."

Quoting fairy tales. He must have drunk a whole pint of something. She knew it was the drink talking, but her heart went out to him anyway. She'd been so mean to him the last time they'd talked. Why did she do such things? Why did he bring out all her defenses and insecurities?

"I need you," he shouted now. "I mean it, Riley. I really need you." He waved his hands in the air again. "Oh, and I really, really need to go to the bathroom, too."

Riley shut the window and grabbed her fleece hoodie. Another midnight meeting didn't suit her, but she couldn't let him stand out there and scream all night.

She hurried down the stairs and opened the front door. "Jackson?"

He moaned to her right. And there he sat in one of Aunt Verde's white rocking chairs, his whole body slumped while he rocked with one booted foot.

"Jackson, you can come inside."

He pushed at getting up then fell back in a heap. "Don't feel so good."

"I wonder why." She walked over to him and lifted his head. "Jackson, you can't pass out. I won't be able to get you inside."

"Just leave me then. I can freeze for all you care."

"That thought had crossed my mind," she admitted.

"You'd like that, huh? No more Jackson to compli-
cate things. Never needed me anyway. Most independent woman on God's green earth."

That admission knocked Riley back a step. Was
that truly how he saw her? Could that be part of their
problems?

"Let's get you inside," she said, her hand out to him.

He grabbed her hand and with his other arm, tugged
her into his lap. Before she could get away, he turned
her with a hand on her chin and planted a big kiss right
on her open, startled lips. The kiss shifted and changed
from playful to demanding and serious, sobering Riley
enough that she sighed and leaned into his embrace.

But apparently it hadn't sobered him at all.

"And a Happy, Happy New Year to you, Mrs. Ex-
Wife-of-Mine-Mother-of-My-Child-Sinclair. You look
beautiful in the moonlight."

Riley regained control enough to stand up. "Come
inside so I can get you sober. Uncle Fred will be home
soon. He'll give you a ride back to the lodge."

Jackson stood, unsteady and unrepentant. "Don't
want to sleep in that drafty old lodge. Want my own
bed. Want you there with me."

The thought of that flashed white-hot inside Riley's
troubled mind. "Jackson, be reasonable. You're drunk.
We're not married. I can't… I won't—"

Car lights filled the driveway, their beams washing
over Riley and Jackson.

He snuggled into her arms. "Uh-oh. Busted."

"Yes," she said, pushing him away. "And time for

you to either come in and let me make you some coffee or hitch a ride home."

"Coffee," he said, his eyes dark with whiskey and regret. "A warm bed," he added on a soft whisper.

"Not my bed," she retorted, shivers moving with telltale precision down her spine.

Then she turned to face her aunt and uncle.

JACKSON WOKE TO bright sunshine and a stern-faced Aunt Verde.

"You've overslept your welcome," she said, a full cup of black coffee in her hand. She held the coffee an arm's length away and averted her eyes.

He sat up, pushed at his hair, saw the familiar rectangular room where he'd spent most of his youth. "My old bedroom. How'd I get here?" Then he groaned. "I haven't gone back to the future or something like that, have I?"

"No," she said, her frown warring with a grin. "You're still in the here and now. But you were a little confused at one this morning. Floyd marched you right in after you tried to make a beeline to Riley's room."

He grimaced and motioned for the coffee. "Sorry about that. Did I do anything to disgrace myself or y'all?"

"No more than usual," Verde retorted, a twinkle in her eyes. "But you certainly tied one on last night."

He drank deeply from the big mug. "Haven't done that in…since…since I don't know when."

"Well, you fell off the wagon, no doubt. So now you need to get up and get back on track."

"I'm an idiot," he said to no one in particular. "I guess Riley is fit to be tied."

Verde neither verified nor condemned. "She's still in her room. She didn't get much sleep last night." Her stern gaze told him he might be the reason for that.

"I'm sorry," he said, meaning it. "I messed up yet again."

Verde walked to the door. "You're human—I think. Just try to cut her some slack, Jackson. She's not as in-control as you might think."

"I'll bear that in mind when I'm figuring out how to make this up to her."

"Breakfast is on the stove," Verde replied. Then she turned at the door. "And we're having the usual New Year's Day dinner later—black-eyed peas and corn bread, turnips, cabbage—"

"Stop, stop," Jackson begged, one hand going up in the air while his stomach did somersaults of agony. "I can't…think about that now."

"I know," Verde retorted with a sweet smile. Then she left without another word.

"They are all so cruel," Jackson mumbled to himself. After downing the coffee, he got up and took a long shower then put back on the clothes he'd slept in—a now-rumpled white shirt and black dress pants.

"Time to pay the piper," he said, his reflection looking back at him with puffy eyes and blotchy skin.

Jackson made his way down to the kitchen and opted for dry toast. Really dry toast.

He got that and a steaming-hot mad stare from the woman sitting at the breakfast table.

"THE PRINCE IS awake."

Riley didn't want to be catty, but it was early and she was in a mood. "Did you sleep okay, my prince?"

"Cute," Jackson said, his gaze zoomed in on the coffeemaker. "I need more caffeine before we go at it, darlin'."

She remained quiet. Which alerted him to get ready. An ill wind was a'coming.

"Where's everyone?" he asked, just to make conversation.

"I think Verde and Floyd had the good sense to give us some space to…uh…talk."

He turned away from the too-bright January sunshine and faced her square on. "Look, Riley. It was New Year's Eve and I was mad and lonely. I'm sorry."

She didn't smile but she didn't frown, either. "I understand."

He waited for the rest of the statement but when she didn't speak, he ventured a little closer. "Are you all right?"

She took a bite of her fruit and yogurt. "Why wouldn't I be?"

"Riley, I…uh…kinda stormed the castle last night. I was drunk and…I want to apologize."

"I said I understand."

While she remained completely calm and indifferent, his blood pressure started simmering to a heated boil. He wanted to fight with her, wanted her to scream and rage and tell him he was worthless and immature.

"Do you really?" he asked, testing the waters. "I mean, do you understand how I feel, how I want to make things right? Or do you just want me to leave?"

"You can eat your toast first," she said, her ink pen in one hand and her infuriating smart phone in the other.

"So just like that. I show up here in a drunken stupor and you decide now is the time to be civil? Why don't you tell me how you really feel?"

She stood, looking beautiful in spite of the dark circles underneath her blue eyes. "I feel sad, Jackson." She moved to the sink to put away her breakfast dishes. "I feel let down and angry. I feel miserable." She turned, swayed against the sink.

"Riley?"

"Jackson, I don't feel so good."

"I'm sorry," he said, hoping to finally have a heart-to-heart with her. "Truly sorry."

Her head tipped forward. "I mean it, Jackson. I… something feels wrong. My stomach—" She turned, panic in her eyes as her hands went to the little rounded bump. "Jackson, something's wrong with the baby."

CHAPTER TWENTY-SIX

"SHE'S GOING TO be fine, but you did the right thing, bringing her here."

Jackson nodded and then scrubbed a hand down his face. "She wanted to call her doctors in Atlanta—"

"I've already talked to Dr. Reynolds," the local E.R. doctor explained. "We're pretty sure this is a false alarm."

"You mean, she's okay? The baby's okay? Is that what you mean by saying she's fine?" Jackson asked, his hands still shaking. He had to get a grip before Riley's parents got here. He'd called them on the way to the nearby hospital.

The young doctor pulled Jackson over to the seating area near the Sinclair Hospital Emergency Room double doors.

"We're at a wait-and-see phase but some cramps and spotting can occur at this stage in a pregnancy."

Jackson's heart hit his throat. He wished he could feel as confident as this smug doctor seemed. Jackson could barely move. "Are you saying my—Riley—isn't going to lose this baby?"

"I don't think she's losing the baby, no." The doctor shook his head. "We think she just had some uterine spotting and some strong cramping, but we want to keep her overnight just to be sure."

Jackson gulped a breath and tried to stay focused. "So this is something that can happen during a pregnancy? Something that might go away or get better."

"Yes. She was in pain and that scared her, but I'm pretty sure she's going to be fine. Getting her to the emergency room was the best thing to do, though."

Jackson wanted more than a *pretty sure* diagnosis. He hadn't listened very well during Riley's first pregnancy because he'd taken for granted that everything would work out. He knew better now. "You do know her history?"

An indulgent smile covered the doctor's face. "Dr. Reynolds brought us up to speed, yes. That's why we want to keep her overnight."

"Should I take her to Atlanta for a checkup just to be sure?"

"Not yet. Dr. Reynolds wants her to rest and calm down right now. If she's not better by morning, we'll decide then, but I wouldn't worry too much about it. I think she'll be okay after a good night's rest."

And if she stayed calm, Jackson thought after the doctor left. Jackson was about to go in and see her when the outside doors opened and Bettye and Charles rushed up the hallway.

"Tell me—not again?" Bettye's eyes were red-rimmed. "I can't take much more of this."

Charles didn't speak. He just stood there holding his wife.

"She's okay," Jackson explained. Then he told Riley's parents what the doctor had told him. "A false alarm, as far as they can tell."

"Thank goodness." Bettye headed toward the emergency room.

No one questioned that Bettye Buckingham was going to see her daughter.

"Have you talked to her yet?" Charles asked.

"Not since they took her in," Jackson replied. He thought back over their conversation this morning. Had he somehow upset Riley? Was she mad that he'd come to her door, drunk and wanting to hold her?

"What caused this?" Charles asked.

Jackson hoped he was imagining the bit of accusation in that question. "I don't know. We were at Southern Hill, talking in the kitchen—"

"This morning?"

"Yes, sir." Jackson shrugged. "I…uh…stayed there last night. In the guest room. I'd been drinking and Verde didn't want me driving."

He left out the part about leaving his car at the country club and walking to Riley's. He wouldn't have remembered that if Verde hadn't filled him in when he'd rushed outside for his car and couldn't find it.

Charles let out a grunt. "Verde, you say? Or maybe Riley?"

"She didn't want me to drive but she didn't want me to stay there, either." He shrugged. "I don't remember everything, but I'm pretty sure Floyd offered to drive me home and I refused. So they put me in a room and shut the door, sorta."

"Uh-huh."

Jackson walked to the window. This was serious. He couldn't do that to Riley again. He'd obviously upset her but she'd tried to hide her worries from him, all the same. Had she done that all throughout their marriage, until she couldn't take it anymore? How could he have been so stupid?

"I shouldn't have done what I did last night," he finally said. Then he turned to face Riley's father. "She wants me to stay out of her life. I think it's time I do that."

Charles gave him a long, measuring look. "And what about the baby?"

"I'll be doing that kid a favor by staying away, don't you think?"

"Honestly, I don't know what to think," Charles replied. Then he sat down in a chair and hung his head.

Jackson gave one last glance toward the double doors into the emergency room before he turned to leave.

"Jackson?"

He whirled at the sound of Bettye's voice. "Yes, ma'am?"

"She's asking for you."

RILEY LAY PERFECTLY still, willing her body to stop whatever it was trying to do. The doctors had assured her that her baby was safe. The ultrasound had shown that, too. But she didn't trust any of that. She didn't dare move. She wanted her baby to stay still and well. She wanted to hold her baby in her arms and know that they had made it through.

The curtains around her swished open and Jackson came into the little closed-off room. He pushed at his unruly hair and put his hands in the pockets of his jeans. "How ya doing?"

"Okay," she said. "Scared." She swallowed back the fear. "They keep telling me it's a false alarm, but it sure felt real."

"Riley, I…I didn't mean for this to happen."

"I know that." She looked into his eyes and saw the guilt eating at him. "You didn't do anything, Jackson."

He slid a glance toward her stomach then fixed his gaze on her. "I crashed your house at one in the morning."

She nodded. "Yes, but you can't think by doing that that you somehow caused this. If this is just me being paranoid, then I'll be okay. The baby will be okay."

He stepped closer. "But you've asked me to stay away, to give you some space—and what did I do? I went and got drunk and hassled you. You should have had a good night's sleep but because of me, you didn't. We both know we're not good for each other. I can't be responsible for—"

"For this baby," she finished. "I never asked that of you."

"I was about to say, I won't be the cause of any more grief for you. I can't go through losing another child.

I won't put you through that again. I guess I finally understand what you've been telling me all along."

Trying to stay calm, Riley frowned up at him. "We both did things before that we want to change. I blamed you a lot back then, but now, we're different people. Even though I'm not so sure we can be a family again, I believe you'll be a great father." She let out a little sigh. "And I intend to see this pregnancy through to the end—so you can prove that to me."

"I want to be a good father." He came an inch closer. "I decided while I was out there hoping and praying our baby would be okay—I can't do this to you again."

She held back the pain of that declaration, too. "Do what, Jackson?"

"Irritate you, worry you, make you get all upset."

"I wasn't upset this morning," she retorted, wishing she could make him understand. "I was aggravated and worried, but I've been those things before."

"That's what I'm saying," he replied. "I caused you to get that way before and we—you—can't be getting all hot and bothered and angry during this pregnancy. If that means I need to stay away, then I'll do it."

She lay there, her fingers curling into the covers, and saw the determination in his eyes. His words tore through her. Why was it that he was offering to do the very thing she'd asked him to do—stay away—and yet in her heart, she so wanted him with her. Wanted him to pull her into his arms and tell her it would all be all right.

Riley had to wonder which would be worse, letting him go or begging him to stay.

Reminding herself that she had to do what was best for this baby, she said, "We had parted ways, before last night."

He gazed into her eyes, his expression harsh and ragged. "Yes, but I didn't honor that agreement. I wanted to see you, wanted to be with you."

Riley didn't dare tell him she wanted the same. As much as she craved a future with Jackson, she had to put their child first. And after the baby was born, well, then she'd have to see what happened. Maybe with time and space, they could compromise enough to raise this baby together. Or maybe there would be no compromise between them.

"I understand," she said. "And I agree it's probably for the best that we stick to our decision for now."

He moved his head in agreement. "So you need to get someone to drive to Atlanta with you—for your checkups."

She held on to the blankets. "Mama said she'd go with me."

"Good. And you need a birthing class partner."

"Allison and Margie Sue can help there."

He moved to the side of the bed and took her hand. "Will you at least keep me updated on how things are going?"

"Yes." She blinked away the telltale tears she felt coming. "Of course." Then she touched his hand. "Jackson, after the baby is born—"

"We'll talk about things then," he said. "About me having time with…my child. That's all I ask. Just some time to be a daddy to this baby. A real daddy. I need that, Riley."

"Yes."

Jackson leaned down and kissed her on the forehead, his lips warm as he lingered close. "I'm so sorry, baby."

Riley wasn't sure if the endearment was meant for her, or for their unborn child. "Me, too."

"You do everything the doctors tell you to do, okay?"

"I will, I promise."

Jackson kissed her again. "I'll see you around."

"Okay."

She waited until he'd left the room and then Riley lay silent and unmoving, while the tears ran down her face.

Why did it have to hurt every time she told Jackson goodbye?

And why did they keep pushing each other away when in her heart, she knew they belonged together?

Because, right now, this baby was more important than trying to fix a broken marriage.

But then, what if this baby *could* fix their broken marriage? What if, one day they could be the family she'd always dreamed about?

Riley held her hand over her stomach and wished it to be so.

THE NEXT MORNING, Jackson waited by the fireplace in the lodge, listening for the sound of Floyd's truck. When he heard the motor revving and shutting down, he sprang toward the back door and was halfway to the truck before Floyd looked up. "Floyd, how is she?"

Floyd grabbed his hat and thick canvas work jacket from the truck's seat. "Give a man time to shake off the dust, will you?"

Jackson stomped against the early-morning cold. "Well, you just left the house. What have you heard? Did they call? Is she coming home today?"

Floyd nodded. "She's fine, Jackson. Doc said she can go home but she needs to rest for a couple more days. No stress, no distractions. Bed rest and a calm environment. Verde has declared herself marshal and bouncer."

That directive hit Jackson square in the face. "That means I can't be near her, then."

Floyd gave him a sympathetic, silent nod. "Probably better that you don't go over there for a while. You know how women get."

Jackson nodded. "I need to respect that. Like for maybe five or six months, at least."

Floyd headed toward the lodge then turned back. "For what it's worth, I think you two need to work through this before that baby is born. I'm old-fashioned, I know. But that child needs both its parents. And you need to make an honest woman out of the little mama."

"I know," Jackson said. When Floyd waited for him, he motioned toward the door. "I'll be there in a minute."

Floyd stomped up the porch steps and went inside.

While Jackson stood there in the early-morning mist, a new idea playing through his head.

He did need to make an honest woman out of Riley Sinclair. They needed to be married again before the baby was born. But how in the world could he do that when he'd been banished until *after* the baby was born?

CHAPTER TWENTY-SEVEN

HE TRIED A new tactic. Instead of harassing Riley or trying to see her every day, he sent her cards of encouragement and flowers to cheer her up. He worked hard at the lodge and sent her weekly email reports of all activities and expenses. He got reports back from her about her checkups and her birthing classes. Yes, Allison was helping. She'd gone up to Atlanta with Riley and she'd helped with the first of the birthing classes. Yes, Margie Sue was keeping an eye on her and the baby, reminding Riley not to work too hard and sending her home early to rest. Yes, her mother was always checking up on her and pampering her.

I'm fine, Jackson. Really.

He wondered if she ever thought about him.

Their correspondence was very cut-and-dried and businesslike. Just the facts. Nothing personal. Nothing about how much he missed her and longed to be with her. Nothing about her true feelings for him. It wasn't enough but it would have to do for now.

Jackson was living vicariously through Riley's friends and family since the whole town knew their situation. He figured the community had a betting pool going on as to who would win this tussle. Jackson didn't care about that. He had to make Riley fall in love with him again before she had that baby. They needed to be married sooner than later.

That was his number-one goal. That had been his goal since day one, baby or no baby. He'd come home hoping to fix his life and reunite with Riley. The baby only added pressure to that particular goal. He wanted his wife back. He wanted his baby, and not just every other weekend and some holidays.

So he started writing her longer, more personal emails, telling her more about his adventures out in the world and trying to explain why he'd felt the need to leave in the first place.

I had a good life with you, Riley. A life I took for granted. When it all fell apart, I didn't know what to do. So I left—I didn't run away. I'm not a coward. I left to give us both some space and peace. Even though I had a kind of crisis after we lost the baby, I think getting away changed my perspective and brought me out of my self-absorbed existence. You changed during that time, too. You grew into yourself, found your strength. So did I. I think we're both better people now. I always wanted to travel, but obligations here held me back. I know you took over a lot of those obligations because you thought I didn't care. I cared but I couldn't breathe, couldn't move. I was in a state of grief that left me paralyzed and unsure. First, my parents die in a car accident and I have to leave college and take over this massive operation and then three years later we lose our baby. I'd never just walk away from you without a fight. But back then, I was fighting to hang on to my sanity. You think I didn't care. Honey, I cared. So much. I'd wake up in the middle of the night, in the middle of the ocean, tears running down my face. I wanted you and our son. I still want you and our child.

He hoped the letters weren't too much. Half the time, he deleted and started all over. Riley responded to the ones he actually sent, at least.

I wish you had talked to me about your grief. After you lost your parents, you seemed okay. You were so strong, so willing to keep Southern Hill alive. I felt there was more but you'd never talk about your mom and dad. You were still Jackson—carefree and fun-loving. Maybe you took that image to a new extreme in order to hide your pain. I should have forced you to open up, to get help. When I tried to talk to you, you always left and went to the lodge. Right across the lake, but I couldn't reach you. You'd use the lodge as your excuse. And that's why I don't like that place.

She was right about that. He'd shut down his emotions and pretended everything was all right after his parents died. But after the baby…it all became too hard. He couldn't pretend and he couldn't break down. He was a Sinclair, the last of his kind. He had to keep on going, no matter the pain. And yet, he'd left it all behind. Even Riley.

Riley probably realized she really didn't know him at all.

I never knew you wanted to travel, she replied. I know we talked about it, but I just figured it was you, doing your daydreaming thing. I didn't have the urge to explore the way you did. But you never followed through with any of your aspirations so I let that slide, didn't push you on doing something you wanted to do. I think I wanted to be queen of my domain and I could only do that right here in Sinclair, where I ruled the roost and had my way about everything. But I didn't have my way when we lost little Jack Thomas. And I lost my confidence and my security when we buried him and when you and I turned away from each other. I had to rebuild from the bottom, Jackson. I'm still doing that. I believe you have changed, but I also believe coming back here had to be hard for you. I'm glad you did come home even if your timing was bad. We'll get through this. You will always have a place in our baby's life.

She'd slowly changed her tune over the month of January, her stance careening from wary and guarded to open and honest. She kept repeating that he'd have a place in the baby's life.

But not her life. She didn't mention that, ever.

Jackson kept the notes and letters and flowers coming. He also sent her expensive chocolate and healthy foods—vegetables and fruit, gift cards to a nearby spa and poetry books to read to the baby. As Valentine's Day approached, he sent her a card that offered her a cup of hot chocolate, made by him, along with some light sugar cookies from a recipe he'd found in his travels.

"I'll come over on Valentine's Night and make you some hot cocoa and we'll bake the cookies together. If you like that idea."

She said she'd let him know.

"SO ARE YOU gonna take him up on that offer?"

Riley glanced at the four other women sitting at the table with her. Margie Sue had insisted she take a break for a long lunch at the Hamhock and she'd invited Dorothy Lyn, Mary Ann and even Allison to help her keep Riley seated and full.

"Better decide quick. Valentine's Day is two days away," Mary Ann pointed out. "Of course, I'll be at the country club, overseeing a romantic Valentine's dinner for everyone else."

"I saw Fred Marshall checking you out at church the other day," Allison said, grinning at Mary Ann. "You ought to go for it."

Mary Ann looked embarrassed. "I wasn't sure if he was a free agent." She shot Riley a pointed look.

Riley sat up straight, her mind off Jackson for a few seconds at least. "Oh, I'm sorry. I should have made it clear that Fred and I are not an item. We never were, really. Go for it, Mary Ann."

Mary Ann smiled and winked. "I will. What can it hurt?"

"He's kind of boring," Dorothy Lyn pointed out with a frown.

"Boring can be good, though," Mary Ann replied. "I've had a bad boy and a power-hungry man. Now, I just want someone to dance with, to watch a movie with, and to maybe make me a cup of coffee and bring *me* some cookies." Her wistful gaze wrapped around the table. "I want a man who is not threatened by me or my career, a man who's comfortable in his own skin and comfortable with me the way I am."

"Fred would do all of those things," Riley said before biting into her tiny slice of coconut pie. "I wish I could have fallen for him, but—"

"But you have always loved Jackson," Allison said on a timid drawl. New to being included in Riley's inner circle, she looked shy and unsure. "You do still love him, right?"

Riley didn't want to say it out loud. "I care about him, a lot. He's the father of my baby, after all."

"She loves him," Dorothy Lyn said, swiping a bite of her own chocolate pie. "Why can't men be as easy as pie?"

"Why can't pie be less fattening?" Margie Sue retorted, her own key lime nearly gone.

Allison giggled. "How often do y'all get together to eat pie anyway?"

"Not nearly enough if you ask me," Mary Ann said. She gave Allison a long stare. "You're fun when you smile, you know that, girl?"

Allison shrugged. "I'll admit I've been a tad uptight for a while now."

"Like most of your life," Riley teased, comfortable with this new relationship. "I don't know why it took us so long to just get over ourselves, but I'm glad you came today."

Margie Sue snorted. "Y'all had this unspoken competition going on. Delton and I used to laugh about it."

Allison bobbed her head. "I wanted to outdo Riley."

Riley laughed. "And I sure wanted to outdo you."

Then Allison turned serious. "It took our grief to make us see we were just being silly. Who would have thought we'd have that kind of shared grief—losing our babies."

Margie Sue gave Riley a pointed look. "Grief can do that. It either brings people together or pushes them apart."

Riley got the message. The conversation made her think of Jackson. He'd been hit with a lot of tragedy but he'd held it all at bay. No wonder he'd come crashing down. Then he'd learned about his own brother dying at birth. She was still afraid that they'd wind up hurting each other over their grief.

"Sometimes, it's hard to get past the pain but, Allison, you've helped me a lot in the past few weeks." Then she looked out the window. A brisk February wind played through the live oaks out in the city park. "Maybe it's time I try to really get over my grief. Maybe let go of being so bitter, too."

"Does that mean hot chocolate and sugar cookies?" Allison asked, her brown eyes hopeful.

"I think it does," Riley replied. Then she wiped her mouth. "What should I wear?"

SHE HAD ON a loose-fitting slinky red sweater that hugged her curves and fluttered over her round belly. Underneath, she had on tight creamy leggings with black flat shoes that sparkled and winked each time she walked past Jackson.

Still surprised that she'd accepted his invitation, he gave her a sweeping look. "Nice," he said to cover the need pooling in his gut. "Pregnancy becomes you, darlin'."

"I'm getting bigger and bigger," she replied, a soft smile on her face.

"That's the idea, isn't it?"

She nodded. "I…uh…brought home dinner from the Hamhock. Steak and potatoes—your favorite."

Jackson rubbed his hands together. "Yes, ma'am. Dorothy Lyn knows I like my steak rare."

"We all know that," she replied, her diamond earrings winking at him.

She presented the meal on the best china. The pattern she'd picked out when they got married. He was surprised she still had the stuff.

They ate the food in a sweet calm, talking about the weather, the farmland, the lodge and Riley's shop.

After they'd run out of things to say, he got up. "Time to make those cookies."

"And your famous hot chocolate," she reminded him.

"Where are our chaperones?" he teased, glancing around for Floyd and Verde.

She laughed. "Oh, you know how it is. They always seem to have something better to do whenever you drop by."

"They either don't like me very much or they very much want you and me to have some privacy."

"You know they like you. Floyd sings your praise every night at dinner, although I think he's exaggerating a bit for my benefit."

Jackson copped a swaggering smile. "It ain't bragging if it's the truth, sweetheart."

While he went about gathering the needed ingredients for the cookies, she rinsed the dishes and stacked them by the dishwasher.

"I can see the truth each time I go past the lodge. You've cleaned the place up. The landscaping looks great even if it is the dead of winter."

He shone in her praise. "I'm gonna plant more azaleas this spring, to replace the few we lost to the drought last year. And we're trimming some of the lower branches on the magnolias and old oaks so we can set out picnic tables. Make the place more family oriented, so we can hold events during the off-seasons."

She watched as he measured flour, sugar and butter. "Great idea, but Mary Ann might frown on that. You'll be drawing people away from the country club."

"A little competition can't hurt," he retorted, comfortable with this business talk.

She brought the cookie sheets to the counter. "Allison and I were talking about being competitive the other day. We both admitted we kind of had a thing going for a while there, trying to outdo each other."

"Ya think?"

She grinned at that. "I guess it got a little out of hand at times, but the day she announced her last pregnancy, it went deeper. I don't think she meant to hurt me, but it did hurt. It felt so unfair then. But now—"

He turned to stir the batter. "But now, you're carrying a healthy baby and she's still dealing with having a miscarriage."

"Yes, and who said that's fair?"

"I don't know about fair," he replied, his hand skirting around hers, "but I've decided we just have to roll with the punches. We're blessed." He waved his hand in the air. "We have Southern Hill. You have this huge network of people who love and adore you, even when you're in full diva mode. You're safe here, Riley. Secure. Loved."

He cut the cookies with a biscuit cutter and placed

them on the pans. Riley opened the oven and slid the cookie sheets inside. "Fifteen minutes?"

"More like ten or twelve."

She set the timer then put her hand on his arm, surprising him, the jolt of awareness sharpening the haze of his need. "Jackson, listen to yourself. You said I have a network of support. What about you?"

He looked down at her hand, saw the pretty silver charm bracelet wrapped against her wrist. "I never thought about it that much. I was with you, so I had people around."

"And then you didn't."

He saw the flash of awareness cresting like a great wave in her blue eyes. Awareness and guilt. "No, I didn't have much of anything after I lost you."

"You were lonely."

He didn't want to have this conversation, not tonight when he only wanted to make things special for Valentine's Day. So he gathered the chunk of rich chocolate and started shaving slices into the milk he'd placed on the stove. "I got by."

She handed him the sugar and vanilla. "Yes, by drinking and flirting and…being the life of the party."

He shrugged. "I'm that guy, you know."

She moved closer. "Jackson, talk to me. Tell me how you really felt after your parents died, after we lost Jack Thomas, after everything was over and gone."

He lowered the burner heat then leaned back against the counter, his hands pressing into the hard granite. "It doesn't matter how I felt, Riley. It never mattered how I felt. That's the way things were handled in my family. We brushed any type of distress right under the hundred-year-old rug. We had to be the pillars of the community that rested on our name."

She watched the hot drink bubbling and foaming. "You, you mean. You had to be that."

"Yes. That was certainly drilled into me from birth. Think about our name, Jackson. Think about our reputation. A Sinclair always does what needs to be done."

"And now, you found out you weren't the first. That there should have been another brother before you."

"Yeah." He didn't dare move toward her, so he just held tight to the cold granite. "A big secret about a little baby. But a secret that could have changed my life if anyone had bothered to tell me. But I didn't matter enough for that."

She yanked the hot chocolate off the burner just before it started to bubble over. "Maybe they planned to tell you but then...they were in that awful accident."

"Doesn't matter," he said, fighting to control his anger. "Doesn't matter. They had plenty of time to tell me. Never mattered."

She moved toward him, her fingers stroking his jawline. "It all matters, Jackson. You matter. You have to know that."

He lifted off the counter and tugged her close. "Do I, really, Riley? This whole scenario is all warped and crooked inside my mind. My mother was probably pregnant when they got married but had a miscarriage and I never knew. You lost a baby and instead of bringing us together, it pulled us apart. You tried to fix your grief by having another baby with our embryo. *Without* me. That's the pattern. My parents went about their business without telling me what had made them so cautious and bitter. You went on with your life and made this huge decision without telling me. Now you want to raise this baby without me. And you expect me to believe I'm worth something to you?"

He stared down at her, taking in her eyes, her hair, her lips. He wanted to punish her with a thorough kiss. He wanted to cherish her with a life of forgiveness and constant love. This night he'd so carefully planned sure hadn't turned out the way he'd expected. But then, nothing in his life had.

"Yes, you mean the world to me. I want to find a way…a way back to us," she said, her words shaky and strained. "I want my carefree, caring Jackson back. But—"

"I've always been the life of the party because I don't have any life without a party."

"Oh, Jackson." She moved toward him, reaching, her lips parting, her eyes telling him what words couldn't express.

And Jackson knew if he pushed, she'd be his again tonight.

But he wasn't ready for that. He'd thought he was ready but he'd been so wrong. The terms of this agreement had changed now. He wanted more. He didn't just want to win. He wanted to win her back—her heart, her soul, everything about her.

"Jackson?"

He held her there. "The hot chocolate is ready."

She cut her gaze to the stove. "The cookies are going to burn."

Not nearly as hot as he was burning right now.

He gave her a chaste kiss on the cheek. "We'd better get two mugs and a cookie plate so I can make good on my Valentine promise—hot chocolate and sugar cookies. Doesn't get any sweeter than that, darlin'."

Riley backed away, shock widening her eyes. Disappointment coloring her blush. "Okay. All right."

He poured up the steaming cocoa while she placed the crisp cookies on a pretty tray. But neither one of them seemed to enjoy the fruits of their labor.

Later, Jackson stood at the window and stared out into the night.

He'd had her in his arms, had her right there where he wanted her. Now he'd probably hurt her again by shutting down, by refusing to show her his deepest, darkest pain.

But as much as he wanted Riley back, he couldn't risk going that deep until he knew he could trust her to still love him even after he'd bared his soul.

Could she love that broken, angry, bitter man who hid beneath the good ole boy?

Could he be the man she needed him to be, after all the revelations between them?

Or had he pushed her away one time too many?

CHAPTER TWENTY-EIGHT

"SO HOW DID it go with Jackson on Valentine's night?" Margie Sue asked the next Monday morning.

Seeing the hope and encouragement in Margie Sue's eyes, Riley wasn't sure how to respond. "We had a nice dinner and then we made the cookies and hot chocolate and then he left."

Margie Sue grunted. "That's about as exciting as flossing my teeth," she said on a huff. "You're not telling me the whole story, are you, suga'?"

Riley closed the computer file she'd been trying to work on all morning. "There is no story. We…had a nice evening but we both still agree we need to give each other some space."

"Space?" Margie Sue shuffled her hand through a rack of new arrivals, rearranging the slinky spring blouses and lightweight capri pants. "Since when do y'all want space? You two were always joined at the hip."

"Well, not anymore," Riley said on a snap of frustration. "And that's part of the problem. Everyone around here thinks Jackson and I should just let bygones be bygones and jump right back in with both feet. We've changed. We can't be the couple we used to be. I'm not sure we can ever get past all the bitterness and blame."

Margie Sue slung three bright-colored cardigans over the matching floral tunics. "I don't see why not. The man can't take his eyes off of you. And I see you watching him, looking at him in that Riley way."

"There is no Riley way," Riley retorted. "There is no more Riley and Jackson." She shrugged, gave in. "We were making progress through email and a few phone calls. Then I agreed to have dinner with him the other night. We had a good, serious talk but he did that thing again. That thing that drives me nuts."

"What…he flirted with you?"

"No. That's just it. He refused to flirt with me. I practically threw myself on the man and he just turned off and shut down." She got up to stomp around the office. "That sure did make the hot chocolate a little bittersweet."

Margie Sue headed her off at the office door. "That doesn't sound like Jackson."

Bitter and discouraged, Riley threw some old papers into the recycle basket. "No, that *is* Jackson at his finest. That's the Jackson I know, the one who shut down when I got pregnant and didn't open up again, even…even after we lost the baby."

Margie Sue frowned then scratched her head. "Are we talking about the same Jackson Sinclair?"

Riley turned, her hands slicing through her hair. "Yes, the very same. The fun-loving, laughing, drinking, rowdy Jackson Sinclair. He can hang with the best of them until the going gets tough. And then he closes down like a bar in a dry county. Locked up and not open for discussion."

Margie finished with her display ensembles. "If that don't beat all. Explains a lot, though."

"Yes, it explains why I don't think Jackson and I will ever get any closer than we are now. We simply can't find a compromise. So I'll just go on with my life same way I have for the past five years."

"And what about the baby?"

"Why does everyone always ask that?" Riley retorted, her anger boiling as hot as her skin felt. "I have every intention of taking care of my baby. That will not change, regardless of the many moods of Jackson Sinclair."

"All righty then," Margie Sue replied. "Speaking of moods, would you like some hot tea?"

Riley sighed and shook her head. "No. I'm sorry. It's just…I thought I had this all figured out and I don't. Jackson coming back has put a strain on this whole pregnancy."

"I think he's put a strain on your whole life."

"Yes, that, too. I want it over. I want to be able to relax and enjoy the last few months of this pregnancy."

Margie Sue glanced at the calendar on Riley's desk. "No wonder you're in a mood. You're five months and counting now but you were right at six months when—"

Riley sat down and stared up at her sister-in-law. "When I lost Jack Thomas."

And she didn't dare tell Margie Sue that her stomach had felt strange all morning.

JACKSON HAD A weird feeling in his gut. He'd been up half the night dealing with trespassers around the back perimeter of the lodge. They were after wild hogs and small game, probably wanted the meat to feed their families, but if Jackson let one get away with illegally hunting on his land, he'd soon have a never-ending stream of squatters messing up his property. Not to mention the dangers of hunting feral hogs. They weren't the friendly, shy type. A feral hog didn't bother with getting to know a hunter. They'd usually run away, but sometimes they'd just plow headfirst toward anything they considered a danger. He couldn't risk someone getting hurt on his land then suing him.

With his dogs Gertrude and Sport running ahead, he trudged toward the lodge but turned automatically to stare across the big lake toward the house. A morning mist covered the water like a woman's veil, making it hard for him to get a bead on the turret room windows. He hadn't heard a word from Riley since their dinner last week. Probably wouldn't hear from her until she wanted him to know something. Or share something.

He'd messed up their big date by choking instead of taking matters into his own hands. And why hadn't he just seized the day? He had every right to pull the woman into his arms and lay claim on her. And he'd wanted nothing more. But something was holding him back. Something left unsaid, undone.

Riley knew him too well. He was holding back. He'd always held things inside, hidden his true feelings behind a smile and a round of drinks. Now that he'd backed off that particular cover, he felt exposed and raw, vulnerable and shaky.

And admitting that, even to himself, didn't set well with Jackson. No wonder he felt a burning in his gut. He needed a good breakfast and a strong cup of coffee. He had a lot to do today. Even though deer season was over, he still had hunters booked for turkey and quail hunts as well as small game day hunts. Nature always provided, no matter the season.

When his phone buzzed, he turned away from the big house to answer it. "Hello?"

"She'll be mad that I called you, but Riley's not doing good. I'm at the doctor's office with her."

Margie Sue.

He started at a trot toward his truck. "What happened?"

"She wasn't feeling good at work this morning. Then she got sick in the bathroom. She said she felt feverish."

"I'm on my way."

He hung up then tapped Floyd's number. "Get the dogs in the kennel for me, will you? I have to go. It's Riley."

Floyd didn't ask any questions. But then, Jackson had hung up before giving him time.

MARGIE SUE AND Riley's mother met him at the hospital.

"They're transporting her to Atlanta," Bettye said, her words calm even though her hands shook. "We've called the family. You can drive me up there."

"What happened?" he asked, torn between going to Riley now and getting a head start on the trip to Atlanta so he could be there when they brought her in.

"She started having contractions." Bettye guided him back toward the parking lot. "Cervix effacement."

That sounded familiar. He stopped on the pavement. "That's what happened last time."

"Yes and we didn't catch it in time," Bettye replied, her cell phone in midair. "But Riley knows the signs. She didn't waste a minute getting here. They called Dr. Reynolds and he told them to put her in an ambulance and get her to Emory. They want her there so they can monitor her."

Jackson followed his ex-mother-in-law to her big Cadillac. He stopped when she handed him the keys. "The baby, Bettye? What about the baby?"

She fumbled with her purse then gave him a sharp-eyed glare. "Trying to be born, but it's too soon. The doctor said each day is precious from here on out."

"What can they do to stop it?"

She got in on the passenger side and waited for him to crank the car. "Drugs, I imagine. And complete bed rest for the duration of the pregnancy."

Bed rest. Riley wouldn't like that. She'd be so isolated and she wouldn't be able to work. But she'd do it for this baby.

Bettye gave him a slanted stare. "She's already complaining but she's a smart girl. She knows what has to be done."

"Will they keep her at the hospital all that time?"

"Not if she can stop them, no."

"YOU DIDN'T HAVE to come."

Riley lay surrounded by machines that beeped and recorded her every move. She gave Jackson a quick glance then looked out the window. Outside her room, a brisk winter wind tossed what remained of the dry leaves in a swirling dance toward the ground.

"Margie Sue called me," he said. "Then I found your mom on her way out. She solicited me to drive her up here."

"Of course she did."

Tired and trying not to show it, he bristled. "Do you want me to leave, Riley?"

She finally looked at him again, fear darkening her blue eyes. "No."

So he stayed and held her hand and talked to her and sat by her bed and waited for the doctors to tell her whether she had to remain here in the hospital in Atlanta or whether she could finish out the pregnancy at home.

"I'M SO GLAD to be home," she told Jackson three days later. She sat surrounded by fluffy pillows and floral comforters and sheets. "Even if I do have to sleep downstairs for a while."

Jackson did one last run-through of the patient's new room.

"I think you have everything you'll possibly need." He walked to the control center she'd insisted they set up by her bed. "You have a place for your phone and laptop, some files and a printer." He turned and pointed his finger at her. "You know, of course, you can't get up or lift anything too heavy. And Verde has orders to make you rest several times a day."

"I understand."

He saw the flash of a pout on her lips. She didn't like him being here to oversee things, but he wasn't going to back down or shut up.

"You can only get out of bed for a quick bath and for bathroom breaks. And I mean quick."

She worried with her hair, twisting it into a puffy updo held together by a big clip. "I heard every word the doctor said, remember." She dropped her hands down onto her lap. "I won't do anything to cause me to go into early labor."

"Good." He sat down and looked around the downstairs room that had once served as his mother's office. It wasn't bad for a sickroom. "You do have a nice view of the pool and gardens. With spring coming, that should be a distraction."

Riley looked out the row of windows. "Yep. But it's so cold out there today."

"The Ides of March," he said, his hand tapping on

the desk that used to be his mother's. He glanced at the bookshelf across the carpeted room. "Well, you have plenty of books in here. My mama loved to read. Shakespeare was one of her favorites."

Riley stopped fidgeting. "You never told me that. She never told me that."

He leaned forward. "In case you didn't notice, we weren't very talkative in the personal department."

"And you still aren't," she replied. "You talk all around yourself, but you never really reveal anything."

He shrugged. "I didn't know I had to."

"To me, Jackson." She sank back on the pillows, her lacy bed jacket fluttering around her in pastel array. "You need to reveal yourself to me. I think that's what was missing in our marriage." She shrugged. "Me, I'm an open book—I let people have it, good or bad. I don't hold anything back."

Except your feelings for me, he thought.

Jackson got up, already uncomfortable with this turn of events. "Look, you don't need to be getting your dander up about anything right now, remember?"

She gave him a hard stare. "And you weren't supposed to be here today. Or at the hospital the other day. But you are here and I'm glad. I don't want to want you here, but it makes me feel better about things that you are. I just want you to talk to me."

"I have talked to you," he replied, his hand tugging against his hair. "I stayed at the hospital day and night and I intend to be here as much as possible. I told you from the beginning that I would be a part of this baby's life. And now I'm starting early on that plan, regardless of how you feel about me. I want this baby to be born healthy. End of discussion."

"End of any discussion regarding you and your real feelings, right?" She leaned up, careful of her growing stomach. "I mean, we can shoot the bull, discuss the weather and the crop reports, talk about updates on the lodge and another coat of paint on the shutters, even talk about our friends and family, but we are never, ever to discuss what really makes Jackson Sinclair tick."

He shot out of his chair, ready to exit. "You used to know what makes me tick."

Riley didn't get angry. She stayed still and quiet. "No, I never knew what *really* made you tick. I knew what got you mad or upset. I knew how to push your buttons and flirt with you and make you want to be with me. But what we had didn't last because it was built on a shallow foundation. Regardless of how you and I feel about each other, this child needs a solid foundation."

"Oh, and I'm the one who will have to provide that?"

"We, Jackson. You and I can provide that."

He watched her face. She knew she had him up against the wall. If he intended to come and see her every day then she intended to drill him until he spilled his guts. "You think you're so smart, don't you?"

She leaned back, all the amusement and confrontation gone from her expression. "I have at least three months to sit here and do not much of anything. And I have you to keep me company during a lot of that time. But here's the deal. If you insist on hovering over me and making sure I behave, then I need something in return. I need you to finally let me in. Just let me in."

Mad, he walked over to the bed and leaned so close he could almost taste her perfume. "And do you think this will be good for the baby?"

She stared up at him, her mouth open in awe and longing. "I think it will be good for us, and yes, that makes it good for the baby. He or she will be right here, listening in, hearing his daddy talk about things we all find hard to talk about."

He got close, his mouth practically touching her ear. "That's a tall order, Riley. We'll see who caves first."

CHAPTER TWENTY-NINE

SHE WOULDN'T CAVE.

Riley pretended to study the open file on her mini laptop but really, she was more fascinated by studying Jackson. True to his word, he was here part of almost every day. After they'd gotten her settled, he'd brought a suitcase over to the house and announced he'd be staying upstairs in the guest room.

No one argued with him.

Verde and Floyd wanted him there since they were concerned for Riley and afraid they'd do something wrong or not hear the alarm if she needed them.

Now Riley was too afraid to send him away. If she shut him out and something happened to this child, they'd never be together again. And in spite of everything, she wanted to be with her husband again. She just couldn't tell him that until later, when she had time to deal with him. Later, when she was holding her healthy baby in her arms. Then…maybe then.

Right now, she had a lot of other things to deal with—first and foremost keeping her baby healthy.

"Do you need something?"

"What?" Riley blinked. She'd been staring at Jackson for a full five minutes. "Oh, no. I'm fine. The home health care nurse said my vitals were good. And the doctors assure me the baby is growing strong every day. We're almost through March."

"April showers to come," he quipped. "The garden is beginning to show signs of life."

She glanced out the window. "I wish I could go out there and walk around, piddle with the azaleas bushes, maybe plant petunias. I need to smell the gardenia and magnolia blossoms. I miss riding my horse."

He gave her a reassuring smile. "All in due time, darlin'."

Riley didn't enjoy being confined, but she couldn't do anything about that now. But she had to admit, this quiet time with Jackson, both of them working between her rest periods, helped to pass the days. She would behave and follow the doctor's orders. For the baby. For her future. For Jackson.

Closing her laptop and laying it aside on the bed, she settled back and took in the sight of the man she loved. Jackson wore his usual outfit of boots, jeans and a button-up shirt. His dark shaggy hair glistened in the early-morning light pouring through the windows. His eyes sparkled in that way that always made her heart clutch. In spite of his charisma and fun-loving reputation, the man had a way of being mysterious, as if he held a secret he couldn't share.

And she believed he did.

"Jackson, tell me about your mama."

He fidgeted, stalled, rolled his ink pen through his fingers. "You knew her. What else do you want to hear?"

"Yes, I knew her, but I'm beginning to see that you

are a lot like her. She didn't share much, didn't talk about herself."

He put down the farm magazine he'd been reading. "But I'm different from her, too. I like being the center of attention. My mama didn't. She stayed in the background, always in my daddy's shadow."

Riley saw that hint of disappointment and sadness in his eyes. Now he had a tiny shadow haunting him. Maybe two—his brother and his son, both long gone but both ever-present in his mind.

Turning back to his mother, she hoped he'd keep talking. "But she loved to read and she sewed. She was such a seamstress. Remember how I used to get her to make me clothes from patterns? Everyone said they looked as good as any Neiman Marcus designer clothes. I still have some of the outfits she created for me."

"She always talked about fashion a lot," he said. "I'd forgotten that about her." He nudged the covers at the foot of the bed. "You learned a thing or two from her. Your shop is amazing, even if I don't get it."

Score one for Riley. In the time since she'd settled in here, she tried a different question each day. Tried to draw him out, so she could find that dark place he guarded so heavily. Maybe one of these days, he'd tell her everything—all his fears, all his hopes, all his dreams.

And maybe one day, they'd work things out and be together again.

She grinned at his compliment. "Thanks. I did work hard on that place. I wanted something to call my own. I know that sounds cliché and silly, but I'm proud of what I've accomplished. It helped me to stay focused after—"

Concern danced across his features. "After you lost everything."

She nodded, pushed at the floodgate of emotions. "Yes. Everything."

"Ready for lunch?"

Shocked, she watched as he got up and was halfway to the door. Ready to run, ready to abandon any show of real emotions. "We just had breakfast."

"Oh, right." He paced toward the windows. "The robins are out. Spring's on the way."

Riley put her hand across her growing belly, this connection to Jackson holding her tight. "And so is our baby." When a little bump hit against her palm, she let out a gasp.

That brought Jackson running. "What's wrong?"

"Nothing," she said, reaching out for him. "Here, hold your hand right there."

He sat down on the bed and did as she asked while she held her hand over his. Riley watched his face. He went from worried to amazed to…joyful. She'd never seen pure joy in his expression before. It floored her and filled her with so many different feelings, she could barely breathe.

"Wow." He grinned from ear to ear, a look of awe in his expression. "Wow. Kicks like a boy but could be a girl. Feisty, like her mama."

"Are you mad that we decided to wait to find out which we're having?"

"We?" He brightened even more. "That's the first time you've ever said *we*. *We,* as in me and you, together."

Riley realized he was right but she didn't know how to move past the wall she'd built up to protect herself and this baby. "Do you want to know what we're having?"

His grin got bigger each time he felt a little kick. "Heck, no. Healthy, honey. *We* want a healthy, full-grown baby."

Her heart did that little clutch. "You mean a fully developed baby, right?"

He kept his hand on her stomach then leaned down, nose to nose with her. The way his fingers and palm splayed across her stomach sent little electrical charges throughout Riley's overly sensitive body. "You better believe it—a healthy, happy baby and a healthy, happy mama."

"And a happy daddy, too," she said, meaning it. Riley took a deep breath and accepted that she was still in love with Jackson. Accepted it and let it cover her with a warm hope.

Jackson seemed to sense the shift in her. His gaze held hers, his eyes going dark with want, with that joy she'd witnessed, dark and rich with love. For her. He still loved her.

He put his other hand on her neck and lifted her closer to him. "Daddy's very happy right now, sweetheart."

"Jackson…"

He nuzzled her ear. "I know, I know. This isn't allowed, but I need to touch you, feel you. I want to remember this, Riley. Just this one special moment."

She couldn't push him away now. Not after she'd badgered him and tugged at him to show her the real Jackson Sinclair. She didn't want to let him go. So she lifted her head and waited for him to kiss her.

Jackson tugged her against him, his hand still holding her stomach. His other hand tore through her hair while his lips tore over hers, drawing her in, filling her with need, making her feel cherished and precious and secure.

"Jackson," she whispered against his lips.

The baby kicked again, there between them, there with them, there in them. And that burst of joy surrounded Riley.

Jackson lifted his mouth to lighten the kiss. "My baby," he said. "Mine, Riley. We're having a baby." Then he put his lips to her tummy and kissed her stomach through the fabric of her cotton gown. "Mine."

"Yes," she said, a single tear tracing down her cheek, her fingers tugging through his hair. "Your baby. Always."

HE'D ALMOST PROPOSED to her right then and there.

But he'd held back. Jackson had big plans on how he wanted to present his case to Riley. A little more time to bring her around, a little more togetherness to remind her that they could be a family again.

But oh, that kiss, that kick of a little foot, that movement of a little hand. How he'd loved that. They'd connected, like the old days. With just a breath, just a look. Really connected. He couldn't mess with that.

He just needed a little more time. So he stayed close, hovering over Riley, making sure she rested, making sure she had everything she needed. He could tell she was changing, shifting toward him, toward a true reconciliation, a true marriage.

And he knew in his heart that he'd failed at that the first time around. They'd been married, but he'd never actually listened to her heart or the vows they'd made to each other.

To love and to cherish, to honor, through sickness and health...

He had not honored his marriage or his wife. He had not honored becoming a father.

But he would now. He would forever.

He woke up in the middle of the night and hurried barefoot down the stairs. Then he tiptoed into Riley's room and watched her sleep. She lay on her side, protecting her rounded stomach, her soft blue nightgown fluttering around her shoulders, her hair glistening like dark gold against the white pillow.

Jackson stood in the shadows, counting her soft breaths, counting each minute and each hour that their baby grew inside her. And he prayed, willed, the baby to be healthy.

Then he leaned down and kissed Riley, just a brush of his lips against her warm skin.

She let out a soft, satisfied sigh.

"I'm not going anywhere this time, darlin'," he whispered through the moonlight.

Then he grabbed an afghan and settled back on the chaise lounge, his last thoughts before he drifted off to sleep centered on Riley and their baby.

RILEY WOKE TO the sunshine moving through the trees, the floating shadows of nature dancing against the sheers covering the window. She stretched, touched her stomach and breathed a sigh of relief that the baby had made it through yet another day and night.

Then she sat up and blinked.

Jackson lay curled in what looked like a tortured position on the way-too-feminine chaise lounge he'd brought from upstairs, her fake-fur afghan gathered around his plaid pajama pants. His hair inked its way across his forehead, fluttering each time a soft snore hissed out of his nose.

Riley laid back and enjoyed looking at him. He looked relaxed, even on the uncomfortable chair. He looked right, being there. He would look even better sleeping beside her.

"What am I gonna do?" she whispered.

She wanted Jackson back.

She wanted her baby to be born healthy.

Her heart hurt, pumping both joy and trepidation.

How could she want so many contradictory things all at the same time?

Because those things shouldn't be in conflict, she thought. What she wanted now, what she'd always wanted since the day she'd fallen for Jackson so long ago, was to be married, with a family. Married to Jackson, with his children.

His child.

She would make it happen. After all, she was Riley Priscilla Buckingham Sinclair. She had single-handedly saved this precious old house and this land that she and Jackson both loved. She'd created her own small business out of a few dreams and an old run-down storefront. She'd helped the local economy and made Sinclair a must-see stop for serious shoppers all over the region. And she'd taken a bold step in order to have a child—just one child—to love and cherish.

"Surely I can figure out how to make this work," she whispered against her pillow. "What's one more thing to the mix?"

That one more thing woke up and sat straight up to stare wide-eyed at her. "Suga', are you talking to yourself?"

"Yes," Riley replied. "I am."

Jackson chuckled then closed his eyes again. "Okay, then. Hope you're giving yourself a good talking-to."

"Oh, I am," she replied, smiling. "I certainly am."

He chuckled again then dozed right back to sleep.

While Riley planned and plotted and pondered how she would get through to him and truly make him hers again.

CHAPTER THIRTY

APRIL DID BRING showers.

Baby showers.

Riley was surrounded by gifts from friends and family. Cute little outfits, most of them leaning toward a girl's wardrobe and all of them returnable if she had a boy.

"Looks like a girl to me," Bettye said, grinning as she handed Riley another frilly package. "Don't get to see her standing up very much but when she does I've noticed she's round and high." She demonstrated with one hand curving over her own stomach and the other hand held underneath her bosom. "Round and high."

"But I bet Jackson wants a boy," someone in the crowd of about a dozen women chirped. "Most men want a son to carry on the name."

Margie Sue winked at Riley. "I think Jackson would love a sweet little girl. He'd spoil her to death, that's for sure."

Riley smiled and remained quiet. Jackson would love a girl. She knew that because he talked to the baby as if it was a girl, promising the moon and a pony and daring her to date before she turned at least thirty.

Allison came to sit down beside the hospital bed.

"Only Riley could have a shower from her sick bed and still make it frilly and glamorous."

Riley pointed a finger at Margie Sue and Mary Ann. "Those two came up with the theme. I just sat here and nodded."

"She's been a very well-behaved girl," Bettye said in a beaming smile. "Won't be much longer now."

"Two more months or so," Riley replied. Her doctors had bragged on her during her last checkup.

Jackson had taken her up to Atlanta, placing her in the back of her mother's big Cadillac with blankets and pillows and magazines. "Stay down and rest," he'd ordered. "Unless, of course, you need something."

Somehow, in spite of all her rules to keep him at a distance, Jackson had worked his way right back into her good graces. Riley had stopped protesting since her protests usually only resulted in a touching and kissing session.

She let him in, let him hover, let him see that she could be willing and able. Soon. But not before the baby was born. She had to hold him off until the baby was home and thriving.

And Jackson had become the gallant, considerate, charming man she'd always loved.

Things were almost perfect, except she couldn't let him take that very last step. Not yet. After the baby was born and safe, then she'd think about what to do with Jackson.

Dorothy Lyn came by with a hunk of rich white cake. "This is so good. Hmmm. I need to start up a cake counter in the restaurant. Then I could be like the Cake Boss."

"You're already bossy," Mary Ann quipped as she dug into some more corn dip and chewed thoughtfully. "But girls, let's get down to the question of the day."

"What's that?" Riley asked from her spot in the bed, her floral lounge suit draped around her.

"When is Jackson Sinclair gonna make an honest woman outta you, honey?"

Riley almost choked on her cake. "I don't know. We haven't discussed that. We're trying to be agreeable for the baby's sake."

"The baby's sake is good and all of that," Dorothy Sue replied before slurping down some lime-green sherbet-laden punch. "But if y'all don't stop making goo-goo eyes at each other, I fear you'll be knocked up all over again."

Riley set down her cake. "Please, not in front of the baby."

They all laughed until they heard the distinct sound of masculine boots hitting the aged hardwood floors of the foyer.

"Man on the floor," Mary Ann called out, cackling with glee.

Riley couldn't stop the jitters in her heart.

Jackson walked into the roomful of women, his masculine scent and demanding presence clouding out the feminine giggles and perfume. "How you ladies doing today?"

"We are all just fine," Margie Sue said. "And we were all just about to leave."

"Don't run off on my account," he replied, his gaze settling on Riley. "I see the queen is holding court."

"Silly, it's a baby shower," Allison said as she hurried to pick up discarded wrapping paper. "There's cake and punch in the kitchen."

"I might get some later," Jackson said, still staring at Riley. "Have you behaved?"

"She's been a perfect patient," Verde said. "Hasn't moved from her spot. Even let her mama open up the heavy stuff."

Riley sensed some heavy stuff behind his charming smile.

"What are you doing here so early?" she asked around the chaos of the shower shutting down.

He glanced at Bettye and Margie Sue. "I…uh… wanted to talk to you."

Wondering what he had to say, she nodded. "Just give us a few minutes. Mama told me it was nap time anyway."

Riley lay still as her mother began shooing everyone toward the kitchen. "Now, Jackson, don't keep her up too long. She's had a lot of excitement today. Needs her rest."

"I'll make sure she takes a load off," Jackson said, looking impatient through a polite restraint. His gaze washed over Riley like a warm rain.

Soon the room was empty and Riley felt the weight of his gaze still on her. "What's wrong?"

He came toward the hospital bed then. "I wasn't truthful with your mom. I'm gonna keep you up for a while." He started moving the wheeled bed. "Do you trust me?"

"Yes," she said, wondering what kind of mood he was in. "But, Jackson, why are you moving my bed. I like it right here near the bathroom and the windows."

"Hang on, darlin'," he said, maneuvering the bed toward the double French doors of the sunroom.

"Are we going for a ride?" Riley asked, giggling.

"Yes, ma'am. A surprise. Just sit tight."

Riley held on while he carefully and gently pushed the bed through the open double back doors and out onto the stone patio near the pool.

"Ah, sunshine," she said, sighing into the blue sky. "This is so nice, so nice. What a beautiful afternoon."

"Look around," he said, his tone low and hopeful.

Riley lowered her head and stared at the yard. The rain a few days ago had caused the yard to burst into color. The pecan trees were budding tender green shoots. The azaleas were going wild in shades of purple, salmon and hot pink. The camellias bloomed in a lush, seductive pink. The dogwoods had opened their delicate white blossoms. They shone like white fire beneath the tall pines and old oaks. And the magnolia trees held the beginnings of thick white flowers that would soon perfume the night.

"It's beautiful," she said, breathing deeply and enjoying the calmness of this day. "Thank you, Jackson. It's so sunny and warm out here."

When he didn't say anything, she tried to see where he'd gone. "Jackson."

"Coming," he said. "One minute."

He came around the bed then, his hand behind his back. "I wanted to do this over a candlelight dinner, but today is such a beautiful day, I thought why wait. A new beginning, just like spring."

Riley watched his face. "What on earth are you talking about?"

He fidgeted and pushed his hand through his hair. "I'm talking about a second chance, Riley. I'm talking about how it's so hard for me to open up and show you how I really feel and I know you've been waiting for that to happen. I'm talking about how even though I can't talk about certain things, I always feel safe when I'm with you. I know you love me. I know you're holding on until you have that little baby in your arms."

Riley felt the tears springing to her eyes. "I am, Jackson. I'm holding on. You need to hold on, too, okay."

He bent down then, and brought his other hand forward.

He held a tiny black box with a dogwood blossom taped to the top.

Riley tried to find a breath. "Jackson, what are you doing?"

Jackson opened the box, his expression full of hope. "I'm trying to ask you to marry me, again."

The solitaire diamond sparkled in the bright sunshine with a thousand shards of light.

Riley put a hand to her mouth. "I don't believe this."

"Believe it," Jackson said, smiling up at her. "I finally got up the nerve. What do you think?"

"I think this is a big diamond," she said, her breath shaky. "I think this is a crazy idea."

"Yeah, darlin', but what do you say about…you and me…becoming we, us, Riley and Jackson, and baby makes three?"

"Oh, Jackson."

He tugged at the dogwood blossom and handed it to Riley. "Don't get all scared on me, Riley."

She gripped the pretty white flower like a lifeline. "I'm not scared. It's just…so much…so much can go wrong. We messed up before."

"But we get a do-over. We won't mess up this time. Not if we hold tight." He stayed on his knee but held her hand in his. "Riley, I'm not that complicated. I was an only child who doubted myself most of my life. I brought that doubt into our marriage and when you started in about having babies, I panicked. I wasn't sure I would be a good father. So I blew it by acting like I didn't care when deep down inside I cared way more than you will ever know. Then I left to get myself right and then I came home and I wanted to win you back and there you were, pregnant again, with my baby and, well, it threw me all over again. Like you didn't really need me after all. Then I found out my parents had lost a baby before I was born, and again, it threw me. I didn't feel worthy but at least I understood why. I tried to talk to you about it, but, I was ashamed and embarrassed, and well, all I can say is that I love you and I want you and I'll try to learn to talk about my feelings more." He took a breath and lifted the ring out of the box. "Riley, will you marry me so I can be an honest man?"

"Jackson...."

"Just say yes, darlin'. My knee's going to sleep."

"Yes," she said, tears falling down her face. "Yes, I'll marry you. Again."

He put the ring on her finger and kissed her, his hands lifting to caress her face.

Then Riley heard shouting and clapping. Jackson laughed and tugged the bed around toward the house.

Her mother and all the other ladies were standing in the sunroom, cheering.

Jackson waved at them then winked at Riley. "I had a little help getting this together. But now we got us a wedding to plan, darlin'. And we need to have it done and over before that baby is born."

Riley wiped at her eyes and stared up at him. "I can't possibly plan a wedding right now."

He grinned again. "Don't worry, sweetheart. I think they've already got it planned."

"How am I going to tell him, Mama?"

A week later, Bettye stared across at Riley, her arched brow twitching with concern. "You mean, you don't want to marry Jackson until the baby is born, or never at all?"

Riley shook her head. "I want to marry him. But I can't marry him until after the baby is here."

"You mean here and in your arms?" Bettye got up to come and sit on the bed. "Honey, do you love Jackson?"

"Yes. I've always loved Jackson."

"Then why wait? Are you afraid he'll get you all hot and bothered—"

"Mother!"

"Well, I'm just saying. You two light up a room, is all."

"It's not that." Riley didn't know how to explain. "I planned this pregnancy by myself and I intended to have the baby as a single parent. And now he's back and he's better and he wants me to marry him again and I want that, too, but what if we're rushing into this to fix what was broken? To put a bandage on a wound that can't be healed?"

"Love heals all wounds, honey."

Riley wanted to believe that. "I hope so. He has changed. He's been with me all the way on this pregnancy even though I tried to push him away. He's opened up to me and told me about his travels and how seeing other people struggle and still manage to be happy has shown him we were wrong to give up."

She lay back on the pillows and stared up at the intricate medallion design around the chandelier. She couldn't tell her mother everything she and Jackson had talked about, but he truly had shown her a new side. And since he'd discovered the truth about his infant brother, he seemed almost relieved and ready to take things from here. "What if he's just pretending?"

Bettye got up and did a little twirl. "Pretending? What I've seen of the man is the real deal, Riley. You know I believe in the sanctity of marriage. If that man is willing to go to the ends of the earth to change for the better, well, then you need to give him a second chance. Plan the wedding and do it quick. That baby needs its daddy."

Riley thought about her mother's words after Bettye had helped her bathe and then gone home. Why couldn't she just go with it and be happy, Riley wondered.

Jackson called a few minutes later. "How are you today?"

"I'm good. Everything's fine."

"You don't sound fine. I'll bring some of that frozen yogurt you love."

"Okay."

"Okay."

He was there in thirty minutes, with a big bowl of the low-fat concoction. "Vanilla with chocolate cookies."

She took it, hoping her smile showed her appreciation. "Thanks."

Digging into his own bowl, he smiled. "So the license is secure and we had our counseling session with the minister. All systems are go for our wedding. So when do you want to get married?"

Riley swallowed too much frozen yogurt and got

a brain freeze. "Oh," she said, holding a hand to her head. "I…uh…I don't know. I mean, I'll have to stay in bed, of course." She shrugged, stared at her bowl of yogurt.

He sank down on the nearby chair, his gaze on her. "Okay, sweetheart, out with it."

Riley looked up to find him frowning at her.

"Out with what?"

"For someone who's supposed to be planning a wedding and about to have a baby, you don't look so happy."

She put down her yogurt. "I am happy. And that's the problem."

"Okay, you're gonna have to explain that one to me."

"I want us back together, Jackson. I do."

"But?"

"I'd rather wait until after the baby is born."

He leaned back in his chair and gave her a confused look. "Honey, the whole idea is to be married *before* the baby comes."

"I know and I think you believe that."

"You should want that, too, Riley. You should believe that."

She leaned up. "I have to take care of the baby."

His expression changed from concerned to guarded. "And marrying me will cause something to go wrong? Is that what you're saying?"

"No." Frustrated, she tugged at her hair and pushed it away from her face. "I think if we wait until we're sure the baby is healthy then…I'll be more relaxed about the wedding."

He got up and came to sit on the bed. "Riley, I want to marry you because you are carrying my child. I need to make things right. We'll keep things simple, if that'll help, but we need to get married as soon as we can."

She looked up at him, her heart trembling and tugging. "When were things ever simple between us, Jackson?"

CHAPTER THIRTY-ONE

RILEY COULDN'T GET settled.

A week after she'd informed Jackson that she wanted to wait to get remarried, she still wondered if she'd done the right thing.

"Do you love me?" he'd asked, his heart in his eyes.

"I love you," she'd replied. "I want to marry you. We've got plenty of time. And in the meantime, you will be with me every step of the way."

He got up to pace around the room. "So I've at least moved up in rank. That's good, I reckon."

His sarcasm hadn't been lost on Riley. She'd hurt him, again. But she had to take that risk to insure she brought this baby to full term.

"We'll talk about this more later. Maybe we can reach a compromise and get married the week before the baby's expected to come." He came to the bed and pulled her into his arms. "Honey, I want to make this right. I can accept that you're still a little gun-shy, but…I've tried so hard to prove myself to you and… you say you love me—"

"I do." Then she took his hand in hers and said, "But right now, I love this baby more."

That statement seemed to floor him. He pulled away,

nodded, ran a hand through his hair. "I see." Then he'd said something that had haunted her thoughts in the days since. "I guess some things haven't changed at all."

He'd kissed her, long and hard, then he'd smiled at her. "You're right, of course. The baby comes first. I can wait."

Now Riley lay awake wondering what he'd meant by that. In her mind, everything had changed. But he didn't seem to think that.

She turned out the lights but kept tossing and turning while she tried to find a comfortable position for the baby.

"Just a few more weeks, little bit. Hang on."

But the night grew darker and she still didn't feel right.

The first sharp hiss of pain hit her around two in the morning. Riley came up off the pillows, her hands clutching her stomach. "No," she moaned. "It's not time yet."

But as the minutes ticked by she realized the baby was coming too early.

Just like last time.

And there in the flash of an intense pressure on her spine and stomach, Riley saw everything with a brilliant clarity. Jackson was right. One thing hadn't changed at all.

She'd always put the baby first.

And rightly so.

But she'd done that at the risk of alienating her husband. Her doubtful, unsure, worried husband.

The man who'd told her she made him feel safe hadn't felt safe at all. She'd left him out there, lost in the woods, in a darkness that had haunted him since birth.

Second-best.

Had she made Jackson feel second-best by pushing him away so she could nurture little Jack Thomas? Had her actions added to his doubts and fears about being a father?

"Some things never change."

"Oh, Jackson. Jackson."

She cried out for him. He should be upstairs. She reached for her cell phone, but another round of cramps hit her.

Her hands shaking, Riley dialed 911 and explained her condition. "My baby is coming too early."

Then she found the walkie-talkie he'd put by her bed. "Jackson? Jackson, can you hear me?"

No answer. Still trembling, still on the phone with the 911 operator, she made sure she had the walkie-talkie on the right channel. She'd call Verde.

Verde came running across the house. "I'm coming, honey."

Riley had the light on, but she lay curled into herself. "The baby's coming, Verde. I've called 911." Then she rolled toward Verde's outstretched hand. "Where is Jackson?"

HE'D GOTTEN THE call around midnight.

The security guard they'd hired to watch the outer regions of the lodge property had seen some trespassers. Then he'd heard gunshots. Someone was illegally hunting on Sinclair land.

After checking on Riley and finding her asleep, he'd left a sticky note on Verde and Fred's bedroom door. He'd let Riley sleep and be back before she ever knew he'd left.

Now Jackson and the guard were traipsing through the woods, looking for the intruders. Jackson intended to call the sheriff as soon as he got a bead on where the illegal hunters were located. So far, he'd seen nothing but a lot of dark shadows cast out in the moonlight like hulking giants.

The guard, an older man named Harry, walked with an expert stealth through the woods. "Think they left maybe?"

"Probably," Jackson whispered, stepping lightly so he didn't snap a twig. "I'm still gonna alert the sheriff that we've had some more problems out here."

"People will take what they want as long as they can get away with it," Harry replied.

That statement caused Jackson to stop and think about his own life. "I reckon so." He'd been taking life as it came, but he'd never taken his life too seriously. And he'd certainly taken Riley and the life she tried to provide for them for granted. And he'd gotten away with it, until something more important than Jackson Sinclair had come along.

Jack Thomas Sinclair.

Like a flash of gunpowder, it came to him what Riley had been trying to say. The baby was more important right now. Because the baby was a big change and the baby was a part of both of them and their love.

Jackson stood there in the woods, the night creatures scurrying here and there around him, and realized he had to go and see his wife. Right now. He had to tell her that he'd been selfish and petty when he should have put her and their child above all else. He could still do that now. He had a chance to make things right this time.

"Harry, let's call it a night—"

A gunshot rang out. Then Jackson felt it, a sharp pain in his lower right leg.

Harry rushed toward Jackson. "You okay, son?"

Jackson stared down at the dark stain covering his jeans. "I think I've been shot. Harry, call the sheriff. I have to go check on my wife."

He turned to find his way back to the lodge.

And another shot rang out.

RILEY COULD HEAR the nurses gossiping.

"Busy night tonight. Paramedics got two calls tonight and both out at the Sinclair place."

"What?" Riley tried to sit up, but all the wires and plugs surrounding her held her back. The wide band across her belly monitored the baby's heartbeat for any signs of stress.

Bettye rushed to her daughter. "What's wrong, honey?"

"Two ambulances. They said two."

"It's okay," Bettye replied, pushing Riley back down. "Dr. Reynolds is on his way from Atlanta. Meantime, they're trying to hold you off with drugs."

Riley tried to rest but her mind was too wrapped up in why she couldn't reach Jackson. "It's happening again, Mama."

"Suga', you're gonna be just fine this time," Bettye replied, her hand on Riley's brow. "I've alerted the minister and he'll make sure everyone is praying for you and the baby."

Riley grabbed her mother's denim jacket. "The minister. We need the minister."

"Riley, you're scaring me, honey."

"Married," Riley spurted through her pain. "Find Jackson. Find the minister."

Bettye's mouth opened and then closed. "You want to get married now? Right now?"

Riley bobbed her head. "Yes. Before I have the baby."

"Just hang on, Harry," Jackson told his friend as the ambulance pulled into the emergency room. "We're here now."

Those darn poachers had gone and shot both Jackson and his security guard. But the sheriff had rounded up the interlopers so he hoped they wouldn't come on Sinclair land again.

As the paramedics helped Jackson onto a stretcher, he motioned toward Harry. "He's worse off than me. They got him in the shoulder."

Harry lifted his head. "Just a flesh wound." A nurse pushed him back down.

"Make sure he's okay," Jackson told the nurse.

"Okay, Mr. Sinclair. But we need to look at your leg, too."

"I'm fine," Jackson hollered. "Take care of Harry."

"We need to clean your wound," a nurse told him as they wheeled both men into the emergency room.

Jackson looked up and saw Riley's daddy walking down the hall. "Charles?"

Charles Buckingham turned in surprise. "Jackson? What on earth? Son, we've been trying to reach you."

Jackson felt for his phone. It was bundled in his inside jacket pocket. "I silenced the phone. Poachers."

"What?" Charles rushed toward him. "Are you hurt?"

"Poachers," Jackson said again. "Harry heard 'em and we went to investigate."

"Mercy," Charles said. Then he grabbed at Jackson's arm. "Then you don't know."

"Know what?" Jackson asked, dread pulling inside his stomach.

"Riley's here. The…the baby is trying to come early."

Jackson slid off the stretcher and held up a finger at the nurse who tried to get him back on it. "I have to see my wife. Right now."

"HE'S NOT COMING," Riley moaned. "It's happening again."

"Dr. Reynolds will be here, honey," Bettye said on a soothing tone. "He has privileges at this hospital so it's okay."

"Jackson," Riley said through a grimace. "He's left me again."

JACKSON HOBBLED OUT of the elevator and headed toward the maternity ward. He dared another doctor or nurse to tell him he needed to be looked at. He didn't care that blood was drying on his jeans or that he looked like a madman in his dirty clothes and windblown hair. He had to get to Riley.

He'd promised her.

Bettye met him in the hallway. "I heard they found you. You better get in there."

A nurse rushed over. "He can't go in there like that. He needs to wash up."

Jackson nodded and allowed the woman to take him to a nearby bathroom. A few minutes later, he begrudgingly let the stern nurse wrap his wound.

Once she'd clamped off the gauze, he was up and walking, hobbling, again. "Where is my wife?"

Bettye took him to Riley's room. "Jackson, there's something you need to know—"

"No, I have to see her. I have to tell her—"

"She wants to get married, right now."

Jackson stopped, his hand on the door. "What?"

"She's ready, right now. Changed her mind completely." Bettye leaned close. "I think she's scared. She needs you there. And…she needs you to marry her."

JACKSON HURRIED INTO the room. "Riley?"

"Jackson?"

He saw her lying there, tubes and cords all around her. She looked pale and frightened. "I'm here, darlin'. I told you I'd be here."

"But where have you been? I was worried."

"Out in the woods. Trespassers. Long story." He kissed her to quiet her. "I hear you need someone to marry you."

"I need you," she said through her tears. "I need you, Jackson."

"Where's the preacher?"

"He's out in the hallway," Bettye replied. "I'll get him."

Riley touched Jackson's cheek. "You are so important to me. I can see that now. Love you as much as I love our child. Always. You've always been first with me, Jackson."

Jackson kissed her face, her lips. "And I get it now, Riley. I took too much. You had to take care of the baby. I took too much. You had to make a choice."

She started crying. "I want you both. I do."

"Me, too," he said, his hand in hers. "We'll be okay, you hear me?"

"Yes." She smiled up at him. "I love you."

THE NEXT FEW minutes were a blur to Riley. Somehow, between her parents and the hospital administrators, the necessary arrangements were made.

And then, in between contractions and with doctors and nurses and her mother and father as witnesses, Riley said her vows again and pledged to love, honor and trust the man she loved. And Jackson did the same, holding her hand, standing close, telling her over and over how much he loved her.

Two hours later, Dr. Reynolds oversaw a team that delivered a tiny, premature baby girl by cesarean birth.

Over the next two weeks, Abigail Louise Sinclair made her presence known by fighting until she was big enough to take home. In the meantime, her parents spent every waking minute in the neonatal nursery, touching her, rocking her and loving her.

On a warm early-summer day, Abby arrived at Southern Hill plantation and slept in the frilly nursery across from her parents' bedroom for the first time.

And at long last, Riley Priscilla Buckingham Sinclair could find some peace and sleep a restful sleep in her husband's strong arms.

"THAT WAS CERTAINLY a nice reception," Jackson told Riley two days later. "A combination wedding reception and…what's that thing you ladies called it?"

Riley giggled from her perch at her vanity table then sent Killer to his little bed in the corner. The dog gave Jackson a "good-night" glance and curled up in a furry ball. "A sip-and-see. We provide refreshments and everyone can see the baby—sip and see."

"Mercy, a coming-out party at birth? I guess that

means we will definitely be involved in cotillion in about sixteen years."

"Don't you know it!" Riley got up, her hair fluttering around her neck, her white satin gown folding around her legs. "Think you can handle it, Jackson?"

He tugged her into his arms and stared down at her. "Having a daughter? I'm terrified. But I've never loved anyone the way I love her. Except you, of course."

Riley looked up at him and smiled. "We're home. We're all home together. It's amazing."

Jackson put his arms around her and held her there. "Promise me you'll tell her about Jack Thomas, as soon as she can understand."

"Of course. We'll talk about him to her a lot."

"And we'll tell her how much we love her and how blessed we are to have her, right?"

Riley pulled her hand through his hair. "Every day."

Jackson tugged her toward the nursery. "Let's go look at her."

And so they did. They stood together and watched each little breath Abby took and marveled at how perfect she looked. Then they came back to the turret room and settled down in bed.

"I want to try one more time," Riley said, lying there in her husband's arms.

Jackson grunted then let out a breath. "Oh, now I don't know about that, honey. I don't think my heart can take it."

She rolled over and crushed her body against his. "Are you sure?"

"Right now, I think I'd agree to anything, but are you sure?"

Riley giggled. "Only if we can do it the old-fashioned way. Sometimes that does work, in spite of everything. And I think now, we both can go at it with a better perspective."

Jackson flipped her and held her tight. "A better perspective? Hmm. I don't mind trying, not at all." Then he nuzzled Riley's neck. "But we have a long time to worry about that."

Riley nodded. "You're right. It's too soon right now." She pulled his head down so she could kiss him. "But in the meantime—"

He reached for the lamp and turned it out. "In the meantime, we've got a lot of catching up to do."

Riley certainly agreed with that plan. Her life, the life she'd worked so hard to create, was finally complete.

* * * * *